THE RĀMĀYANA
(VOLUME I)

LECTOR HOUSE PUBLIC DOMAIN WORKS

THE RĀMĀYANA
(VOLUME I)

VALMIKI,
MANMATHA NATH DUTT

ISBN: 978-93-5420-345-9

Published: -

LECTOR HOUSE LLP
E-MAIL: lectorpublishing@gmail.com

THE RĀMĀYANA
(VOLUME I)
BĀLA KĀNDAM.

BY

VALMIKI

TRANSLATED INTO ENGLISH PROSE FROM THE ORIGINAL SANSKRIT OF VALMIKI

EDITED BY
MANMATHA NATH DUTT, M. A.

Rector, Keshub Academy.

IN SEVEN VOLUMES,
VOL. I.

THE RĀMĀYANA IN AN ENGLISH GARB.

The immortal Epic of Valmiki is undoubtedly one of the gems of literature,—indeed, some considering it as the Kohinur of the literary region, which has for centuries, and from a time reaching to the dim and far past been shedding unparalleled and undying halo upon the domain presided over by "the vision and the faculty divine." The burthen of the bard's song is the perpetual contest between good and evil,that is everywhere going on in this mysteriously-ordered world of ours,and which seemingly sometimes ending in the victory of the former,and at others in that of the latter,vitally and spiritually results in the utter overthrow and confusion of evil and in the triumph and final conquest of good. Rāma sprung from the bright loins of the effulgent luminary of day, and bringing his life and being from a long and illustrious ancestry of sovereigns, Rāma taking birth among the sons of men for chastising and repressing rampant Iniquity and Injustice, typifies the spirit of good that obtains in this world,—Rāvana, that grim and terrible Ten-headed one, a Rakshasa by virtue of birth, and worthy to be the chief and foremost of Rākshasas by virtue of his many misdeeds and impieties, who challenges and keeps in awe the whole host of the celestials—"to whom the Sun did not shine too hot, and about whom the Wind did not dare to breathe," represents the spirit of unrighteousness and evil. Lakshmana, disregrading the pomp and splendours of princely life, to follow his beloved brother Rāma into the forest, and cheerfully undergoing there a world of trials and privations, and daily and nightly keeping watch and ward over his brother and his spouse in their cottage,—and Bharata, stoutly and persistently declining, despite the exhortations of the elders and the spiritual guides, to govern the kingdom during Rāma's absence in the forest, and holding the royal umbrella over his brother's sandals,are personations of the *ne plus ultra* of fraternal love, and consummate and perfect ideals of their kind. The righteous Bibhishana, who for Rāma's cause forsook his royal brother, and set small store by the splendours of royalty, who suffered no earthly considerations to interfere with his entire and absolute devotion to his friend, embodies in his person the sterling virtues going under the precious name of friendship. The ever-devoted Hanumana glorying in the appellation of Rāma's servant,—ever-prompt at the beck and call of his master to lay down his life—is the grandest and loftiest conception of the faithful servant that is to be found in all literature. Shall we say aught of Rāma and Sitā, or keep silence over themes too sacred for babblement and frofane mouthing? The kingdom is astir and alive with the jubilations of the populace at the prospect of Rāma's coronation; pennons by thousands are streaming like meteors in the air at the tops of stately edifices; and drums and *panavas* and other musical instruments are sounding forth the auspicious anouncement. The royal household swims in a sea of bliss surging and heaving on all sides. Delight and Joy move about and laugh and talk under the names of Daçarātha and Kaucalya. Anon a thunder-clap bursts in the midst of the Merry-making, and converts delight into dole, the sounds of laughter and hilarity into loud wails and lamentations issuing from hearts knowing no consolation. All is lost! Rāma is to be banished into the woods for fourteen years. He cheerfully makes up his mind and repairs to the forest in consonance with his father's promise. Sitā steps forth—a divinity clad in flesh—Sitā would follow the fortunes of her lord. She considers it as the height of undutifulness to remain behind, continuing to enjoy the pleasures of the palace, while her beloved Rāma is leading a life of toils and privations in the remote woods. The daughter as well as the daughter-in-law of kings, brought up in the lap of luxury and amidst the soft ministrations of those pleasures that pertain to a royal household, Sitā, the idol of every one's love and regard, boldly and with alacrity faces all the toils and terrors of a forest-life, in preferance to remaining in Daçarātha's residence, bereft of the company of her sweet lord.

All these and various other characters that figure on the fascinating and enchanting boards of Valmiki, have been developed fully and elaborately, and with and perfect consistency of portraiture through the length of his gigantic poem of Rāmāyana. Rāvana standing before us in stupendous proportions as the personation of terror and wrong-doing, before whom the human spirit trembles as Sitā in the Asoka wood; the lotus-eyed Rāma self-forgetful and heroic, and possessed of the highest perfections that can adorn humanity, and through the extremes of misery and misfortune ever abiding by righteousness and truth; Sitā the best and fairest of her sex, the embodiment of all loveliness and grace physical and mental, she who rose from the sacrificial fire of inspiration—a goddess in all her manifold perfections and unsurpassed exellences, whose name carries in the very mention a world of pathos; the faithful Lakshmana, aye cleaving to his brother on the perilous edge of raging battle, and in the dreary forest leading a life lorn and desolate,—these and others whom we forbear reluctantly to name, have been pourtrayed to the life; they are quick with the Promethean spark and occupy prominent positions in that ideal world brought into being by those mighty intellectual wizards—the poets; and are the perennial fountains of our joy and sorrow, never suffering the good and the beautiful to degenerate into cant and commonplace in our minds. Oh! the privilege of genius.

The influence exercised by the Rāmāyana upon the Hindus reaching down to the lowest strata of the society, is literally and in actual fact immense. Truly of the Rāmāyana it can be said in Baconian language that it has come home to the business and bosoms of all men. If there is one test which more than another distinguishes the true from the false in Art, it is the circumstance of a work influencing or not influencing life: a work that assimilates itself with the mental constitution of a nation, lending energy to impulse, contributing to clearness of thought, and ennobling and spiritualis- ing the higher emotions and aspirations, must by the very reason of its doing so, be true; while that which fails in doing so, is not the real and genuine thing and can well be spared. The Rāmāyana has become a household-word in Hindu Society, and expressions embodying the memories of incidents celebrated in the epic, pass current amongst all ranks of the people, being mouthed alike by high and low, by prince and peasantry the aristocracy and the nobility of the land, by merchants and mechanics, by cultivators ploughing the field, and by shepherds keeping the flock, by princesses and high-born dames in towering edifices, and the women of the peasantry plying their daily tasks, religionists and politicians and men of letters,—in short by the community universally. Such absolute and all-commanding and comprehensive sway and influence of literature is perhaps unknown in the West, with the single exception of the Bible. *Rāma's regime* embodies the popular conception of administrative perfection—the ideal of a monarchy. Rāvana is remembered not only in consequence of the prominent part he plays in the Rāmāyana, but also on account of his famous advice to Rāma immediately before his death,—namely that the execution of evil projects should be deferred, but that good ones should be promptly executed,—a very sage counsel doubtless, answering partially to Macbeth's observation on hearing of Macduff's escape:

> "— — — — —From this moment
> The very firstlings of my heart shall be
> The firstlings of my hand— — —"

"The vow concerning the bow-breaking," applied sarcastically to a case of contumacy, "The war between Rāma and Rāvana is matched by that war alone," "Rāvana's family." "Rāvana hath been ruined by domestic disclosure," "Lankā hath met with destruction in consequence of excess of pride," "That won't render the Rāmāyana incorrect,"—these are some of the adages universally current in Hindu society, mixing constantly into common talk. Does not this unequivocally and unmistakably prove that the influence of Valmiki has entered into the pith and marrow of the nation, and vitally sways its intellectual and emotional tendencies?

Sitā has become the grand exemplar to Hindu women as the embodiment of purity, chastity, and wifely fidelity. She has furnished Hindu ladies with the highest and noblest conception of their duties in their various and manifold relations in life. Her empire is both wide and deep over the hearts of her sex, performing for their eternal behoof spiritual services of incalculable worth. She should be looked upon as one of the greatest teachers of her kind—as a teacher in that highest and best sense in which Christ and Chaitanya, Nanat and Socrates are called teachers. Ah, who can say how many women have turned away in the budding prime of youth from the primrose path of dalliance, and have in preferance followed virtue, who alone is truly fair,—how many stirred and influenced by the example of her matchless self-sacrifice have firmly made up their minds to tread in her foot-steps? In like manner it may be said of almost all the principal characters of the Rāmāyana, that they have more or less deeply influenced the thoughts and sentiments of the people.

Further, the Rāmāyana has been all along a reservoir upon which subsequent writers have drawn ceaselessly. Indeed most of the succeeding poems owe to the Mahabharata and the Rāmāyana for their subjects. Not to mention writers of less note, even Kalidasa's self has dunk deep of that fountain. Bhababhuti not less celebrated has composed a poem treating of the latter part of Rāma's life and saturated with a pathos which perhaps no other pen has surpassed.

To the antiquary and the student of oriental literature and manners, a knowledge of the Rāmāyana is simply indispensable. Together with the Mahabharata with which it is joined in popular parlance, and with which it goes hand in hand in compass and variety of information, but to which its superiority is pronounced in point of epic excellence and consistency and uniformity of execution, the Rāmāyana constitutes the great repository of wisdom and learning, the manners and customs of the ancient Hindus. Indeed, the adage current in our socity with regard to the Mahabharata, "What is not in *Bharat* (Mahabharat), is not in *Bharat* (India)" applies to Ihe Rāmāyana as well. In it, cosmogony and theogony, the genealogies of kings and princes, — of human and extra-human beings, of *Ashuras* and *Dānavas*, of *Yakshas* and *Gandharvas*, and *Shiddhas* and *Charanas*; folklore and anecdotes and legends, and stories half- mythical and half-historical; descriptions of cities existing at a period long anterior to the age of Troy and Memphis, and the chronicles of kings that reigned before Priam and Busiris, — all these with others too numerous to enumerate, have been woven into the mighty web and woof of the magic drapery evolved by the so potent art of Valmiki.

Nor is the poem less interesting in a political point of view. It can hardly be questioned that all progress to be real and intrinsic must be developed out of the inherent tendencies of a nation—the feelings and sentiments and idiosyncracies into which it is born as well as those which have been stamped on its life and mind by the stress and exigencies of circumstances, social and political. For a nation, therefore, to govern another with such an object as that with which England has taken upon herself the Government of this country—namely, the progress and advancement of the children of the soil—a close and wide study of its laws, and institutions manners and customs, modes of thought and emotional proclivities becomes a thing of paramount interest. It is clear, hence, that to our rulers an acquaintance with such works as the Mahabharata and Rāmāyana is most important for wise and beneficient adminstration. Nor can it avail one to advance the seemingly unanswerable objection that treating of as they do a state of society divided from the real present by a huge and abyssmal gulf of time, such works can by no means serve as useful and faithful guides to the life and manners of Hindu society existing at this day. "In India," as Professor Monier Williams justly remarks, "the lapse of centuries is powerless in effecting radical changes in the foundation and constitution of Hindu society." The conservative character of the Hindu nation is proverbial. In India usages and observances, the rituals prescribed by the scriptures and the customs sanctioned by hoary age, are clung to with a tenacity that is proof against time and innovation; and those who think that England has materially swayed and influnced the social life of the people, labour, we make bold to say, under a lamentable delusion.

Having regard alike to the surpassing and matchless excellence of the poem itself both in its dramatic and lyric character, the extreme interest it possesses for antiquaries and students of oriental literature, and the importance with which its study is fraught politically to Englishmen, it is most desirable that the Rāmāyana should be presented before the public in an English garb. In consequence of its being composed originally in Sanskrit, it literally remains a sealed book to the majority of students. Few are the persons that can devote their time and energies to master Sanskrit—a language which of all languages existing on earth, is, in consequence of its highly complex and complicated grammar, as well as the indefiniteness which characterises it on account of its possessing countless synonyms, most difficult to master by a foreigner. Nay, we can perhaps safely go so far as to assert that very few amongst those Western scholars who have devoted their lives to the study of Sanskrit literature, have been able to enter into the spirit of that part of its vocabulary in which are couched those peculiarly Hindu ideas and sentiments that constitute the unique genius of the people. To translate, therefore, such a work as the Rāmāyana from the dead and indefinite Sanskrit into the living and real English, is, like unearthening a fossil and inspiring it with life; or rather like transferring a light from a bushel in which it has been hidden, to a mountain-top,—so that men may behold it and the surrounding objects by help of its grateful rays. Surely, to render a work from a dead tongue into a living language and specially such a language as English with all its resources, is literally taking it from its narrow and circumscribed sphere of influence, and placing it before the world at large—in fact, making it the common property and heritage of all mankind. The utility, therefore, we flatter ourselves, of this present literary undertaking, will recommend itself to all thinking-minds without any further elaboration on our part. Indeed, it would argue no common hardihood in him who despite common sense and reason, would endevour to maintain that the Epic of Valmiki published in an English garb (always provided that the execution do not fall far short of the requirements) would prove valueless as a contribution to the case of literature and culture.

In translating the Rāmāyana into English, we are concerned with a work composed by an illustrious ascetic passing his days in a hermitage in devout contemplation and the practice of rigid austerities and self-denial. It behoves us, therefore, to approach the task in a becoming spirit, with minds duly prepared and fitted. Let us, accordingly, begin by invoking Him whose presence can convert the foulest and the most unclean spot, pure and clean, "like the icicle that hangs on Dian's temple," or the hearts and aspirations of the Vestal Virgins, or pious saints ever engaged in meditating the Most High. May He in His infinite and eternal grace vouchsafe to purge our minds of all ignoble feelings and motives,—may He enable is to find delight in duty and doing His will! May our energies never flag while carrying the burden we have taken on our shoulders! May He enlighten our understanding to interpret aright and convey in clear and adequate language the great thoughts and sentiments of the sublime bard,—so that the English Rāmāyana being read by all the subjects of a Monarch on whose dominions the sun never sets, it may contribute to their constant profit and delight.

CONTENTS

Page

THE RĀMĀYANA IN AN ENGLISH GARB. v

BĀLAKĀNDAM.

1. SECTION I. 1

2. SECTION II. 5

3. SECTION III. 6

4. SECTION IV. 8

5. SECTION V. 10

6. SECTION VI. 11

7. SECTION VII. 12

8. SECTION VIII. 13

9. SECTION IX. 14

10. SECTION X. 15

11. SECTION XI. 16

12. SECTION XII. 17

13. SECTION XIII. 18

14. SECTION XIV. 20

15. SECTION XV. 22

16. SECTION XVI. 24

17. SECTION XVII. 25

18. SECTION XVIII. 27

CONTENTS xi

19. SECTION XIX. 29

20. SECTION XX. 30

21. SECTION XXI. 31

22. SECTION XXII. 32

23. SECTION XXIII. 33

24. SECTION XXIV. 35

25. SECTION XXV. 36

26. SECTION XXVI. 37

27. SECTION XXVII. 38

28. SECTION XXVIII. 40

29. SECTION XXIX. 40

30. SECTION XXX. 42

31. SECTION XXXI. 43

32. SECTION XXXII. 44

33. SECTION XXXIII. 45

34. SECTION XXXIV. 46

35. SECTION XXXV. 47

36. SECTION XXXVI. 48

37. SECTION XXXVII. 49

38. SECTION XXXVIII. 50

39. SECTION XXXIX. 51

40. SECTION XL. 52

41. SECTION XLI. 54

42. SECTION XLII. 55

43. SECTION XLIII. 56

44. SECTION XLIV. 57

45. SECTION XLV. 58

46. SECTION XLVI. 60

47. SECTION XLVII. 61

48. SECTION XLVIII. 62

49. SECTION XLIX. 63

50. SECTION L. 64

51. SECTION LI. 65

52. SECTION LII. 66

53. SECTION LIII. 67

54. SECTION LIV. 68

55. SECTION LV. 69

56. SECTION LVI. 70

57. SECTION LVII. 71

58. SECTION LVIII. 72

59. SECTION LIX. 73

60. SECTION LX. 74

61. SECTION LXI. 75

62. SECTION LXII. 76

63. SECTION LXIII. 78

64. SECTION LXIV. 79

65. SECTION LXV. 80

66. SECTION LXVI. 81

67. SECTION LXVII. 82

68. SECTION LXVIII. 83

69. SECTION LXIX. 84

70. SECTION LXX. 85

71. SECTION LXXI. 87

72. SECTION LXXII. 88

73. SECTION LXXIII. 89

74. SECTION LXXIV. 91

75. SECTION LXXV. 92

76. SECTION LXXVI.. 93

77. SECTION LXXVII. 94

BĀLAKĀNDAM.

SECTION I.

The ascetic Vālmiki asked that best of sages and foremost of those conversant with words, ever engaged in austerities and Vaidika studies, Nārada saying,—"Who at present in this world is alike crowned with qualities, and endued with prowess, knowing duty, and grateful, and truthful, and firm in vow,—who is qualified by virtue of his character, and who is ever studious of the welfare of all creatures? Who is learned, hath studied society, and knoweth the art of pleasing his subjects? And who alone is ever lovely to behold? Who hath subdued his heart, and controlled his anger, is endowed with personal grace, and devoid of malice; and whom, enraged in battle, do even the gods, fear? Great is my curiosity to hear of such a person. Thou canst, O *Maharshi*[1] tell me of a man of this description." Hearing Valmiki's words, Nārada, cognizant of the three worlds, said with alacrity,—"Do thou listen! Rare as are the qualities mentioned by thee, I will, O sage, having duly considered, describe unto thee a person endued with them. There is one sprung from the line of Ikshwāku, known by the name of Rāma. He is of subdued soul and exceeding prowess; effulgent; endowed with patience; having senses under control; intelligent; learned in morality; eloquent; crowned with grace; the slayer of foes; broad-shouldered; possessed of mighty arms, a conch-shaped neck, fleshy jaws, and a broad chest; a powerful bowman; the repressor of foes; having plump shoulder-blades; of arms reaching down unto his knees; with a beautiful head, and a graceful forehead; and endowed with excellent might; having symmetrical limbs; and of a cool hue; and possessed of prowess; and having a well- developed chest; with expansive eyes; crowned with auspiciousness and favourable marks; knowing duty; firm in promise; aye engaged in the good of his subjects; of accomplished renown; furnished with knowledge; pure in body and spirit; modest towards superiors; versed in self-knowledge; like unto Prajāpati himself; blest with prosperity; protecting all; the destroyer of enemies, and supporter of all living beings; and the stay of order, practising all the duties of his class; and preserving those cleaving unto him; versed in the profundities of the Vedas and the Vedāngas; accomplished in archery; gifted with a good memory; ascertaining with rapidity the truth of things; the darling of all; unreproved; of unvanquished spirit; discerning; proficient in every branch of learning; ever resorted to by the good even as the ocean is, by the rivers; worthy of being honored; having an equal regard for all; and capable of filling the heart with ever-new sensations.

---

[1] Lit, a great saint. The word, however, signifies one belonging to a particular order of saints.—T.

Crowned with every grace; he enhanceth the joys of Kaucalya; being like unto the sea in gravity, and unto the Himavat in patience. In prowess, he is like unto Vishnu, and boasteth of the personal attractions of the Moon. In anger he resembleth the fire raging at the dissolution of all; and in forgiveness, he is like unto the Earth. In giving away, he is like unto (Kuvera) the Bestower of riches, and in truth, he is like another Dharma.

"Desirous of doing that which would be acceptable to subject, king Daçaratha, from fulness of affection, wished to instal as his associate in the kingdom his beloved and meritorious eldest son, Rāma, of infallible prowess, and endued with sterling virtues, and ever intent on the welfare of the people. Beholding the provisions for the installation, that lady the king's consort, Kaikeyi, who had previously been promised two boons, even asked for these, *viz.*, the exile of Rāma, and the installation of Bharata. Bound by the ties of duty in consequence of that promise of his, king Daçaratha banished his favorite son Rāma. In pursuance of his father's promise, and with the view of compassing the pleasure of Kaikeyi, that heroic one, commanded by his sire, wended into the forest. And on the eve of his departure for the forest, that enhancer of Sumitrā's joy and favorite of his brother (Rāma), his dear brother Lakshmana, endowed with humility, displaying brotherliness, followed him out of affection. And as Rohini followeth the moon, Rāma's beloved spouse, sprung in Janaka's line—like unto an embodiment of Divine power—dear (unto Rāma) as life itself, and engaged in acts of good, and furnished with every auspicious mark, and the best of wives, followed Rāma. Having been followed far by his father Daçaratha along with the citizens, Rāma met with the virtuous and beloved king of the Nishādas; and then in company with Guha, Lakshmana,and Sitā, dismissed his charioteer on the banks of the Ganges at Sringaverapura. Then wending from one wood to another, and having crossed many broad rivers, they, in accordance with Bharadwāja's directions, arrived at the Chitrakuta; and constructing a romantic abode, the three began to live there as they listed. And they spent their days in delight, even like gods and Gandharbhas. And when Rāma had reached the Chitrakuta, king Daçaratha, distressed on account of his son, went to heaven, bewailing the latter. And when Daçaratha had ascended heaven, the mighty Bharata, although pressed by the Brāhmanas headed by Vasistha, to rule the kingdom, did not wish for dominion. And that hero went after Rāma into the forest, with the view of propitiating that worshipful one. And having come to the high- souled Rāma, with truth for his prowess, he besought his brother, with every mark of respect. And Rāma said unto Bharata these words,—"Thou too, O thou conversant with duty, art king." And the exceedingly generous, illustrious and mighty Rāma of a cheerful countenance did not wish for the kingdom, in consonance with his father's injunction. And having made over unto Bharata, as his substitute on the throne, his own sandals, Bharata's elder brother repeatedly forbade him. And then Bharata,finding his desire not obtained,touched Rāma's feet, and began to rule at Nandigrāma, expecting the return of Rāma. And when the auspicious Bharata, firm in promise and of subdued sense, had gone away, Rāma again perceiving there the influx of citizens and others, eagerly entered Dandaka. And having entered that mighty forest, the lotus-eyed Rāma slew the Rākshasa, Virādha, and saw Sarabhanga, Suitikshna, Agastya and Agastya's brother. And he then, directed by Agastya, gladly possessed himself of Indra's bow, the inexhaustible arrows, the scimitar, and the quiver. And while Rāma was dwelling there with the rangers of woods, the sages came to him in a body for the destruction of the Asuras and Rākshasas. Thereupon in the presence of those ascetics like unto flaming fire, inhabiting the Dandaka forest, he promised to slay those Rākshasas in battle. And it was while he was living there that, that dweller of Janasthāna, the Rākshasi Surpanakhā, capable of assuming any form at will, was disfigured. And it was while living there in the society of the inhabitants of Janasthāna, that Rāma slew in battle the Rākshasas Khara and Tricira and Dushana, together with their followers, who all had been stirred up by the words of Surpanakhā. And fourteen thousand Rikshasas were slain in that battle. And learning of the destruction of his relatives, Rāvana wrought into frenzy by anger, sought the aid of a Rakshasa named Māricha. And although strongly dissuaded by Māricha,saying "Thou ought not to enter into hostilities with that powerful one. Do thou, therefore, O Rāvana, excuse me!" Yet, disregarding those words of his, Rāvana, urged on by Fate, went into that asylum in company with Māricha. And that one (Māricha) commanding illusions, having drawn far the king's sons (Rāma and Lakshmana) he (Rāvana) carried away Rāma's wife, slaying the vulture Jatāyu. And beholding the vulture slain and learning of the carrying off of Mithilā's daughter, the descendant of Raghu, deprived of sense, bewailed in grief. And having with unassuaged sorrow burnt the vulture Jatayu, as he was searching for Sita in that wood, he fell in with a Rākshasa, Kāvandha by name, of a dreadful and deformed shape. Having slain him, the mighty-armed one burnt his body,—and thereupon he went to heaven. And the Rākshasa addressed Rāma, saying, "Do thou, O descendant of Raghu, repair unto the female ascetic, Savari, conversant with all systems of morality." Reparing to Savari, that destroyer of foes, gifted with exceeding energy, Rāma, the son of Daçarātha, highly honored by Savari, met with Hanumān on the banks of the Pampā. Then, agreeably to Hanumān's advice, the exceedingly powerful Rāma saw Sugriva and detailed unto him all, specially touching Sitā. Then the monkey Sugriva, having heard all from Rāma, was well pleased with Rāma and in the presence of fire, made friends with him. Then the king of monkeys, out of friendship, mournfully related unto him all about his hostilities with Vāli. And then Rāma vowed that he would slay Vāli. Thereupon the monkey described unto Rāghava the prowess of Vāli, and he feared lest Rāma should not prove a match for Vāli. And with the view of convincing Rāghava (as to Vāli's might), Sugriva showed unto him the huge corpse of Dundabhi, resembling a large hill. And looking at the skeleton, Rāma endued with exceeding prowess, smiling the while, with his toe cast it off at the distance of full ninety miles. And with a single mighty shaft he pierced seven palmyra palms, a hill, and the sixth nether world, carrying conviction into Sugriva. Thus convinced, the mighty monkey well pleased went with Rāma towards the cave called Kishkinda. And having arrived there, that best of monkeys Sugriva of a tawney and golden hue, set up loud roars. And at those mighty sounds, out came the lord of monkeys and having obtained Tāra's consent, came before Sugriva for battle. Then Rāghava killed Vāli on the spot with a single shaft. And, in compliance with Sugriva's request, having slain Vāli in battle, Rāghava conferred the kingdon on Sugriva. Then that best of monkeys having summoned all the various monkeys, sent them in various directions it search of Janaka's daughter. Then at the suggestion of the vulture Sampāti, the mighty Hanumān crossed the salt sea extending for a hundred *yojanas*. And arriving at the city of Lankā, ruled by Rāvana, he found Sitā in the midst of an Asoka wood, absorbed in thought. And then having shown her the sign, he related unto her all about the friendship between Rāma and Sugriva, and having cheered Videha's daughter, he smashed the gate of the palace. Then having slain five generals, and seven counsellors' sons, and grinded the heroic Aksha, he was bound fast (by the arms of Indrajit). Then knowing that in virtue of the grand-sire's boon, he was free, he forgave those Rākshasas that were leading him (to Rāvana). Then having burnt down the city of Lankā, with the exception of the place occupied by Mithila's daughter, the mighty one returned, with the intention of delivering the glad tidings unto Rāma. And that one of immeasurable soul having come before the high souled Rāma, and circled him, addressed him, saying, — "I have truly seen Sitā." Then accompanied by Sugriva, Rāma repaired to the shore of the mighty ocean, and with shafts resembling the sun, vexed the deep. Then that lord of rivers — the Ocean — showed himself. And agreeably to the advice of the Ocean, Nala constructed a bridge (over the water). By that bridge Rāma went to the city of Lankā, — and slew Rāvana in battle. And having recovered Sitā, Rāma experienced high shame (in consequence of Sitā's having lived so long in Rāvana's place), and used harsh language towards Sitā in the presence of all. Incapable of hearing it, the chaste Sitā entered flaming fire. Thereupon assured by Agni as to the sinlessness of Sitā, Rāma became exceedingly pleased, and was honored by all the deities. And at the great act of Rāma's, the three worlds with all that was mobile and immobile in them, as well as the sages and gods, were well pleased with the mighty-souled Rāghava. Then installing that foremost of Rākshasas, Bibhisana, on the throne of Lankā, Rāma was perfectly easy, and rejoiced exceedingly. Then Rāma, obtaining a boon from the celestials, revived the monkeys fallen in battle, and surrounded by friends, set out for Ayodhyā on the car Pushpaka. And repairing to Bharadwāja's hermitage, Rāma, having truth for his prowess, despatched Hanumān to Bharata. Then talking over past affairs, accompanied with Sugriva, Rāma, mounted on the Pushpaka, departed for Nandigrama. Having arrived at Nandigrama, the sinless Rāma sheared himself of his matted locks along with his brothers, and, laving regained Sitā, got back his kingdom. And Daçarātha's son, the auspicious Rāma, lord of Ayodha, hath been ruling those happy subjects of his, even like a father. (During his reign) his subjects will enjoy happiness, and contentment, and become hale, and grow in righteousness, and be devoid of mental disquietude and disease, and free from the fear of famine. And no person is to witness his son's death, and women will be ever chaste, and never bear widowhood. And no fear of conflagration (will exercise people), nor creatures be drowned in water. And no danger will come from the wind, — nor any suffer from fever. And no fear will come from hunger, Or from thieves. And cities and provinces will be filled with corn and wealth. And all will live happily as at the Golden age, And having performed with countless gold an hundred horse sacrifices, and bestowed with due rites *ayutas* and *kotis*[2] of kine on learned persons, and countless wealth

---

[2] *Ayuta* is ten thousand; and *koti* is ten millions. — T.

on famous Brāhmanas, Rāghava will establish an hundred royal families, and will employ each of the four castes in its own duties. And having reigned for ten thousand and as many hundred years, Rāma will depart for the regions of Brahā. He that readeth this sacred, sin-destroying, merit-bestowing history of Rāma like unto the Veda itself, becometh cleansed from all sin. And the man that readeth this Rāmāyana conferring length of days, after death, is honored in heaven, along with his sons, and grandsons, and relations. If a Brāhmana readeth it, he attaineth excellence in speech; if a Kshatriya, he acquireth lordship over landed possessions; if a Vaisya, abundance of wealth in trade; and if a Sudra, greatness."

SECTION II.

Hearing those words of Nārada, that one of virtuous soul, skilled in speech, together with his disciples, worships that mighty sage. And having received due honors, the celestial asking for and receiving permission (to depart), went to the etherial regions. And when Nārada had left for the celestial regions, that holy person went to the banks of the Tamasā hard by the Jahnavi. And having arrived at the banks of that river, the pious one, observing a holy spot devoid of mud, spoke into his disciple standing by, saying, — "O Bharadwiya, behold this holy spot devoid of mud. And it is beautiful, and contains pleasant waters, even like the minds of good men. Do thou, child, put down thy pitcher, and give me my bark. I will bathe even in this Tamasā, the best of holy spots." Thus accosted by the high- souled Vālmiki, Bharadwāja ever intent upon serving his spiritual guide, presented the sage his bark. And that one of subdued senses, having received his bark from his disciple, began to range around, surveying that extensive forest. In the vicinity of the wood, that worshipful one espied a pair of Kraunchas, emitting melodious notes, and ranging around in perfect peace of mind. At this juncture, a wicked-minded fowler, singling out the male without any cause of hostility, slew him in the very presence of the holy man. And observing him struggling on the earth, bathed in blood his help-mate began to bewail in piteous accents, at the prospect of her separation from her copper-crested oviparous husband, engaged in sport with extended plumage. Finding the oviparous one thus brought down by the fowler, the piety of that pious and righteous-souled Rishi was excited exceedingly. Then considering it to be an unrighteous deed, with a heart moved with pity, that twice-born one, beholding the weeping Kraunchi, spoke these words, — "O fowler, since thou hast slain one of a pair of Kraunchas, thou shalt never attain prosperity!" Having uttered this, he thought within himself, "What is this that I have said, afflicted with grief for the bird?" Revolving thus in his mind, that highly-wise one and best of sages addressed his disciple, saying, — "This speech that I have uttered is of equal feet and accents; and is capable of being chaunted according to measure to stringed accompaniment. Let it therefore go forth as a *sloka* as it has come out of my sorrow!" When the sage had spoken thus, his disciple, well pleased, assented to his excellent speech; and thereat that pious person was gratified. Then having duly performed his ablutions at that holy spot, the reverend sage retraced his steps, pondering over the incidents touching the *sloka*. And his disciple also, accomplished in learning, and of I meek demeanour, followed Valmiki, carrying on his back a pitcher filled with water.

Having entered the hermitage along with his disciple, that one knowing duty, while apparently engaged in diverse kinds of talk, revolved in his mind the circumstances connected with the verses. And it came to pass that desirous of seeing the best of sages, there arrived that lord and creator of all, the effulgent Brahmā, furnished with four countenances. Beholding him, Vālmiki rose up suddenly and, wondering greatly, humbly and silently stood before him with folded hands. And duly bending low in reverence Vālmiki offered that deity water to wash his feet, and other things for reception. And having sat down on a highly-honored seat, that worshipful one enquired after the welfare of that sage Vālmiki knowing no deterioration; and then asked him to be seated. And having been seated in the presence of the Grand-sire of all, Vālmiki, his mind running upon the self-same subject, became plunged in thought. "What a sin hath been committed by that wicked-minded one, incited by hostile feeling, when he without cause slew that sweetly-singing Krauncha!" And thereupon, again lamenting that female Krauncha, he, in grief of heart, mentally recited those verses. Then smiling, Brahmft spoke unto that excellent sage, — "Those verses of thine which thou hast composed shall attain celebrity: no doubt need be entertained on this head. It is because I had intended so, that those verses had come out of thy lips. Do thou now, O best of saints, compose the entire history of Rāma. Do thou relate unto the world the history of the righteous-souled and intelligent Rāma crowned with qualities. And do thou, and thou hast heard it from Nārada, relate all that is known, and all that is unknown to thee, O wise one, concerning Rāma, and Lakshmana, and Videha's daughter, and all the Rākshasas. And even what is not known to Nārada, shall be unfolded unto thee. And no words of thine in this poem shall contain an untruth. Do thou, therefore, compose into verses this delightful story of Rāma. And as long as the mountains and the seas exist on earth, thy history of Rāmāyana will spread among men. And as long as this story of Rāmāyana shall retain currency, thou shalt reside both in this world and in mine." Having said this, the worshipful Brahmā disappeared there. And thereat the sage and his disciples marvelled greatly. And his disciples sang those verses again and again; and, momentarily experiencing pleasure, said unto him with exceeding wonder, — "Those verses, composed of equal accents, and furnished with four parts, have been sung by the mighty saint, have, in virtue of frequent repetition, been associated with a world of pathos, and have attained the eminence of a *sloka*. And now it is the intention of that illustrious and self centered sage to compose the entire Rāmāyana in this metre."

The great ascetic Vālmiki of gracious appearance and unparalleled renown has composed hundreds of verses in melodious measure, couching the significance of the history of Rāma's line. Listen to the annals of the foremost of Raghu's race, and the destruction of the Ten-headed one composed by the ascetic, with *Samasas*, *Sandhis*, *Prakritas*, and *Pratayas*; and lucid with sweet and equally-accented words.

SECTION III.

Having heard the entire history of the intelligent Rāma, capable of conferring religious merit and the two other cognate objects, as well as emancipation, Vālmiki again sought to get insight into it. And, seating himself facing the east on a cushion of *kusa* grass, and sipping water according to the ordinance, he addressed himself to the contemplation of the subject through *yoga*. And by virtue of his *yoga* powers, he clearly observed before him Rāma, and Lakshmana, and Sitā, and Daçarātha together with his wives in his kingdom, laughing, and talking, and acting, and bearing themselves as in real life. And he saw into all that was endured by Rāma firm in promise, with his wife for the third. And like an *emblic myrobalan* on his palm, that righteous-souled one, by virtue of his yoga, perceived all that had happened as well as all that would happen in future. And having truly seen everything by virtue of his contemplation, that magnanimous one set about recording the charming Rāma's history. And agreeably to what had been related by the mighty-souled Nārada, that worshipful saint composed the history of Ragu's line, conferring profit and pleasure, and impregnated with qualities fraught with them, and, like unto the ocean, abounding in riches, and captivating ear and mind. And Rāma's birth, and mighty prowess, and kindness to all, and popularity, and forbearance, and good- ness, and truthfulness, and the wonderful converse he had with Viswāmitra; and the nuptials of Jānaki; and the snapping of the bow; and the hostilities of Rāma with Rāma (Parasurāma); and the noble qualities of Daçarātha's son; and Rāma's installation; and the enmity of Kaikeyi; and the obstacle in the way of the installation; and the exile of Rāma; and the king's grief, lamentations, and departure for the other regions; and the grief of the subjects, and their dismissal by Rāma to Ayodhyā; and the tidings of the lord of Nishādas; and the charioteer's return; and the crossing of the Ganges; and Rāma's interview with Bharadwāja; and his arrival at Chitrakuta in consonance with Bharadwāja's injunction; and Rāma's building a mansion there and sojourn; and Bharata's arrival, and his propitiation of Rāma; and Rāma's offering oblations to the manes of his father; and the installation of the sandals; and Bharata's dwelling at Nandigrāma; Rāma's removal to Dandaka and destruction of Virādha; Rāma's interview with Sarabhanga and meeting with Sutikshna; and Sitā's companionship with Anusuyā, and the latter's painting the former; and Rāma's interview with Agastya, and his obtaining the bow from him; and the story of Surpanakhā and her disfigurement; and the slaughter of Khara Tricira; and the exertions of Rāvana; the destruction of Māricha, and the carrying away of Vaidehi; Rāghava's lamentations, and the death of the king of vultures; Rāma's encounter with Kavandha, (a headless demon) and his view of Pampā; Rāma's interview with Savari, and his subsistence there on fruits and roots; Rāma's lamentations, at Pampā, and meeting with Hanumān; the former's sojourn to the Rishyamukha, and interview with Sugriva; Rāma's raising the confidence of Sugriva, and his friendship with the latter; and the encounter between Vāli and Sugriva; the destruction of Vāli, the establishment of Sugriva on the throne; and Tārā's lamentation; the understanding between Rāma and Sugriva as to the time for commencing the march; Rāma's stay during the rainy season; and the ire of the lion of Raghu's race; the levying of forces; and the despatch of envoys in different directions; and the assignment by Sugriva of different quarters to the monkeys; the making over of his ring by Rāma to Hanumān; Jāmbubāna's discovery of the cave; the fasting of the monkeys on the shore of the ocean; Hanuman's interview with Sampāti; Hanumān's ascension of the mountain, and his bounding over the main; and his sight of the Maināka at the injunction of Ocean; the ring of Rāksha-

sis; Hanumān's meeting with the Rākshasa Chyāgrāha; Hanumān's destruction of
Sinhikāya; and Hanumān's sight of Lankā, and his entrance by night into Lankā;
his ascertaining of conduct in times of helplessness; his journey to the tavern; and
his sight of the inner apartments; and his sight of Rāvana and of his car Pushpaka;
his walk to the Asoka wood, and sight there of Sitā; his presentation of the ring
to Sitā and converse with her; and the roaring of the Rākshasis; and dreaming of
the dream by Trijata; Sitā's handing a gem to Hanumān; and the breaking down
of trees; and the flight of the Rākshasis, and slaughter of the slaves; and the wind-
god's Son being taken captive; and his terrible roars while burning down Lankā;
and his bounding back over the ocean; and the forcible possession of honey; and
Hanumān's consoling Rāghava, and handing him the gem; Rāma's interview with
Ocean; and Nāla's constructing the bridge, the army's crossing of the ocean; and
the nightly seige of Lankā; and Rāma's interview with Bibhishana; the communi-
cation as to the means of destruction; and the destruction of Kumbhakarna and
Meghanānda; and the destruction of Rāvana, and the recovery of Sitā in enemy's
city; and the sprinkling of Bibhishana, and the sight of Pushpaka; Rāma's return
towards Ayodhyā, and meeting with Bharadwāja; despatch of Hanumān; and Rāma's meeting with Bharata; and the installation of Rāma; and the dismissal of all
the forces; and Rāma's pleasing his subjects, and renunciation of Sitā,—all else
besides concerning Rāma on earth, that hath not yet taken place,—have been dealt
with by the worshipful sage in the last book.

SECTION IV.

When Rāma had obtained his kingdom, that worshipful sage Vālmiki, composed the entire history [of that hero] in excellent metre and fraught with high
meaning, saint recited twenty-four thousand *slokas*; and it consists of five hundred
sections, and is divided into six *Kandas* with the Uttara. And having composed it,
including as well fut incidents to happen afterwards, that lord reflected as to who
should publish the same before assemblies. And as that great sage of purified soul
was thus pondering, in came Kusi and Lava, in the guise of the sons of ascetics,
and touched his feet. And he found those illustrious princes, the brothers Kusi
and Lava, knowing morality, and living in a hermitage, and endowed with sweet
voices,—apt at taking in the meaning of poetry. And finding them of a retentive
endowment, and initiated into Vedic studies, that lord taught them how to interpret the Vedas, and that vow-observing one taught them the great Rāmāyana in
full, treating of Sitā's life, and the destruction of Paulastya. And those sweet voiced
brothers, resembling Gandharbas in grace, accomplished in music and dancing,
and cognizant of *Sthana* and *Murchhana*, began to chant this poem delightful in
recitation and in singing, set in three measures, and seven notes, and sung according to time to the accompaniment of stringed instruments, and fraught with the
sentiments of love, pathos, risibility, the irascible, the terrible, and the heroic. And
knowing the characteristics that go to make up the Drama, and gifted with mellifluous voices, those blameless princes, coming from Rāma's body, and resembling
him, even as the reflection of the solar or the lunar disc resembles that disc, got by
heart that excellent and moral story in its entirety; and those princes versed in the
Fine arts, with a concentrated mind chanted it as they had learnt it, in the assem-

blies of ascetics and Brāhmanas and good men.

Once upon a time, those high souled and pious ones, furnished with every auspicious mark, chanted this poem in an assembly of ascetics of purified souls. Having heard this music, all the ascetics were seized with surprise, and with eyes flooded with tears, exclaimed, "Well done! Well done!" And well pleased, those saints cherishing Duty, praised the praiseworthy Kusa and Lava as they sang, saying—"Ah! what charming music! What sweetness of the verses! All this happened long ago, yet it seems as if we saw it before us." And unified with the theme, both of them singing together sweetly, and at a high pitch, by means of *saraja* and the other notes, they entranced the audience. And the two thus went on sweetly singing at a high pitch, praised by those mighty sages priding in their asceticism. Some one in the assembly pleased with them presented them with a water-pitcher; and some one of high fame, being delighted, made them a present of a bark garment; and some one gave them a dark deer skin;—and some holy thread,—and some, a *kamandalu*[3] and some great saint conferred on them a *maunja*[4] made girdle; and some person granted them a *vrishi*,[5] and some, a *kaupina*.[6] And then some ascetic, well-pleased, gave them an axe; and some, a red cloth; and some, a thread for tying up their matted locks; and some gladly gave a twine for binding faggots with,— and some, ascetic presented them with a sacrificial pot; and some, a quantity of fire-wood; and some, a seat made of *adumvari*[7]. And some exclaimed, "Swasti;" and some joyfully cried,—"May ye be long-lived!" And all those ascetics of truthful speech conferred on them blessings. And the sages said,—"Wonderful is the story! And, O ye accomplished in all kinds of music! beautifully have ye chanted and finished this poem, charming ear and heart, and conferring long life and prosperity,—which will afford themes to poets." And admired everywhere, on one occasion those singers were seen by Bharata's elder brother, in a street of Ayodhyā, sparsely scattered with stalls. And having had the brothers Kusa and Lava brought under his roof, that destroyer of enemies, Rāma, accorded those ones worthy of honor, a respectful reception. And having seated himself on a throne of excellent gold, in the midst of his brothers and counsellors, that lord, Rāma, beholding both the brothers, handsome and of modest demeanour, spoke unto Lakshmana, Bharata and Satrughna, saying,—"Do ye listen to the story, fraught with excellent sense and composed in excellent measure, as sung by these ones endowed with the divine afflatus." And then he ordered the singers to begin. Thereupon causing the down of the audience to stand on end, and ravishing their minds and hearts, they began to sing melodiously and distinctly and in as high a pitch as they could command, and in strains rivalling the notes of a Vina. And that song of theirs enchanted the ear of that assembly. And Rāma said,—"Although these Kusa and Lava, of rigid penances, look like ascetics, yet they bear on their persons the signs of royalty. And, besides, the story conduces to my fame. Do ye, therefore, listen to that history fraught with great worth!" And then commanded by Rāma, they

---

[3] An earthen or wooden water pot used by an ascetic.
[4] A kind of grass.
[5] The seat of an ascetic.
[6] A small piece of cloth worn by ascetics.
[7] The glomerous fig tree.

began to chaunt according to the *Marga* mode, and Rāma seated in the midst of his court, was drawn to the music, anxious for the perpetuation of his history.

SECTION V.

This great story of Rāmāyana treats of those victorious kings commencing with Prajāpati, and having Ikshwāku for their founder, who ruled the entire earth as no other kings had done so before them, and in whose line Sagara was born — Sagara who dug the ocean, and whom, while out in progress, his sixty-thousand sons followed. We shall now chaunt the entire history of that dynasty from the beginning. Do ye, with minds free from ill will, listen to that story conferring merit, profit and pleasure.

There is on the banks of the Sarayu a great and flourishing country called Kosala abounding in corn and wealth, in which the inhabitants passed their days pleasantly. And the capital of that country was Ayodhyā famed among men which was founded by Manu himself — that foremost of men. And that beautiful and mighty city was twelve *yojanas* in length and ten in breadth; and was intersected outside with spacious roads laid out orderly. And scattered with blown blossoms, and regularly sprinkled with water, the well- arranged broad high-ways looked beautiful. And that one bringing prosperity unto mighty kingdoms, King Daçarātha, lived in that city, like unto the lord of the deities inhabiting the celestial regions. And the city was furnished with doors and gates, and well-arranged rows of shops. And it contained all kinds of instruments and arms, and was inhabited by all classes of artizans. And that graceful and matchlessly brilliant city abounded in eulogists and genealogists. And it was crowned with stately edifices with flags, and guarded by hundreds of *Sataghnis*[8]. And the mighty city contained theatres for females, and gardens, and mango-groves; and was enclosed by a wall. And encircled by a deep moat, the city was accessible neither to friend nor foe. And it abounded with elephants and horses, and kine and camels and asses. And it was thronged with neighbouring kings come to pay tribute, and inhabited by merchants from various countries, and adorned with mountain-like palaces glittering with gems, and filled with sporting-places for females, and like unto Indra's Amaravāti. And the city was wonderful to behold, gleaming with gold-burnished ornaments, and inhabited by troops of courtezans, and abounding in all kinds of gems, and graced with royal places. And it abounded in paddy and rice, and its water was sweet as the juice of the sugar-cane. And it resounded with the sounds of *Dundubhis* and *Mridangas* and *Vinas* and *Panavas*. And that foremost spot of all the earth was like unto an aerial car obtained in heaven by the *Siddhas*, through force of ascetic austerities, and thronged with the best specimens of humanity. And that city was filled by king Daçarātha with thousands of such Mahārathas[9] light-handed and accomplished in fight, as could by force of arms or sharpened shafts slaughter infuriated lions and tigers and boars roaming in the forest; yet as would not pierce with arrows persons lorn or abandoned or hiding or fugitive. And it abounded mostly in excellent Brāhmanas, lighting the sacrificial fire, and crowned with qual-

[8] A weapon commonly described as a stone set round with iron spikes. — T.

[9] A warrior coping with ten thousand persons, and protecting both his charioteer and steeds. — T.

ities, and versed in the Vedas and the Vedāngas, and giving away thousands, and ever abiding by truth, and high-souled, and resembling mighty ascetic.

SECTION VI.

And in that city of Ayodhyā resided king Daçaratha versed in the Vedas, commanding all resources, far-sighted, of mighty prowess, dear to the inhabitants both rural and urban, an *Athiratha*[10] in the Ikshwāku line, performing sacrifices, engaged in the performance of duties,self-controled like unto a *Maharshi*, a royal saint famed in the three worlds, possessed of strength, the destroyer of foes, having friends, of subdued senses, comparable unto Sakra and Vaisravana by virtue of accumulated riches and other possessions, and protecting people even as the highly energetic Manu protected them. And as Indra rules Amarāvati, that one firm in promise, and following duty, profit, and pleasure, ruled that best of cities. And in that excellent city, the men were happy and righteous-souled, and widely-read, and each contented with his possessions, and devoid of covetuousness, and speaking the truth. And in that prime of cities, there was none who had not at his command a plenteous supply of the good things, and there was no householder who was not well off in horses and kine, and corn and wealth. And one could see nowhere in Ayodhyā persons given up to lust, or unsightly, or crooked-minded, or unlettered, or atheistical. And all the men and all the women were of excellent character, and subdued senses and a happy frame of mind, and both in respect of occupation and conduct spotless like unto *Maharshis*. And all wore ear-rings and tiaras and garlands, and abundantly enjoyed the good things of life. And all were clean, daubing their limbs, and perfuming their persons, and feeding on pure food, and giving away, and wearing *Angadas* and *Nishkas*[11] and hand-ornaments, and repressing passions And there were not in Ayodhyā persons not lighting the sacrificial fire, or not performing sacrifices, or mean-minded, or thieving, or engaged in improper occupations, or of impure descent. And the Brāhmanas of subdued senses were always engaged in the performance of their own duties, giving away in charity, and studying, and receiving gifts with discrimination. And none of them was atheistical or untruthful or slenderly-read or detracting or incompetent or illiterate. And there was no Brāhmana who was not versed in the Vedas and Vedāngas, or not observing vows, or not giving away by thousands, or poor-spirited, or of insane mind, or afflicted. And no man and no woman was seen devoid of grace or beauty, or lacking in reverence for their monarch. And the four orders with Brāhmanas at their head contained persons serving gods and guests, and endowed with gratitude, and munificent, and heroic, and possessing prowess. And the men were long-lived; and ever abode by duty and truth; and lived in that best of cities, always surrounded by sons and grandsons and wives. The Kshatriyas were obedient unto the Brāhmanas, and the Vaicyas followed the Kshatriyas, and the Sudras, occupied with their proper vocations, ministered unto the three other orders. And that city was ably governed by that lord of Ikshwāku's line, even as that foremost of men, the intelligent Manu, had governed it before him. And as a mountain-cavern abounds with lions, it was filled with warriors resembling flam-

---

[10] A warrior fighting ten thousand Maharathas.—T.
[11] A bracelet worn upon the upper arm.—T.

ing fire, of straight ways, unforbearing, and of accomplished learning. And the city abounded with excellent horses sprung in Kāmvoja, and Vāhlika, and Vanāyu, and the banks of the Sindhu, and like unto that best of horse, Hari's charge; and with fierce elephants sprung on the Vindha mountain, and the Himavat, filled with juice, and of exceeding strength, and resembling hills; and with Bhadra,[12] Mandra, and Mriga elephants; and those sprung from the mixture of the three, and from the mixture of Bhadra and Mandra, and from Bhadra and Mriga, and from Mriga and Mandra,—superior like unto Airavata, and coming from Mahāpadma, Anjana, and Vāmana breeds; fierce, and looking like hills. And that city was over two *yojanas*; and truly it was called Ayodhyā.[13] And repressing enemies, that city was governed by the great and the exceedingly powerful king Daçaratha, even as the Moon sways the stars. And that lord of earth resembling Sakra governed that city of Ayodhyā bearing a true name, furnished with strong gates and bolts, and auspicious, and graced with excellent edifices, and teeming with thousands.

SECTION VII.

That high-souled one of Ikswāku's line had competent counsellors, capable of administering business, of diving into the motives of others, and ever intent upon the good of the monarch. And that heroic king had eight famous counsellors, pure and devoted to the royal service,—*viz.*, Dhrishti, and Vijaya, and Surāshtra, and Rāshtravardhana, and Akopa, and Dharmapāla, and Sumantra the eighth, conversant with profit. And he had two family priests after his heart; *viz*, those foremost of saints, Vasistha and Vāmadeva. And he had other counsellors besides; *viz.*, Suyajna,and Javali, and Kācyapa, and Gautama, and the long-lived Markandeya, and the regenerate Kātyāyana. Ever associated in counsel with these Brahmārshis, his priests and counsellors serving the dynasty from father to son, learned yet modest, and bashful, and conversant with policy, and of subdued-senses, and auspicious, and high-souled, and accomplished in the art of arms, and of high renown, cautious, and acting according to their word, and possessing energy, forgiveness and fame, and ever preluding their speech with a smile, and never committing themselves a lie either from anger or interest or desire, and ever employing spies noting what was doing or done in the midst of their own or a hostile party. And they were adepts in intercourse with people, and well-tried in friendship by the monarch. And they were ever busy in replenishing the exchequer and in levying troops. And they did not cherish ill will even towards enemies, when innocent. And they were heroic, and ever high-spirited, following policy, and protecting those citizens that were pure, and not bearing ill will towards Brāhmanas and Kshatriyas, and filling the treasury, by inflicting punishments according to the offences of the persons guilty. And during the time when those pure ones of one mind presided over the justice of the kingdom, there was neither in the city nor the provinces any that was a liar, or wicked, or going after others' wives. And peace reigned all around the city and the provinces. And the ministers wore excellent raiment, and ornaments,

---

[12] Those elephants whose limbs are contracted are Bhadras; those whose bodies are fat, slack, and contracted are Mandras; and those whose bodies are lean and large are Mrigas.—T.

[13] Lit, incapable of being conquered.—T.

and were engaged in observing pure vows, and ever kept their eye of policy open, in the interests of the monarch. And the king considered them as crowned with virtues; and they were famed on account of their prowess, concluding unerringly in consequence of their intelligence of other countries. And in all climes and times they could manifest their noble qualities; and they were cognizant of war and peace, and possessed of goodness, passion and ignorance. And they could keep their counsel, and judge of things finely, and were well-versed in the art of policy, and ever fair-spoken. Surrounded by such counsellors endowed with various qualities, the faultless king Daçaratha ruled the earth, gathering intelligence by means of spies, and righteously protecting the subjects, and preserving the people, and not sacrificing his duties, — famed over the three worlds. And munificent, and firm in promise in battle, that best of men ruled there this earth. Nor did he ever meet with a foe that was either his equal or superior. And possessed of friends, and having obedient commanders, and extricating his thorns by his might, that king ruled the earth, even as the lord of celestials ruleth heaven. And surrounded by those counsellors studious of his welfare, and bearing affection towards him, and clever, and competent, that king, by virtue of his prowess in subduing others, resembled the Sun surrounded by his rays.

SECTION VIII.

And although engaged in austerities with the view of having sons born to him, the powerful and high-souled king, had no son capable of perpetuating his line. And mentally turning the matter over, the high-souled one thought, "Why do I not celebrate a horse-sacrifice with the intention obtaining a son?" And that highly-energetic, pious and intelligent monarch, in consultation with all his counsellors of sedate minds, having made up his mind to celebrate the sacrifice, said unto that best of counsellors, Sumantra, — "Do thou speedily summon my spiritual guides, along with the family priests." Thereupon, going out speedily, Sumantra of swift movements called together all the spiritual guides, as well as others versed in the Vedic ritual; *viz.*, Suyajna, and Vāmadeva, and Jāvāli, and Kācyapa, and Vasistha, and other principal twice-born ones. And having paid homage unto them, the virtuous king Daçaratha then spoke unto them these sweet words, consistent with duty and interest, —"Ever pining on account of a son, I know no happiness, — therefore it is my intention that I should celebrate a horse sacrifice. I intend to celebrate it according to the ordinance. Do ye, therefore, consider how I may attain my object." Thereat, the Brāhmanas with Vasistha at their head, exclaiming ing "Well! Well!" approved the words that had fallen from the lips of the monarch. And exceedingly pleased, they spoke unto Daçaratha saying, — "Do thou order the necessary articles, loose the horse, and prepare the sacrificial ground on the north bank of the Sarayu. And, O king, since with the intention of obtaining offspring thou purposest so piously, thou wilt surely obtain sons after thy heart." And hearing these words of the regenerate ones, the king was highly gratified. And with eyes expanded in delight, he spoke unto his ministers, — "Do ye procure the necessary sacrificial articles, according to the injunction of my spiritual preceptors; and loose a horse protected by a competent person, and followed by one of the chief family priests; and do ye prepare the sacrifical ground on the north bank of the

Sarayu; and do ye in due order and according to the ordinance perform the rites required to secure an uninterrupted completion to the ceremony. This ceremony is incapable of being celebrated by every king. Particular care should be taken that the sacrifice is not defective on account of any serious omission; inasmuch as with learned Brahmā-Rākshasas ever on the look-out to espy shortcomings in the ceremony, the performer thereof speedily perishes, should anything take place not consonant to the Ordinance. And do ye possessed of ability so arrange, that this sacrifice may be completed in harmony with the ritual." Thus addressed with due respect, the counsellors listened to the words of the monarch, and said, "So be it."

Then taking the permission of that best of kings, those regenerate ones knowing duty, having blessed the monarch, returned to their respective quarters. And dismissing those Brāhmanas, the king spoke unto his minister, saying, —"Do ye, even as the family priests have ordered, arrange for the sacrifice!" Having said this, that mighty-minded and best of men dismissed his ministers, and himself entered into the inner apartment. And coming there, that lord of men said unto his favourite wives, —"Do ye know it for certain that in order to obtain a son I am going to petform a sacrifice." And hearing those sweet words, the countenances of those shining dames looked resplendent, like lotuses after the cold season is over.

SECTION IX.

Hearing all about it, the king's charioteer addressed the monarch in private, saying, —"Do thou listen to what is related in ancient history, and to what I have heard myself! This horse-sacrifice is enjoined by the family priests; and I have myself heard the following story celebrated in ancient chronicle. And what the worshipful Sanat Kumāra had said formerly in the presence of the saints, applies, O king, the case of thy having a son. "Kācyapa hath a son known by the name of Bibhāndaka. He will get a son called Rhishyasringa. And he will grow up and pass his days in the woods. And that foremost of Brāhmanas will not know aught else save following his father. And, O king, it is rumoured abroad, and also always said by the Vipras, that that high-souled one will practise the two modes[14] of Brahmācharya life. And he will spend some time in serving the sacrificial fire and his famous sire. At this time, the powerful Romapāda of exceeding strength will be famed as king of the Angas. And in consequence of some default on bif part, there will occur in his kingdom a terrible and dreadful drouth, capable of striking terror into all. And filled with grief on account of this drouth, the king will call about him Veda-accomplished Brāhmanas, and speak unto them, saying, —"Ye are conversant with the Vedic ritual and the social duties. Do ye, therefore, tell me how to expiate for this evil." And thus accosted by the king, those excellent Brāhmanas versed in the Vedas, will say unto that ruler of earth, —"Do thou, O monarch, by all means, bring Bibhāndaka's son. And having, O king, brought that Brāhmana versed in the Vedas, Bibhāndaka's son Rhishyasringa, and duly honored him, do thou, O monarch with a concentrated mind, bestow upon him thy daughter Sāntā, according to the ordinance." And hearing those words of theirs, the king will be-

---

[14] Those that assume the staff and the *kamandalu* are reckoned the first order; while those that continue to live with their wives are considered as next in worth—T.

gin to think as to how he can bring over that one endowed with energy. Then in consultation with his counsellors, the prudent king having come to a conclusion, will, honoring them duly, desire his priest and his courtiers to set out in quest of Rhishyasriuga. Thereupon hearing the king's words, with aggrieved hearts, and with heads hanging down, they will beseech the monarch, saying,—"Afraid of the saint, Bibhāndaka, we shall not be able to repair thither." Anon hitting upon the appropriate means, they say,—'We will search for the Vipra, and no blame shall attach unto us.'—

Thus by help of courtezans, the saint's son was brought by the lord of the Angas. And then the god (Indra) poured down showers; and the king conferred on him Sāntā. And now thy son-in-law Rhishyasringa will help thee in obtaining a son. Now I have related unto thee what Sanat Kumāra had communicated." Thereupon king Daçarātha, well pleased, spoke unto Sumantra,—"Do thou now tell me by what means Rhishyasringa was brought over (by the lord of the Angas)."

SECTION X.

Thus asked by the king, Sumantra said these words,—"I will relate unto thee how the counsellors brought Rhishyasringa. Do thou listen with thy counsellors! The priest together with the counsellors spoke unto Romapāda, saying,—'The means that we have hit upon can never fail of effect.' Rhishyasringa hath been brought up in woods; and is engaged in austerities and the study of the Vedas; and is ignorant of the pleasure that ensueth from contact with women. By help of things agreeably ministering unto the senses, and ravishing the soul, we shall bring him to the city. Do thou, therefore, arrange for them! Let courtezans of comely presence, clad in ornaments, repair thither. And if well treated, they will by various means bring him hither.' Hearing this, the king said unto the priest,—'So be it!' and laid the charge upon him,—who, however, made it over to the courtiers. And the latter acted accordingly.

And in accordance with the instructions, the courtesans entered that great forest; and remaining at some distance from the hermitage, endeavoured to meet with the sober son of the saint ever dwelling in the woods. And satisfied with serving his sire, he never strayed from the hermitage; and consequently had never seen men and women, or any other creatures living in cities and towns. And it came to pass that on one occasion, walking about at will, Bibhāndaka's son came to that spot and beheld the courtezans. And excellently attired, and singing in sweet voices, the women said unto the saint's son,—'Who art thou? And what dost thou, O Brāhmana? We wish to learn all this. And why is it that thou rangest alone this far-off forest? Beholding these beautiful damsels never seen before, he from delight hastened to inform them of his lineage, 'My father is Bibhāndaka; and I am his son, having sprung from his loins. My name is Rhishyasringa; and my occupation is known the world over. And this auspicious hermitage hard by belongs to us; and there I shall receive you all in due form.' Hearing the words of the saint's son, they all consented, and the women went to behold that asylum. And when they had come there, the saint's son received them hospitably, saying,—'Here is *Arghya*,'

'Here is water for washing the feet,' 'Here are fruits and roots.' And thereupon they readily received his hospitality. And actuated by the fear of the saint, Bibhāndaka, they bent their minds upon departing soon. And they said,—'Do thou also, O twice-born one, receive from us these excellent fruits! And, good betide thee, O Vipra, do not tarry!' And thereupon, embracing him joyfully, they gave unto him sweetmeats and various kinds of savoury viands. And tasting those things, that one of exceeding energy took them for fruits, never tasted before by the dwellers of the forest. Then, having accosted him, the women, feigning the observance of some vow, went away, inspired with the fear of his father. And when they had gone, that twice-born one, Kācyapa's son, became sad, and from grief of heart went this way and that. And the next day his mind momentarily running upon it, the graceful son of Bibhāndaka, endowed with prowess, came to that spot where he had encountered the comely courtezans, adorned with ornaments. And as soon as they observed him coming, they came forward, and said,—Do thou, O Brāhmana, come unto our hermitage! There are in that asylum diverse kinds of fruits and roots; and there thou wilt surely feed thy fill. Thereupon, hearing those words of theirs capable of influencing the heart, he became bent upon going,—and the women brought him away. And when that high-souled Vipra had been brought over, the good, Indra, suddenly poured forth plenteous showers, enlivening the spirits of men. And when the ascetic had arrived, with showers, the king approached him in humble guise, bending his head to the ground. And he offered him *Arghya,*in due form, and with a collected mind; and asked for his favor, so that wrath could not influence the Vipra. And taking him into the inner apartments, and in due form conferring upon him in sober mood his daughter Sāntā, the king became happy. Thus the highly powerful Rishyasringa together with his wife Sāntā, began to live there, respectfully ministered unto in regard to every desire."

SECTION XI.

And he said again,—"O foremost of monarchs, do thou listen to me as I relate how that intelligent Sanat Kumāra, best of deities, spoke. 'In the line of Ikshwāku will be born a righteous king, named Daçarātha, fair of form, and firm in promise. And that king will contract friendship with the ruler of the Angas. And the latter will have a highly pious daughter, Sāntā by name. And the (old) king of the Angas will have a son, named Romapāda. And repairing unto him, the highly famous king Daçarātha will speak unto Romapāda,—O righteous-souled one I am without issue. Let Sāntā's husband, desired by thee, take charge of this sacrifice of mine, to be celebrated with the object of my obtaining a son to perpetuate the race.—Hearing these words of the king, and having pondered well, he will make over unto him Rhishyasringa of subdued senses, together with Sāntā and his children. And taking that Vipra, that king, his mind free from anxiety, with a glad heart, will prepare for that sacrifice. And king Daçarātha, knowing duty and desirous of fame, with the intention of obtaining offspring and heaven, with joined hands, will appoint that best of Brāhmanas, Rhishyasringa, to conduct the ceremony. And that bringer of good will attain his object at the hands of that foremost of Brāhmanas; and four sons will be born to him of immeasurable prowess, bringing fame unto the family, and known by all.' Thus spoke formerly in the divine age, that worshipful and foremost of deities, Sanat Kumāra. Therefore, do thou, O best of men, repairing thither, accompanied with thy forces and equipage, thyself, O mighty king, bring Rhishyasringa over with due honors." And hearing Sumantra's words, Daçarātha was exceedingly delighted. After hearing these words, and permitted by Vasishtha, he, accompanied with the ladies, and his courtiers, set out for the place where that twice-born one was. And gradually passing by woods and fells, he arrived at the place where that foremost of ascetics was. And coming before that best of regenerate ones, he saw that sage's son near Romapāda, like unto flaming fire. Then the king received him respectfully, and with a delighted mind, on account of the friendship he bore him. And he communicated unto the intelligent son of the saint, the fact of their intimacy, and then the latter paid homage unto Daçarātha. Having passed seven or eight days with Romapāda, receiving high honors, that foremost of men, Dayaratha spoke unto Romapāda, saying,—"Let thy daughter, O king, together with her husband, O lord of men, repair unto my city. I am going to be engaged in a mighty enterprise." Hearing this as to the journey of that intelligent one, the king said unto that Vipra,—"Do thou repair with thy wife!" Thereupon the saint's son, promising to go, said unto the king,—"So be it!" And then with the king's permission, he set out with his wife. And Daçarātha and the puissant Romapāda clasping each other by the palm, and embracing each other in affection, attained excess of joy. Then Raghu's son, bidding farewell unto his friend, set out. And he despatched swift messengers to the citizens, saying,—"Let the entire city be embellished; let it be perfumed with *dhupa*, and watered and decked with pennons." And hearing of the king's approach, the citizens joyfully did every thing as they had been commanded. Then the monarch, with that foremost of Brāhmanas before him, entered the decorated city, to the blares of conchs and drums. And behold irlg that Brāhmana entering the city, duly honored by the prime of men, subservient unto Indra, like unto Kaçyapa's son entering the celestial regions, honored of the thousand-eyed lord of the celestials, ail the citizens rejoiced exceedingly. Then taking him into the inner apartment, and paying him homage according to the ordinance, the king considered himself as having gained his object, in consequence of the presence of that Brāhmana. And all the inmates of the inner apartment, seeing the large-eyed Sāntā thus arrived with her husband, experienced excess of joy. Then honored by them and the king in especial, she happily spent there some time along with that twice-born one.

SECTION XII.

Then after a long while, when the charming spring had appeared on the earth, the king conceived the desire of celebrating the sacrifice. Then bowing down the head unto that Vipra effulgent like a celestial, he appointed him to undertake the ceremony, for the purpose of obtaining offspring to perpetuate his line. Then that Brāhmana said unto that lord of the earth, the king,—"So be it! Do thou order the necessary provisions, loose the horse, and prepare a sacrificial ground on the north bank of the Sarayu." Then the king spoke unto Sumantra, saying,—"O Sumantra, do thou summon speedily Brāhmanas versed in the Vedas and priests professing the Vedānta philosophy—Suyajna, and Vāmadeva, and Jāvāli, and

Kācyapa, and the priest Vasistha, together with other excellent twice-born ones." Thereupon Sumantra endowed with activity, bestirring himself, summoned all those versed in the Vedas. Then, honoring them duly, the virtuous king Daçarātha spoke unto them these amiable words, consistent with duty and interest,—"Aggrieved on account of a son, I have no happiness on earth,—and therefore, I have intended to celebrate a horse-sacrifice. And by the grass of the saint's son, I shall obtain my desire." Thereupon the Brāhmanas with Vasishtha at their head honored the words that fell from the king's lips, saying,—"Well." And the Brāhmanas headed by Rhishyasringa addressed the king, saying,—"Do thou arrange for the provisions, loose the horse, and prepare the sacrificial ground on the north bank of the Sarayu! And since thou purposest so virtuously in obtaining offspring, thou shalt obtain four sons of immeasurable prowess." And hearing those words of the regenerate ones, the king was exceedingly delighted. All cheerfully he spoke these auspicious words to his courtier,—"In accordance with the directions of my spiritual guides, do ye speedily procure these provisions,—loose the horse well protected, and followed by a priest,—and prepare the sacrificial ground on the north bank of the Sarayu. And do ye perform the ceremonies capable of securing the rites from disturbance. Surely every king is competent to perform this sacrifice. Yet care must be taken that no default occurs in it. For flaws in this foremost of sacrifices are watched by learned Brahmā-Rākshasas. And should it come to be celebrated in violation of the ordinance, the performer thereof shall meet with instant destruction. And do ye so order that this sacrifice of mine may be completed according to the prescribed ritual." Thereupon honoring those words of the king, the ministers did as ordered. And having eulogized the king knowing duty, the twice-born ones, with the Monarch's leave, departed for their respective quarters. And when the Vipras had gone, the mighty- minded lord of men dismissing his counsellors, entered the inner apartment.

SECTION XIII.

And when after a full one year, spring had again appeared on the face of the earth, the puissant king, intent upon getting offspring through the horse-sacrifice, saught Vasishtha's side. And having saluted Vasishtha and duly paid him homage, he humbly spoke unto that best of twice-born ones, with the intention of having offspring. "Do thou, O Brāhmana, undertake to perform this sacrifice of mine, according to the ordinance, O foremost of ascetics! And do thou order so that no impediment may happen to the sacrifice! Thou art my kind friend, and prime and mighty spiritual guide. Engaged in it, thou wilt have to bear the entire burden of the ceremony." Thereupon that best of Brāhmanas said,—"So be it! I will do all that thou askest." He then said unto old Brāhmanas well-up in sacrificial affairs, and experienced car-makers, and highly pious aged people, and servants, carrying on the ceremonial operations till the end, and artists, and carpenters, and diggers, and astrologers, and artizans, and dancers, and conductors of theatres, and pure and learned persons variously versed in knowledge,—"Do ye, in obedience to the royal mandate, engage in the sacrificial work! And fetch bricks by thousands! Do ye raise structures for the kings, commanding every convenience! And do ye rear goodly and comfortable buildings by hundreds for the Brāhmanas, replenished with various meats and drinks. Ye should provide spacious apartments for the citizens and the dwellers of provinces,—and separate quarters for the princes, coming from foreign parts; and stables for horses, and dressing- rooms,—and wide apartments for native and foreign warriors. And dwellings filled with diverse kinds of viands, and commanding everything desirable,—and mansions for the lower orders of the citizens, exceedingly beautiful to behold. And meats should be duly dispensed with respect, and not in the indifference of festive occasions,—so that all may regard themselves as honorably entertained. None should be disregarded out of lust or passion. Those persons, and artizans, that will labor eagerly in the sacrifice should by turns, be especially entertained; and servants, who, being entertained with gifts, do every thing completely, and omit nothing. And do ye, with hearts mollified by love, act so, that all our friends be well pleased with us."

Then they approached Vasishtha, saying,—"Everything hath been performed properly, without anything being left out. And what thou sayest shall be performed, and nothing omitted." Then summoning Sumantra, Vasishtha said these words,—"Do thou invite all those kings that are pious,—and Brāhmanas, and Kshatriyas and Sudras, by thousands. And do thou with due honors bring people from all countries. And, with proper honor thyself bring the righteous, truthful, and heroic Janaka, lord of Mithilā. And it is because he is our old friend that I first mention him. Then do thou thyself bring the amiable and ever fair-spoken lord of Kāsi, of execellent character, resembling a celestial. Then do thou bring hither along with his son, the highly-pious, old king of Kekaya, who is the father in-law of this best of monarchs! Then do thou bring with due honors the puissant king of Kocala, and that mighty archer, the illustrious Romāpada, the friend of that lion of a king, and that foremost of men—the heroic, and highly generous lord of Magadha, versed in all branches of learning. And in accordance with the mandate of the king, do thou invite the foremost monarchs! And do thou summon the kings of the East, of the Sindhu and Sauvira countries, and of Saurashtra, and of the South! And do thou speedily bring those monarchs that are attached unto us, together with their friends and followers. Do thou in obedience to the mandate of the monarch, bring over these, despatching dignified emissaries!"

Having heard those words of Vasishtha, Sumantra speedily ordered faithful persons anent the bringing over of the kings. And the virtuous Sumantra, in accordance with the injunction of the ascetic, himself speedily set out for the purpose of bringing the monarchs. And then the servants came and informed the intelligent Vasishtha as to the articles that had been got ready for the sacrifice. Then well-pleased that best of twice-born ones, the ascetic Vasishtha, said unto them,—"Do not give away disrespectfully or lightly. A gift bestowed with disrespect, indubitably destroyeth the giver."

Then for several days, kings began to pour into Daçarātha's city daily and nightly, bringing with them various kinds of gems. Thereupon Vasishtha well-pleased said unto the king,—"O best of men, obeying thy mandate the kings have come here; and I too, according to merit, have received those excellent kings with respect. And ev thing hath been carefully made ready for the sacrifice the persons concerned. Do thou, therefore, repair to ill sacrificial ground, for performing the sacrifice. And, 9 foremost of monarclis, it behoveth thee to view the. platffc filled with all desirable objects, and looking as if preparedly imagination herself."

Then in accordance with the injunctions of both Vasishtha and Rhishyasringa, the king came to the sacrificial spot on a day presided over by an auspicious star. Then, with Rhishyasringa at their head, Vasishtha and the other principal Brāhmanas wending to the sacrificial ground, began the ceremony, according to the ordinance; and in due form. And the auspicious king, in company with his wives, was initiated into the ceremony.

SECTION XIV.

And after the expiry of full one year, when the sacrifcial horse had returned, the sacrifice of the king commenced on the north bank of the Sarayu. And with Rhishyasringa at their head, the principal twice born ones began the proceedings in that mighty horse-sacrifice of that high-souled monarch. And the priests, each duly and according to the ordinance performing his proper part, engaged in the ceremony in consonance with the scriptures. And the regenerate ones, having performed the *pravargya* as well as the *upasada* according to the ordinance, duly completed the additional ceremonies. Then, worshipping the deities with glad hearts, those foremost of ascetics duly performed the morning ablutions and the other prescribed rites. The oblations of clarified butter first having been offered unto Indra, according to the ritual, the king with a purified heart performed his ablutions. And then the mid-day ablutions took place in proper sequence. And those foremost of Brāhmanas, in due form, and according to the ordinance, officiated at the third bath of that high-souled monarch. And the priests presided over by Rhishyasringa, invoked Sakra and the other deities, reciting measured *mantras*. And the sacrificial priests, chaunting sweet *Sâmas* and soft mantras, duly invoking the dwellers of the celestial regions, offered each his share of the oblations. And no part of the ceremony was performed improperly, or left out,—and every thing was satisfactorily celebrated with *mantras*. And on that day no Brāhmana ever felt tired, or hungry; and there was none that was not learned, or that was not followed by an hundred persons. And Brāhmanas, and Sudras having among them ascetics, and Sramanas, and the aged, and the infirm, and women, and children, were continually fed. And although they ate their fill, yet they knew no repletion. And "Give food, and clothes of various kind"—(was heard all around). And those employed in the task gave away profusely. And every day food dressed properly in due form was to be seen in countless heaps resembling hills. And men and women coming from various countries to the sacrifice of that high-souled one were excellently entertained with meats and drinks. And the foremost regenerate ones said,—"The viands have been prepared in the prescribed form, and they taste excellent. We have been gratified. Good betide thee!" All this was heard by that descendant of Raghu. And persons adorned with ornaments distributed the victuals among the Brāhmanas, and they were assisted by others beaming jewelled pendants. And in the interval between the completion of one bath and the beginning of the next, mild and eloquent Vipras, desirous of victory, engaged in various disputations. And every day in that sacrifice, skilful Brāhmanas, engaged in the ceremony, did every thing, according to the ritual. And there was no twice-born one that was not versed in the Vedas and the Vedāngas, or that did not observe vows, or that was not profoundly learned,—nor did any assist at the sacrifice that could not argue ably. And when the time came for planting the *Yupas*, persons cognizant of arts and sacrificial rites, prepared six *Yupas* of *Vilwa*, as many of catechu, and as many of *Palasa*, and one of *Sleshmataka*, and two of *Devadaru* well-made and measuring two outstretched arms. Persons versed in the arts and science of sacrifice constructed these *Yupas*. And at the time of throwing up the *Yupas*, for embellishing the sacrifice, these one and twenty *Yupas*, each measuring one and twenty *Aratnis*, having eight angles, and smooth-faced were decked out in one and twenty pieces of cloth, and were firmly planted with due ceremonies by artizans. And being wrapped up in cloths, and worshipped with flowers, they looked like the seven Rishis appearing in the welkin. And an adequate number of bricks was also duly made (for the ceremony.) And Brāhmanas accomplished in the arts constructed the sacrificial fire-place with those bricks. And that fire-place of that lion among kings, set by skilful Brāhmanas, consisting on three sides of eighteen bricks, looked like the golden-winged Garura. And for the purpose of sacrificing them unto the respective deities were collected beasts and reptiles, and birds, and horses, and aquatic animals. And the priests sacrificed all these in proper form. And to these *Yupas* were bound three hundred beasts, as well as the foremost of the best horses belonging to king Daçarātha. Then Kaucalyā, having performed the preliminary rites, with three strokes slew that horse, experiencing great glee. And with the view of reaping merit Kaucalyā, with an undisturbed heart passed one night with that horse furnished with wings. And the *Hotâs* and *Adhwaryus*, and the *Uâgatas* joined the king's *Vâvâtâ* along with his *Mahishi* and *Parivriti*[15] And priests of subdued senses, well-up in sacrificial rites, began to offer oblations with the fat of the winged-horse, according to the ordinance. And that lord of men, desirous of removing his sins, at the proper time smelt the odour of the smoke arising from the fat, agreeably to the scriptures. And then sixteen sacrificial priests in the prescribed form offered the various parts of the horse unto the fire. It is customary in other sacrifices to offer the oblations by means of a *Plaksha* bough; but in the horse-sacrifice a cane is used instead. The horse-sacrifice, according to the Kalpa Sutras and the Brāhmanas, extend over three days. There after, on the first day was the *Chatushtoma* celebrated; and on the second the *Uktha*,—and on the third the *Atiratra*. And then the *Jyotishtoma*, and then *Ayushtoma*, and the *Atiratra* and the *Abhijit*, and the *Viswajit*, and the *Aptoryama*—all these various great sacrifices were celebrated with due rites. And in this mighty horse-sacrifice founded of yore by Sayambhu, that perpetuator of his line, the king, bestowed the Eastern quarter on his chief sacrificial priest, the Western on his *Adhwaryu*, the Southern on Brahmā, and the Northern on the *Udgath*, as *Dakshinas*. And having completed that sacrifice, that perpetuator of his race, and foremost of men, the king, conferred on the priests the earth; and having conferred it, that auspicious descendant of Iskhāku experienced high delight. And then the priests spoke unto that monarch, who had all his sins

---

[15] The Kshetriya kings could marry wives from among Kshetriyas, Vaishyas and Sudras. The Kshetriya wife is called *Mahishee,* the Vaishya wife *Vâvâtâ* and the Sudra wife *Parivriti.*—T.

purged off, saying,—"Thou alone art worthy to protect the entire world. We do not want the earth; nor can we rule it, being, O lord of Earth, constantly engaged in Vaidika studies. Do thou, therefore, confer upon us something instead, as the price thereof. Do thou confer upon us gems, or gold, or kine, or anything else, for, O foremost of monarchs, we do not want Earth." Thus addressed by the Brāhmanas versed in the Veda, that best of kings bestowed upon them ten lacs of kine, and ten *Kotis* of gold, and forty of silver. Then those priests in a body, accepting the wealth, brought it unto the ascetic Rhishyasringa and the intelligent Vasishtha. Then having receieived each his share, those foremost of regenerate ones were exceedingly pleased, and said,—"We have been highly gratified." Then unto those Brāhmanas that had come there, the king with due regard gave *Kotis* of gold. And unto a certain poor twice-born one that asked for gifts, the descendant of Raghu gave an excellent ornament from his own arm. And, when the regenerate ones were thus properly gratified, that one cherishing the Brāhmanas, with senses intoxicated by excess of joy, reverentially bowed unto them. And thereupon the Brāhmanas uttered various blessings upon that generous king, bending low to the earth. Then having celebrated that excellent and sin-destroying sacrifice, bringing heaven, and incapable of being celebrated by foremost monarchs, king Daçarātha, well pleased, spoke unto Rhisyasinga, saying,—"0 thou of excellent vows, it behoveth thee to do that whereby my line may increase." Thereupon the best of Brāhmanas said,—"Be it so! Unto thee, O king, will be born four sons,—perpetuators of their race." Hearing these sweet words of his, that foremost of monarchs bended low unto him with controlled faculties, and experienced the excess of joy. And then that high-souled one again spoke unto Rhishyasringa.

SECTION XV.

Then that one of capacious intelligence, versed in the Vedas, having pondered for a time, and regained his senses, returned unto the king this excellent answer,—"On thy behalf, and with the view of obtaining sons for thee, I will by help of *mantras* laid down in the Atharva Veda, duly celebrate the famous ceremony, capable of crowning thee with offspring." And then with the view of obtaining sons (for the king), that effulgent one set about the son-conferring ceremony; and in accordance with the ordinance, and with *mantras*, offered oblations unto the sacrificial fire. And the deities, with the *Gandharbas*, and the *Siddhas*, and the principal saints, assembled there duly, with the object of each obtaining his share of the offerings. And having duly assembled there, the deities addressed these words unto Brahmā, the lord of creatures,—"O thou possessed of the six attributes, through thy grace, a Rākshasa named Rāvana oppresses us all by his prowess,—nor can we baffle him. And, O lord, as thou hast well-pleased conferred on him a boon, we always suffer him in deference to it. And the wicked-minded one harasseth the three worlds furnished with prosperity, and beareth ill-will unto them. And blinded by the boon he hath received, that irrepressible one intends to bring down the lord himself of the celestials, and the Yakshas, and the Gandharbas, and the Brāhmanas, and the Asuras. And the Sun doth not burn him, or the Wind blow about him; and at sight of him, that one engarlanded with billows, the Ocean, dares not stir. Therefore, great is the fear that afflicteth us, coming from that Rākshasa of dreadful appearance. And O lord, it behoves thee to devise some means for destroying him." Thus addressed by the deities in a body, he said,—"Alas! I have, however, decided on the means of destroying that wicked-souled one. He had asked,—'May I be incapable of being slain by *Gandharbas*, and *Yakshas*, and gods, and *Rākshasas*!'—whereat I said,—'Be it so!' Through disdain, the Rākshasa did not at that time mention men. Therefore, by men alone he is capable of being slain; nor can his end be compassed by any other means." Hearing this welcome speech uttered by Brahmā, the deities and the Maharshis became exceedingly delighted. At this juncture, that lord of the universe, the highly- effulgent Vishnu, clad in yellow apparel, and bearing in his hands the conch, the discus, and the mace, and adorned with burnished *Keyuras*[16] arrived there, riding Vinatā's son; like the Sun riding the clouds. And worshipped by the foremost of the celestials, he drew near Brahmā, and sat down a collected mind. And bending low before him, the deities spake unto him, saying,—"O Vishnu, for the benefit of the worlds, we shall appoint thee to some work. Do thou, O lord, dividing thyself into four, O Vishnu, become born as sons in the three wives, resembling Modesty, Auspiciousness, and Fame,—of Ayodhyā's lord, king Daçarātha, cognisant of Duty, and munificent, and possessing energy, and like unto a Maharshi. Do thou, O Vishnu, becoming man, slay in battle this thorn of the worlds; the pampered Rāvana, incapable of being slain by the gods; for the foolish Rākshasha, by virtue of sublimated prowess, baffles the deities, and the *Gandharbas*, and the *Siddhas*, and the foremost of saints. And by him bereft of the sense of right and wrong, have saints and *Gandharbas* and *Apsarās* sporting in the groves of Nandana, been wantonly slain. It is to compass his death that accompanied by the ascetics, we have come hither: it is for this that the *Siddhas* and the *Gandharbas* and the *Yakshas* have taken refuge in Thee! Thou O God, art the prime way of us all, O repressor of foes! Do thou, for bringing destruction unto the enemies of the gods, turn thy thoughts to being born as man." Thus besought that foremost of gods and chief of celestials, Vishnu, worshipped of all creatures, addressed the assembled deities, following Duty, with the Grand-sire at their head, saying,—"Do ye renounce fear! For your behoof, slaying in battle the wily and irrepressible Rāvana, dreadful unto the saints and the celestials, together with his sons, and grandsons, and friends, and counsellors, and relatives, and acquaintances, I will abide among mortals, ruling this earth for ten thousand and as many hundred years." Having thus conferred a boon upon the gods, the god Vishnu of subdued soul fell to thinking as to the place where he would be born among men. Then that one of eyes resembling lotus-petals, dividing self into four parts, chose even king Daçarātha for his father. Thereat the celestials and the saints and the *Gandharbas* and the *Rudras* and the *Apsarās* hymned the Slayer of Madhu in excellent hymns:

"Do thou utterly uproot the haughty Rāvana of fierce prowess and enhanced insolence—that foe of the lord of celestials, who is the occasion of the tears of the three worlds,[17] and dreadful unto ascetics; Slaying that one of terrible prowess, who distresses the three worlds, with his forces and friends, do thou, O foremost of gods, thy fever of heart removed, repair unto the celestial regions protected by

[16] A bracelet worn on the upper arm.—T.
[17] Lit. the thorns of pious ascetics.—T.

thee and purged of all its faults and sins."

SECTION XVI.

Thus besought by the foremost of the celestials, that[18] searcher of hearts, Vishnu, although cognizant of the means whereby Rāvana was to be destroyed, spake unto the gods these amiable words, —"What, ye gods, is the means of compassing the destruction of that lord of the Rākshasas, by adopting which I could slay that thorn of the ascetics?" Thus addressed, the deities answered Vishnu, incapable of deterioration, saying, —"Assuming the form of a human being, do thou in battle slay Rāvana! He, O repressor of foes, had for a long course of time performed rigid austerities; and thereat, that creator of all, the first-create Brahmā was well pleased. And propitiated by his penances, the Master conferred a boon on the Rākshasa to the effect that, save man, no fear should come to him from the various beings. And in the matter of that boon-bestowing, man had formerly been disregarded by (Rāvana). And puffed up with pride in consequence of the boon he received from the Grand-sire, he commits ravages upon the three worlds and carries away the fair sex by violence. Therefore, O subduer of enemies, we have even fixed upon man for bringing about his death." Hearing this speech of the celestials, Vishnu of subdued soul chose even king Daçarātha for his father. And at that time, eagerly wishing to have sons, that destroyer of enemies, the effulgent king Daçarātha, who was sonless, was celebrating the sacrifice that conferreth male offspring. Then, having ascertained the course to follow, Vishnu, having greeted the Grand-sire, vanished there, worshipped by the deities and the Maharshis.

And then himself bearing in his hands a capacious vessel made of burnished gold, with a silver cover, —dear like unto a spouse, and resembling the divine Creative energy, filled with celestial *Pāyasa,*[19], from out the sacrificial fire of Daçarātha initiated into the ceremony, there arose a mighty being, of unparalleled prowess, high energy, and huge strength, black, and wearing a crimson apparel, with a red face, uttering the blares of a trumpet, and having a body covered with leonine hair, having whiskers and an excellent head of hair, furnished with auspicious marks, and adorned with celestial ornaments, and resembling a mountain-peak, and bearing the prowess of a flaming tiger, and like unto the Sun or tongues of flaming fire. And with his eyes fixed upon Daçarātha, he addressed the king, saying, —"O monarch, take thou me as a person commisioned by *Prajāpati.*" Hearing him speak thus, Daçarātha, with joined hands, said, —'Lord, art thou welcome? What can I do for thee?" Thereupon, that person despatched by *Prajāpati* again spake thus, —"O king, having adored the deities, thou hast to-day obtained this. Do thou foremost of kings, accept this excellent and divinly-prepared Pāyasa, conferring sons, health, and affluence, —which thou art to give unto thy worthy consorts, saying, —*Partake it.* Through them thou wilt, O monarch, obtain sons, —for obtaining whom thou hast performed this sacrifice." Thereupon, saying, —"So be it," the lord of men delightedly placed that divinely-bestowed golden vessel filled

[18] Nara means a multitude, and Ayana, dwelling-place. He whose dwelling-place is a multitude, is Nārayāna. Metaphorically, the word means evidently, the *Searcher of hearts.*—T.

[19] A preparation of milk, and sugar.—T.

with the celestial *Pāyasa* upon his head. And having saluted that wonderful being of gracious presence, he in excess of joy began to go round him again and again. Then Daçarātha, having received that divinely-prepared *Pāyasa*, waxed exceeding glad; like unto a pauper attaining plenty. Then that highly effulgent being of a wonderful form, having performed that mission of his, vanished even there. And Daçarātha's inner apartment, being graced with the rays of joy, looked like unto the welkin flooded with the lovely beams of the autumnal moon. Then entering the inner apaitment, he spake unto Kausalya, saying,—"Take thou this *Pāyasa*; for this will make thee bear a son." Having said this,the king offered unto her a portion of this *Pāyasa*. Then he conferred upon Sumitrā a fourth of it. Then in order that she might have a son, king Daçarātha made over unto Kaikeyi an equal portion of what remained. And then having reflected, the mighty-minded one gave unto Sumitrā the remaining portion of the *Pāyasa* resembling ambrosia. Thus the king dispensed the *Pāyasa* unto each and all of his wives. And those foremost wives of the king, having received that *Pāyasa*, became exceedingly delighted, and considered themselves as highly honored. Then those excellent consorts of the lord of earth, having separately partaken of that choice *Pāyasa*, shortly bore offspring, resmbling fire or the Sun. And the king, beholding those wives of his bearing children, obtained his desire and became delighted; even as that foremost of the celestials, Indra, while being worshipped by the *Siddhas* and the ascetics.

SECTION XVII.

When Vishnu had accepted the sonship of that high- souled king, the self-create Lord addressed the celestials, saying,—"For assisting the heroic Vishnu firm in promise, always seeking the welfare of us all, do ye create powerful beings, assuming shapes at will, cognizant of illusions, heroic, furnished with the celerity of the wind, versed in morality, possessing intelligence, like unto Vishnu in prowess, unslayable, knowing the ways and means (of war and peace) gifted with excellent bodies, capable of resisting all weapons, and resembling immortals. And from forth the bodies of the foremost *Apsaris*, and *Gandharbis*, and *Yakskis*, and *Panagis*, and *Rikshis*[20] and *Vidhyddharis*, and *Kinnaris*, and *Vanaris*[21] do ye produce sons wearing the shapes of monkeys. Formerly I had created that foremost of bears, Jāmbuvāna, who suddenly came out of my mouth as I was yawning." Hearing this mandate of Him possessed of the six attributes, they began to produce sons endowed with monkey- forms. And high-souled ascetics, and *Siddhas*, and *Vidhādharas*, and *Uragas*, and *Chāranas*, generated heroic sons,—rangers of woods. And Indra begat as his son that foremost of monkeys, Vāli, resembling the Mahendra hill, and that best of those imparting heat, the Sun, Sugriva. And Vrihaspati begat the mighty ape named Tārā, the most excellent and intelligent of the prime monkeys. And the Bestower of riches begat as his son the graceful ape Gandhamādana. And Vicwakarma begat that mighty monkey named Nala; and Agni begat as his son the powerful and graceful Nila in effulgence like unto the fire, who surpassed even his sire in energy, prowess, and renown. And the beautiful Acwins, endowed with the wealth of loveliness, begat Maindra and Dwivida. And Varuna begat the monkey

[20] She-bears.—T.
[21] She-monkeys.—T.

named Sushena; and Paryyanya begat Sarava, possessed of great strength. And the Wind god begat the graceful monkey named Hanumān, endeued with a frame hard as adamant; in fleetness like unto Vinatā's offspring; and the most intelligent as well as the most powerful amongst all the principal monkeys. Thus produced, there suddenly came into being by thousands, mighty bears, and monkeys, and *Gopuchchhas*,[22] of immeasurable strength, and heroic, and powerful, assuming shapes at will, endowed with bodies resembling elephants of hills,—even those who would engage in compassing the destruction of the Ten-headed one. And the sons of the deities retained distinctly the respective hues, forms, and prowess, that characterized their several sires. And those that sprang from the Golangulas,[23] possessed even more than the might of the gods. Likewise, on *Rikshis* and *Kinnaris* were gladly begot thousands upon thousands of monkeys, by gods, and *Maharshis*, and *Gandarbas*, and *Tarkshyas*, and famous *Yakshas*, and *Nagās*, and *Kimpurushas*,[24] and *Siddhas* and *Vidyādharas*, and *Uragas*. And upon the principal *Apsaris*, and the *Vidyādharis*, and the daughters of the *Nāgas*, and the *Gandarbis* were begot by the *Chāranas* as sons, heroic monkeys of gigantic bodies, ranging the forests and living on fruits and roots. And all these monkeys were endowed with strength; and could assume shapes and repair everywhere, at will. And they were like unto lions and tigers, both in pride and in prowess. And they faught with crags and hurled hills. And they faught with nails and teeth,—and were accomplished in all weapons. And they could move the largest hills; and crush the fixed trees; and with their impetus, vex that lord of rivers—the Ocean. And they could with their kicks rend the Earth, and swim over the mighty main. And they could penetrate into the welkin,—and capture the clouds. And they could subdue mad elephants ranging the forest. And with their roars, they could bring down birds singing. Thus came into being *Kotis* of high-souled leaders of monkey-herds, assuming forms at will. And these became the leaders of the principal monkey-herds; and they, in their turn, generated heroic monkeys, the foremost of the leaders of herds.

Some of these monkeys began to dwell on the top of the Rikshavāna mountain; while others inhabited various other mountains and forests. And all the leaders of monkey- herds stayed with those brothers,—Sugriva, the son of the Sun-god and Vali, that of Sakra,—and also with Nala, and Nila, and Hanumān, and other leaders of monkey-herds. And endowed with the might of Garura, and accomplished in fight, they ranged around, pounding lions, and tigers, and mighty *Uragas*. And the mighty-armed Vali of great prowess and redoubtable strength protected by virtue of the energy of his arms *Rikshas*, and *Gopuchchhas*, and monkeys. And this earth, furnished with mountains, and forests, and oceans, began to teem with those heroic lords of leaders of monkey- herds, inhabiting different places, bearing characteristic marks, resembling masses of clouds, or mountain-peaks, possessed of mighty strength, and of terrible bodies and visages,—in order that they might assist Rāma.

---

[22] Cow-tailed monkeys—T.
[23] Cow-tailed monkeys.—T.
[24] Being half-man and half-beast.—T.

SECTION XVIII.

When the horse-sacrifice of the high-souled Daçaratha had been completed, the immortals, accepting each his share, returned whence they had come. And the monarch, having observed all the rules of initiation, entered the palace with his equipage and retinue. And the lords of the earth, having been received suitably by the king, with glad hearts set out for their own countries, saluting that foremost of ascetics (Rhishyasringa). And clad in bright apparel, the delighted forces belonging to those graceful kings repairing to their own homes, looked exceedingly beautiful. When the lords of the earth had gone away, the graceful king Daçaratha re-entered his palace, with the foremost of regenerate ones at his head. And followed by the intelligent monarch with his retinue, Rhishyasringa, having been duly honored, set out with Sāntā. Having thus dismissed them all, the king, his object attained, began to dwell there happily, expecting sons.

And then when tbe six seasons had rolled away after the completion of the sacrifice, in the twelfth month, on the ninth lunar day, under the influence of the Punarvasu asterism, when the Sun, the Moon, *Saturn, Jupiter,* and *Venus* were at *Arius, Capricorn, Libra, Cancer,* and *Pisces,* —and when Jupiter had arisen with the Moon at Cancer, Kaucalyā gave birth to that lord of the universe, bowed unto by all the worlds, Rāma, the descendant of Ikshwāku, furnished with excellent marks,— the one half of Vishnu,—exceedingly righteous, with rosy eyes, and mighty arms, and crimson nether lip, and endowed with a voice like the sound of a kettledrum. Then on having given birth to that son of immeasurable prowess, Kaucalyā looked resplendent, like Aditi on having brought forth that foremost of celestials—the wielder of the thunder-bolt. And then was born of Kaikeyi, Bharata, having truth for prowess, endowed with all the virtues, and the very fourth part of Vishnu. And then Sumitrā gave birth unto Lakshmana and Satrughna, heroic, and skilled in all weapons, and endowed with the half of Vishnu. And Bharata of purged intelligence was born under the asterism *Pushyā,* when the Sun had entered *Pisces;* while the two sons of Sumitrā were born when the Sun arose in Cancer, under the asterism of *Aslesha.*[25]

And thus were separately born four high-souled sons unto the king, crowned with qualities, and graceful, and in loveliness resembling the constellations *Prostha-pada*[26] Thereat the *Gandharbas* began to chaunt sweetly, and the *Apsarās* to dance. And the celestial kettledrums sounded; and there showered down blossoms from the sky. And high festivities were commenced by the multitude in Ayodhyā. And the spacious highways became filled with players and dancers, glittering with all kinds of gems, and resounding with the music of singers and performers on instruments. And the king bestowed gifts upon bards and genealogists and penegyrists, and he also gave kine by thousands to Brāhmanas.

And when the eleventh day had gone by, the king performed the Naming ceremony of his sons. And experiencing great delight, Vasishtha conferred the names. And the high- souled eldest one was called Rāma; and Kaikeyi's son was called Bharata; and Sumitrā's son was called Lakshmana,—and the last was named Sa-

---

[25] The ninth lunar mansion.—T.

[26] Otherwise called *Uttarabhādrapada* and *Purvabhādrapada.*—T.

trughna. And the king fed the Brāhmanas as well as the inhabitants rural and urban; and he bestowed heaps of jewels upon Brāhmanas. Thus did he celebrate the natal rites of the princes. And among all those princes, the eldest, Rāma, like unto Ketu,[27] and the special delight of his father, became the object of general regard, even as the self-create Himself. And all of them were versed in the Vedas, and heroic, and intent upon the welfare of others. And all were accomplished in knowledge; and endowed with virtues. And among them all, the exceedingly puissant Rāma, having truth for prowess, was the desire of every one, and spotless like unto the Moon himself.[28] He could ride on elephants and horses, and was an adept in managing cars. And he was ever engaged in the study of arms, and aye occupied in ministering unto his sire. And even from early youth, that enhancer of auspiciousness, Lakshmana, was ever attached unto his eldest brother Rāma, that delight of all. And like unto another life of Rāma, Lakshmana furnished with auspiciousness was in everything attentive to Rāma's wishes, even at the neglect of his own person. And that foremost of persons did not even attain sleep without Rāma's company,—nor did he partake any sweetmeat that was offered, unless Rāma partook it with him. And when mounted on horse-back, Rāghava went a-hunting, Lakshmana went at his back bow in hand, protecting him. And that younger brother of Lakshmana, Satrughna, likewise became ever dearer unto Bharata than life itself.

And on account of those exalted and well-beloved sons of his, Daçarātha experienced the excess of joy, like unto the Grand-sire on account of the celestials. And when they came to be furnished with knowledge, and crowned with virtues, and endowed with bashfulness and fame, and to attain wisdom in everything, and to be far-sighted,Daçarātha, the father of such powerful and flamingly effulgent sens, became delighted even like that lord of worlds—Brahmā. And those best of men, ever engaged in the study of the Vedas, were accomplished in the art of archery— and always intent upon ministering unto their father.

And once upon a time, when the virtuous king Daçarātha, surrounded by his priests and friends, was reflecting about the nuptials of his sons, unto that high-souled one engaged in thought in the midst of his counsellors came the mighty ascetic Viswamitra. And desirous of seeing the king, he said unto the warders,—"Do ye speedily announce that I, Gadhi's son, sprung in the Kuçika line, have come!" Hearing those words of his, they urged on by them, all hurriedly began to run towards the royal chambers. And coming to the royal apartments, they communicated to Ikshwāku's descendant the arrival of the ascetic Viswāmitra. Hearing those words of theirs, Daçarātha surrounded by his priests, went out delightedly to meet him, like Vāsava going out to meet Vrihashpati.[29] And having come unto that ascetic observing vows and of flaming energy, the monarch with a cheerful countenance offered him the *Arghya*. And there- upon, having accepted the king's *Arghya* in accordance with the ordinance, he enquired of the lord of men as to his continued prosperity and peace. And the exceedingly virtuous descendant of Kuçika

[27] The ninth of the planets.—T.

[28] The Moon is a male in Sanskrit.—T.

[29] The text has *Brahmānam*. Vrihashpati is the Brahmā of the gods—*Vrhashpatir devanam Brahmā*,—according to Sruti—T.

asked the king concerning the welfare of the exchequer, and the provinces; and the peace of his friends and acquaintances. "And are thy captains submissive: and hast thou vanquished thy foes? And hast thou performed well the human and the divine rites?" And approaching Vasishtha and the other anchorites, that foremost of ascetics of exalted piety duly asked them touching their welfare. And having been properly received by the monarch, they with glad hearts entered the royal residence, and sat them down according to precedence. Then gladly worshipping the mighty ascetic, Viswāmitra, the exceedingly generous king, well-pleased, addressed him, saying, —"Like unto the obtaining of ambrosia, like unto a shower in a land suffering from drouth, like unto the birth of sons of worthy wives to him without issue, like unto the recovery of a lost thing, yea, —like unto the dawning of a mighty joy, I consider this thy arrival. illustrious ascetic, thou art well come. What is even that which is nearest to thy heart. What shall I do for thee, experiencing sincere pleasure? Thou, O Brāhmana, art worthy of my best services. By luck it is that, O bestower of honor, I have gained thee. To-day my birth hath been crowned with fruit—to day hath my life attained its object. And truly yesternight hath been succeeded by an auspicious morning, since I have beheld thee. Having first attained exceeding effulgence by virtue of austerities performed for obtaining the title of *Rājarshi*, thou hast afterwards obtained the status of a *Brahmārshi*. Thou art worthy of manifold homage from me. This thy exceedingly holy arrival appeareth wonderful. O lord, by beholding thee, surely my body hath been rendered pure. Tell me, what is it that thou wouldst have, —and what is the purpose of thy coming? I wish that I may be obliged by doing thy will. And, O thou of excellent vows, thou ought not to hesitate. I will every way accomplish thy will for thou art my god. O regnerate one, surely great prosperity cometh to me in consequence of thy coming, in as much as it shall be the means of bringing me entire and excellent merit, O Brāhmana!" Hearing this soul-soothing, ear-charming, and free-humble speech that was uttered, that illustrious prime of ascetics crowned with virtues, and furnished with all perfections, experienced exceeding delight.

SECTION XIX.

Hearing those astonishing words of that lion-like king, the highly-energetic Viswāmitra with his down standing on end, said, —"O foremost of kings, sprung from an illustrious line, and having Vasishtha for thy guide, these words become thee alone on earth and no one else. Do thou, O best of kings, ascertain thy course in respect of the matter I bear in my heart; and do thou prove firm in promise! For celebrating a sacrifice, I, O foremost of men, abide by some prescribed course. And it comes to pass that two Rākshasas assuming shapes at will, have become bent upon disturbing the ceremony. And in that sacrifice which I have determined to bring to a completion, and which is on the eve of being completed, both these Rākshasas, Maricha and Suvihu, accomplished in arms and possessed of prowess, shower flesh and gore upon the altar. And on that ceremony being thus disturbed and my purpose thus frustrated, I considered my labors as all lost, and, therefore, have left my country in dejection. And, O monarch, I cannot bring myself to vent my wrath; for such is the nature of that business, that it is not proper for one engaged in it to utter a curse. Therefore, O foremost of monarchs, it behoves thee to grant me thy eldest son, the heroic Rāma of genuine prowess, with the side-locks. By virtue of his own divine energy, he, being protected by me, is capable of even destroying those Rākshasas disturbing the ceremony. And I will, without doubt,confer upon him manifold blessings,—by means of which he will secure the golden opinions of the three worlds. And encountering Rāma,they will by no means be able to stand him, nor is there any other who dares to slay them. And puffed up with energy, they have become ensnared at the hands of Kāla,[30] —and, O best of monarchs, they are no match for Rāma. Nor, king, ought thou to indulge in paternal affection. For ten nights only Rāma is to remain there, with the object of slaying those foes to my sacrifice, those Rākshasas disturbing the rites. I tell thee, do thou consider the Rākshasas as already slain. I know full well Rāma of sterling prowess,—as also the highly-energetic Vasishtha and the other ascetics present here. And if thou, O king, set thy heart upon acquiring religious merit and high fame on earth, do thou then grant me Rāma! And, O Kākutstha,[31] if thy counsellors together with the Brāhmanas having Vasishtha at their head, consent, do thou then dismiss Rāma! Even this is my wish,—and he also hath come of age. Do thou, therefore, part with thy son, the lotus-eyed Rāma, for the ten days of the sacrifice! Do thou act so, O descendant of Raghu, that the time appointed for the ceremony may not be overpassed. Good betide thee! Let not thy mind indulge in grief!"

Having said these words consistent with virtue and interest, the mighty-minded and highly-powerful Viswāmitra paused. And hearing the auspicious words of Viswāmitra, that foremost of kings shook with a mighty sorrow, and became bewildered. Then, having regained his sense, he rose up and became cast down through apprehension. Having heard the words of the ascetic, capable of rending the mind and heart, the bigh-souled king of men became stricken with grief and shook on his seat.

SECTION XX.

Hearing the words of Viswāmitra, that best of monarchs remained insensible for a time,—and then regaining his sense, spake thus,—"My lotus-eyed Rāma is not yet turned of sixteen; and I do not perceive his fitness to cope with Rākshasas in battle. I am the lord of this *Akshaukini*[32] of forces. Marching with this, will I engage with the night- rangers. And these servants of mine are valiant, and warlike, and accomplished in weapons, and capable of fighting the Rākshasas,—therefore, it behoveth thee not to take Rāma. And myself bow in hand, stationed at the van of the array, will battle with the rangers of the night as long as life is spared unto me. And then well protected, thy sacrifice will hold an unimpeded course. Therefore, I will repair thither,—and it behoveth thee not to take Rāma. And youthful, and unaccomplished, and not knowing what constitutes strength and what not, and not equipped with the energy of science,—and unskilful in fight, he is not a match for Rākshasas,—they being deceitful warriors. Bereft of Rāma, O best of ascetics, I

[30] Yama, the god of death.

[31] From *Kakud*, an emblem of royalty and *Stha*, residing,—meaning a prince, the grandson of Ikshwaku.—T.

[32] A complete army consisting of 1,09,350 foot, 65,610 horse, 21,870 chariots, and 21,870 elephants.—T.

cannot live for a moment. Therefore, it behoveth thee not to take him. If, O Brāh-mana, it is thy intention to take Rāma, then, O thou of excellent vows, do thou also take me along with the *Chaturanga*[33] forces! O Kuçika's son, I am sixty thousand years old; and (at this age) I have obtained Rāma after undergoing extreme trou-bles,—it therefore becometh thee not to take Rāma. And among the four sons of mine, I find my highest delight in Rāma, my first-born, and the most virtuous of them all,—therefore, it behoveth thee not to take Rāma. What is the prowess of the Rākshasas? And whose sons are they? And who, pray, are they? And what are the proportions of their bodies? And who protecteth them, O foremost of ascetics? And by what means shall either Rāma, or my forces, or, O Brāhmana, I myself be able to slay in fight those deceitful warriors—the Rākshasas? Do thou tell me, adorable one, inflated as they are by virtue of their prowess, how can I stand them in fight?" Hearing that speech of his, Viswātmitra said,—"There is a Rakshasa named Rāva-na, sprung from the line of Pulastya. Having obtained a boon from Brahmā, he boldly opposeth himself to the three worlds, being possessed of great strength, and prowess, and backed by innumerable Rākshasas. And, O mighty monarch, I also hear that that lord of the Rākshasas is the very brother of Vacravana and the son of the ascetic Vicravan. And when that one possessed of mighty strength does not stoop to disturb the sacrifice himself, those powerful Rākshasas, Mārich and Suvāhu, being incited by him, disturb the rites." The ascetic having spoken thus, the king then answered him,—"I am incapable of standing that wicked-souled one in fight. Therefore, do thou, O thou versed in morality, extend thy favor unto my son! Of slender fortune as I am, thou art my guide and my god. Even the celestials and the *Dānavas* and the *Gandharbas* and the Birds and the Snakes are incapable of bearing Rāvana in battle—what then is man? He depriveth in conflict even the puissant of their prowess. I cannot fight either with him or with his forces. And, O foremost of ascetics, whether thou art accompanied with my son or my forces, thou wilt not be able to stand him. And how can I, O Brāhmana, make over unto thee my son, of tender years, resembling an immortal, who is ignorant of warfare? I will not part with my son. The sons of Sunda and Upasunda resemble Kāla him-self in battle,—and it is they who are disturbing thy sacrifice. Therefore I will not part with my son. And Māricha and Suvāhu are possessed of prowess, and accom-plished in weapons. But with my friends I will repair to encounter one of them. If thou do not consent to this, I beseech thee with my friends, (do thou desist!)" Hearing these words of the lord of men, a mighty ire took possession of that fore-most of regenerate ones, Kuçika's son; and the fire of the Maharshi's wrath flamed up even like unto a fire fed by fuel and clarified butter.

SECTION XXI.

Hearing those words of Daçaratha, composed of letters faltering with affec-tion, Kuçika's son, stirred up with anger, answered the monarch, saying,—"Hav-ing promised me first, thou endeavourest to renounce that promise of thine. This surely is unworthy of a descendant of Raghu,—and this can bring destruction upon the dynasty. If, king, in acting thus, thou hast acted properly, I will then re-pair to the place whence I had come. O Kākuthstha's descendant false in promise,

[33] An army consisting of foot, horse, elephants, and cars.—T.

do thou attain happiness, being surrounded by thy friends." And when the intelligent Viçwāmitra was exercised with wrath, the entire earth began to tremble, and the gods even were inspired with awe. And knowing that the entire universe was in trepidation, that mighty saint, the sedate Vasishtha of excellent vows, said these words unto the king,—"Born in the line of Ikshwāku, thou art the very second self of virtue. And endowed with patience, and auspicious, and observing excellent vows, thou ought not to renounce virtue. The descendant of Raghu is famed over the three worlds as righteous-souled. Do thou maintain thy habit of adhering to promise; for it doth not behove thee to act unrighteously. If having promised,—'I will do so,' thou dost not act up to thy word, the merit thou hast achieved by digging tanks and by performing sacrifices shall come to naught,—therefore do thou renounce Rāma! Accomplished or not accomplished in weapons, the Rākshasas cannot bear him protected by Kuçika's son, like ambrosia, by flaming fire. This one is Virtue incarnate: this one is the foremost of those possessing prowess. This one surpasseth all others in learning, and is the refuge of asceticism. This one is cognizant of all the weapons that exist in the three worlds furnished with mobile and imobile things; but others do not know him,—nor yet shall know him hereafter. And neither the gods, nor the saints, nor the immortals, nor the Rākshasas, nor the foremost of Gandharbas and Yakshas, nor the Kinnaras, nor the mighty Serpents can know him. And formerly while the descendant of Kuçika was ruling bis kingdom, Sivā conferred upon him the highly famous sons of Kricācwa in the shape of all weapons. And those sons of Kricācwa were the offspring of Prajāpati's daughters. They were endowed with various forms, and were effulgent and dreadful. And Daksha's daughters of elegant waists, Jayā and Suprabhā, brought forth an hundred exceedingly effulgent weapons. And by virtue of her boon, Jayā obtained fifty sons of immeasurable strength and endued with the power of becoming invisible for the purpose of slaughtering the hosts of the Asuras. And Suprabhā also brought forth fifty sons named *Sanhāras*, incapable of being borne, and infallible, and powerful. Kuçika's son is adequately conversant with all those weapons. And that one knowing duty is also capable of creating wonderful weapons. And, O descendant of Raghu, there is nothing present, past, or future which is not known by that foremost of ascetics of high soul, and cognizant of morality. Such is the prowess of that highly famous Viçwāmitra possessed of mighty energy. Therefore, O king, it behoveth thee not to hesitate in the matter of Rāma's going. The descendant of Kuçika is himself capable of repressing the Rākshasas; and it is in order to thy son's welfare that coming unto thee, he asketh for him of thee." At this speech of the ascetic, that foremost of Raghus, the king, well- pleased, became exceedingly delighted. And that famous one, relishing the journey of Rāma, began to reflect in his mind about consigning him unto Kuçika's son.

SECTION XXII.

Upon Vasishtha's representing this, king Daçarātha himself with a complacent countenance, summoned unto him Rāma and Lakshmana. And when the auspicious rites had been performed by both Rāma's father and mother, and when the priest Vasishtha had uttered mantras, king Daçarātha, smelling his son's crown, with a glad heart, made him over unto the descendant of Kuçika. Then there blew a Breeze free from dust and of delicious feel, on witnessing the lotus-eyed Rāma at the hands of Viçwāmitra. And as the high-souled one was about to set out, blossoms began to shower down copiously, accompanied with the sounds of celestial kettle-drums and the loud blares of conchs. Viçwāmitra went first, and next the highly famous Rāma with the side-locks, holding the bow. And him followed Sumitrā's son. And equipped with quivers, and with bows in hand, gracing the ten cardinal points and resembling three-hooded serpents, they followed the high-souled Viçwāmitra, like the two stalwart Aswins following the Grand-sire. And those effulgent ones of faultless limbs went in the wake of the ascetic, illumining him with their grace. And like unto those sons of his, Skanda and Bisākha following the incomprehensible deity, Sthānu, those youthful brothers of comely persons and faultless limbs, Rāma and Lakshmana, highly effulgent, carrying bows in hand, adorned with ornaments, and equipped with scimitars, with their fingers encased in *Guana* skin, flamingly followed Kuçika's son, beautifying him with their splendour. And having proceeded over half a *Yojana*, and arriving at the right bank of the Sarayu, Viçwāmitra addressed these sweet words unto Rāma,— "O Rāma! do thou, O child, take of this water: let no delay occur. Do thou receive the *mantras* Valā and Ativalā,—and thou wilt not feel fatigue or fever or undergo any change of look, and whether asleep or heedless, the Rākshasas will not be able to surprise thee. And, O Rāma, the might of thy arms will be unequalled in this world,—nay, in all the three worlds. There shall be none—thy equal. Do thou, O Rāghava, recite Valā and Ativalā, O child! And, O sinless one, when thou hast secured these two kinds of knowledge, none in this world will equal thee in good fortune, or in talent, or in philosophic wisdom or in subtle apprehension, or in the capacity of answering a controversialist; for Valā and Ativalā are the nurses of all knowledge. And, O Rāma, O foremost of men, if thou recitest Valā and Ativalā on the way. neither hunger nor thirst will exercise thee, O descendant of Raghu! And if thou recitest these, thou wilt attain fame on earth. Those sciences fraught with energy are the daughters of the Grandsire. I intend to confer them upon thee, O Kākutstha; and, O lord of earth, they are worthy to be conferred upon thee as thou art possessed of various virtues. Thou need not entertain any doubt about it. And if thou learn them like unto the exercise of asceticism they will prove of manifold good unto thee." Thereat Rāma with a cheerful countenance sipping water, with a purified body received those sciences from the *Maharshi* of subdued soul. And furnished with the sciences, Rāma of dreadful prowess appeared resplendent, even like the adorable autumnal Sun invested with a thousand rays. Then Rāma having rendered unto Kuçika's son all the duties appertaining to a spiritual guide, the three happily spent that night on the banks of the Sarayu. And although those excellent sons of Daçarātha lay down on an unbeseeming bed of grass, yet in consequence of the sweet converse of Kuçika's son, the night seemed to pass pleasantly away.

SECTION XXIII.

And when the night had passed away, the mighty ascetic spoke unto Kākutstha, lying down on a bed of leaves, —"O Rāma, the best son of Kaucalyā, the first Sandhyā[34] should now be performed. Do thou, O foremost of men, arise! Thou shouldst perform the purificatory rites and contemplate the gods." Hearing those proper words of the ascetic, those foremost of men, endowed with heroism, bathed, and, offering *Arghya*, began to recite the Gāyatri.[35] And having performed these daily duties, those exceedingly powerful ones, greeting Viçwāmitra having asceticism for wealth, stood before him, with the object of starting on their journey. And as those ones endowed with exceeding prowess were proceeding, at the shining confluence of the Sarayu and the Gangā they beheld a noble river flowing in three branches. And there lay a holy hermitage, belonging to ascetics of subdued souls, where they had been carrying on their high austerities for thousands of years. Beholding that sacred asylum, those descendants of Raghu, exceedingly delighted, spake unto the high-souled Viçwāmitra, these words,—"Whose is this sacred hermitage? And what man liveth here? O worshipful one, we are desirous of hearing this. Surely, great is our curiosity." At those words of theirs, that foremost of ascetics, smiling, said,—"Hear, O Rāma, as to whom the asylum belonged in time past. Kandarpa, called Kāma by the wise, was once incarnate (on earth.) And it came to pass that as that lord of the deities, Sthānu, having performed here his austerities in accordance with the prescribed restrictions, was wending his way in company with the Maruts, that fool-hardy wight dared disturb the equanimity of his mind. Thereupon, descendant of Raghu, uttering a roar, the high-souled Rudra eyed him steadfastly. And thereat all the limbs of that perverse-hearted one became blasted. On his body being consumed by that high- souled one, Kāma was deprived of his person in consequence of the ire of that foremost among the deities; and, O Rāghava, from that time forth, he hath become known as Ananga.[36] And the place where he was deprived of his body is the lovely land of Anga. This sacred hermitage belongs to Sivā; and these ascetics engaged in pious acts, O hero, have been from father to son his disciples. And no sin toucheth them. Here, O Rāma, in the midst of the sacred streams, will we spend the night, O thou of gracious presence, crossing over on the morrow. Let us then, having purified ourselves, enter the holy hermitage! It is highly desirable for us to sojourn here,— here will we happily spend the night, having bathed, and recited the *mantras*, and offered oblation unto the sacrificial fire, O best of men!"

As they were conversing thus, the ascetics were highly delighted on discovering them by means of their far-reaching spiritual vision,—and they rejoiced greatly. Then giving Kuçika's son water to wash his feet and *Arghya*, and extending unto him also the rites of hospitality, they next entertained Rāma and Lakshmana. And having experienced their hospitality, they (the guests) delighted them with their talk. And then the saints with collected minds recited their evening prayers. And having been shown their destined place of rest along with ascetics of excellent vows, they happily passed that night in that hermitage affording every comfort. And that foremost of ascetics, the righteous- souled son of Kuçika, by means of his excellent converse, charmed the prepossessing sons of the monarch.

---

[34] Brāhmanas have to perform their daily devotions thrice,—in the morning, at noon, and in the evening.—T.

[35] The solar hymn of the Veda—T.

[36] Lit. the bodiless.—T.

SECTION XXIV.

Then next morning which happened to be fine, those repressors of their foes, with Viçwāmitra who had performed morning rites at their head, came to the banks of the river.[37] And those high-souled ascetics observing vows, having brought an elegant bark addressed Viçwāmitra, saying,—"Do thou ascend the bark with the princes at thy head! May thy journey be auspicious: let no delay occur!" Thereupon saying,—"So be it!", and having paid homage unto those ascetics, Viçwāmitra set about crossing that river with them, which had replenished the ocean.[38] And it came to pass that while thus engaged, they heard a sound augmented by the dashing of the waves.[39] And having come to the middle of the stream, the highly energetic Rāma with his younger brother, became curious to ascertain the cause of that sound. And reaching the middle of the river, Rāma asked that best of ascetics,—"What is this loud uproar that seemeth to come riving the water?" Hearing Rāghava's words dictated by curiosity, that righteous-souled one spake, unfolding the true cause of the noise,—"O Rāma, there is in the Kailāca mountain an exceedingly beautiful pool, created mentally by Brahmā, O foremost of men,—and hence this watery expanse goeth by the name of *Mānasa Pool*, And the stream that issues from that liquid lapse, flows through Ayodhyā: the sacred Sarayu issues from that pool of Brahmā. And as the Sarayu meets the Jāhnavi, this tremendous uproar is heard, being produced by the clashing of the waters. Do thou, O Rāma, bow down to them with a concentrated mind." Thereupon, both of these exceedingly righteous ones, bowed down unto those streams; and betaking themselves to the right bank, began to proceed with fleet vigour. And beholding a dreadful trackless forest, that son of the foremost of men, Ikshhwaku's descendant, asked that best of ascetics, saying,—"Ah! deep is this forest abounding in crickets; and filled with terrible ferocious beasts,and various birds possessed of shocking voices and screaming frightfully; and graced by lions, and tigers, and boars, and elephants; and crowded with *Dhavas*[40] and *Acwas* and *Karnas*[41] and *Kukubhas* and *Vilmas*[42] and *Tindukas*[43] and *Patalas*[44] and *Badaris*.[45] Whence is this dreadful forest?" Him answered thus the mighty asetic Viçwāmitra endowed with high energy,—"Do thou listen, O Kākutshtha, as to whom belongeth this dreadful forest! Here were formerly, O foremost of men, two flourishing provinces, named Malada, and Karusha, built by celestial architects. In days of yore, O Rāma, on the occasion of the destruction of Vritra, the thousand-eyed one came to have hunger, to be besmeared with excreta, and to slay a Brāhmana. And when Indra had been thus besmeared, the deities, and the saints having asceticism for wealth, washed

[37] Ganges.—T.

[38] The legend is that when the saint Agastya had sucked up the ocean, the Ganges replenished it.—T.

[39] The text has *Susrāva*—he heard. Another reading is *Tatas Susruvatus Sabdam*—then they heard a sound,—which I adopt.—T.

[40] Grislea Tomentosa.—T.

[41] Cassia fistula.—T.

[42] Ægle marmalos.—T.

[43] Diospyros glutinosa.—T.

[44] Bignonia suave-olens.—T.

[45] Jujube.—T.

him here, and cleansed his person from the dirt. And the deities, having renounced here the filth that had clung unto the person of the mighty Indra, as well as his hunger, attained exceeding delight. And thereat Indra becoming purified, attained his former brightness, and became devoid of hunger. And mightily pleased with this region, he conferred on it an excellent boon, saying,—"Since these two places have held excreta from my body, they going by the names of Malada and Karusha, shall attain exceeding prosperity and fame among men." And beholding the land thus honored by the intelligent Sacra, the deities said unto the subduer of Pāka,— 'Well!" "Well!" And, O repressor of foes, these two places, Malada and Karusha, enjoyed prosperity for a long lime and were blessed with corn and wealth. Then after a space of time, was born a Yakshini capable of assuming forms at will, and endowed with the strength of a thousand elephants. Her name, good betide thee! was Tārakā, and she was the spouse of the intelligent Sunda—she whose son is the Rākshasa, Māricha possessed of the prowess of Sacra; having round arms, with a huge head, a capacious mouth and a cyclopean body. And that Rakshasa of dreadful form daily frightens people. And, O descendant of Raghu, Tārakā of wicked deeds, daily commits havoc upon these countries, Malada and Karusha . And now at the distance of over half a Yojana, she stayeth, obstructing the way. And since this forest belongeth unto Tārakā, thou shouldst repair thither and, resorting to the might of thy own arms, slay this one of wicked deeds. And by my direction, do thou again rid this region of its thorn; for no one dareth to approach such a place, infested, O Rāma, by the dreadful and unbearable Yakshini. And now I have related unto thee all about this fearful forest. And to this day that Yakshini hath not desisted from committing ravages right and left."

SECTION XXV.

Hearing this excellent speech of that ascetic of immeasurable energy, that foremost of men answered him in these happy words,—"O best of ascetics, I have heard that the Yaksha race is endowed with but small prowess. How can then that one of the weaker sex possess the strength of a thousand elephants?" Hearing this speech that was uttered by Rāghava of immeasurable energy, Viçwāmitra, delighting with his amiable words that subduer of foes, Rāma, and Lakshmana, said,—"Do thou listen as to the means whereby attaining terrible strength, that one belonging to the weaker sex hath come to possess strength and prowess by virtue of a boon. In former times there was a mighty and exceedingly powerful Yaksha, named Suketu. And he had no issue. And he was of pure practices, and used to perform rigid austerities. And, O Rāma, the Grand-sire, well pleased with that lord of Yakshas, conferred upon him a gem of a daughter, by name Tārakā. And the Grand-sire endowed her with the strength of a thousand elephants; yet that illustrious one did not bestow a son on that Yaksha. And when she had grown, and attained youth and beauty, he gave that famous damsel unto Jambha's son, Sunda, for wife. And after a length of time, that Yakshi gave birth to a son, named Māricha, possessed of irrepressible energy—him who became a Rākshasa in consequence of a curse. And, O Rāma, when Sunda had been destroyed, Tārakā along with her son, set her heart upon afflicting that excellent saint Agastya. And enraged with Agastya, she rushed at him with a roar, intending to devour him. And on seeing her thus rushing, that worshipful saint, Agastya, said unto Māricha, "Do thou become a Rākshasa!", and, in exceeding wrath, he also cursed Tārakā. "And, O mighty Yakshi, ince in frightful guise with a frightful face thou hast desired to eat up a human being, do thou immediately leave this (thy original) shape, and become of a terrible form!" Thus cursed by Agastya, Tārakā, overwhelmed with rage, lays waste this fair region, where Agastya carrieth on his austerities. Do thou, O descendant of Raghu, for the welfare of Brāhmanas and kine, slay this exceedingly terrible Yakshi of wicked ways and vile prowess! Nor, O son of Raghu, doth any one in the three worlds, save, thee, dare to slay this Yakshi joined with a curse. Nor shouldst thou, best of men, shrink from slaying a woman; for even this should be accomplished by a prince in the interests of the four orders. And whether an act be cruel or otherwise, slightly or highly sinful, it should for protecting the subjects, be performed by a ruler. Of those engaged in the onerous task of government, even this is the eternal rule of conduct. Do thou, O Kukutstha, slay this impious one; for she knoweth no righteousness! We hear, O king, that in days of yore, Sakra slew Virochana's daughter, Mantharā, who had intented to distroy the earth. And formerly, O Rāma, Vishnu destroyed Kāvya's mother, the devoted wife of Bhrigu, who had set her heart upon making the world, devoid of Indra. By these as well as innumerable princes—foremost of men—have wicked women been slain. Therefore, O king, renouncing antipathy, do thou, by my command, slay this one!"

SECTION XXVI.

Hearing those bold words of the ascetic, the son of that foremost of men, Rāghava firm in his vows, with clasped hands answered,—"In accordance with the desire of my sire, and in order to glorify it, I ought fearlessly to do even as Kuçika's son sayeth. And havingbeen desired to that end while at Ayodhyā by that high-souled one, my father Daçarātha, in the midst of the spiritual guides, I ought not to pass by thy words. Therefore, commanded by that upholder of the Veda, I, agreeably to my father's mandate, will, without doubt, bring about that welcome event—the death of Tārakā. And in the interests of Brāhmanas, kine, and celestials, I am ready to act as desired by thee of immeasurable energy." Having said this, that repressor of foes, with clenched fist, twanged his bow-string, filling the ten cardinal points with the sounds. And at those sounds, the dwellers in Tārakā's forest were filled with perturbation,—and Tārakā also amazed at those sounds, became exceedingly wroth. And, rendered almost insensible by anger, that Rākshasi furiously rushed in amain towards the spot whence had come the report. And beholding that frightful one of hideous visage and colossal proportions, transported with rage, Raghu's descendant spake unto Lakshmana,—"Behold, O Lakshmana, the terrible and hideous body of yonder Yakshini! The sight of her striketh terror into the hearts of even the brave. Mark! - This irrepressible one, possessing all the resources of illusion, will I oppose, and deprive her of ears and nose. But I dare not slay her, she being protected by virtue of her fcminineness. I intend only to oppose her course, and de- prive her of her prowess." As Rāma was speaking thus, Tārakā, deprived of sense through ire, uttering roars, with uplifted arms rushed against him. And thereat the Brahmārshi, Viçwāmitra, uttering a roar, upbraided her, and said,—"*Swasti!*"[46] May victory attend the descendants of Raghu!" And raising thick clouds of dust, Tāraka instantly bewildered both the descendants of Raghu. And then by help of illusion, she began to pour upon them a mighty shower of crags. And thereat Raghu's descendant was wroth. And resisting that mighty shower of crags by vollies of shafts, Rāghava with arrows cut off her hands. And with the fore-parts of her arms lopped off, as she was roaring before them, Sumitrā's son waxing worth deprived her of her ears and nose. Therupon that one capable of assuming forms at will, began to assume various shapes; and to vanish from sight, bewildering her antagonists with her illusory displays. And terribly ranging the field, the Yakshi showered crags upon her antagonists. And beholding them enveloped on all sides by that craggy down-pour, the auspicious son of Gadhi spake these words,—"O Rāma, renounce thy antipathy. This one of wicked ways is exceedingly impious. And this sacrifice-disturbing Yakshi will, by virtue of her power of illusion, come to increase more and more in energy. Do thou, therefore, against the arrival of dusk, slay her! The Rākshasas are incapable of being controlled when evening sets in." Thus addressed, Rāma, displaying his skill in aiming by sounds, enveloped with arrows that Yakshi showering crags. Being thus hemmed in with a network cf shafts, she possessed of the powers of illusion, rushed against Kākutstha and Lakshmana, uttering terrible roars. And as that Yakshi, in prowess like unto a thunder-bolt, was rushing on, Rāma pierced her chest with arrows,—and thereat she dropped down and died. And upon seeing that grim-visaged one slain, the lord of the celestials together with the celestials themselves honoring Kākutstha, exclaimed "Well!", "Well!" And exceedingly pleased, the thousand -eyed Purandara, together with the delighted deities,said unto Viçwāmitra,—"O ascetic, O Kuçika's son, good betide thee! all the Maruts with Indra at their head, have been gratified with this act (of Rāma's). Do thou therefore show affection unto Rāghava! Do thou, O Brāhmana, confer upon Raghu's descendant the sons of Prajāpati Kricācwa, of true prowess, and charged with ascetic energy. And ever following thee, he, O Brāhmana, is fit to receive them of thee. And this son of the king is to accomplish a mighty task in the interest of the celestials." Saying this, the deities, having paid homage unto Viçwāmitra, joyfully entered the celestial regions.

And now came evening on, when that best of ascetics, gratified at the destruction of Taraki, smelt Rami's crown and said these words,—"Here O Rāma of gracious presence, shall we pass the night; and morrow morning wend unto that hermitage of mine." Hearing Viçwāmitra's words, Dacatatha's son, glad at heart, happily passed that night in the forest of Tāraka. And being thus freed from all disturbances from that day forth that forest appeared charming, even like unto the forest of Chaitraratha. Having thus slain the Yaksha's daughter, Rāma, eulogized by celestials and Siddhas spent there that night with the saint, being awakened by the latter at the break of day.

SECTION XXVII.

Having passed that night, the illustrious Viçwāmitra, smiling complacently

---

[46] A particle of benediction, indeclinable.—T.

sweetly spake unto Rāghava, saying,—Pleased am I with thee. Good betide thee, O highly famous prince! With supreme pleasure, do I confer upon thee all the weapons by means of which subduing such antagonists as celestials and *Asuras* backed on earth by Gandharbas and Uragas, thou wilt in battle be crowned with victory. And all those celestial weapons, good betide thee, I will confer upon thee. And I will confer upon thee, O Rāghava, the celestial and mighty Dandachakra,[47] and Dharmachakra, and also Kalachakra. And O foremost of men, I will confer upon thee the fierce Vishnu Chakra,—and Indra Chakra, and the Vajra, and Sivā's Sulavata, and the weapon Brahmāciras, and Aishika, O mighty-armed descendant of Raghu! And, O best of men, I will, O king's son, bestow upon thee the matchless Brahmā weapon, and, O Kākutstha, the two excellent maces, the flaming Modaki and Cikhari. And, O Rāma, I will confer upon thee Dharmapāca,[48] and Kālapāca, and the excellent Vārunapāca. And, O descendant of Raghu, I will bestow upon thee the two *Ashanis*,—Sushka and Ardra, and the Pināka weapon, and the Nārāyana, and the Agneya weapon called Sikhara, and the Vāyavya, called Prathama, O sinless one! And, O Rāghava, I will confer upon thee the weapon called Hayaciras, and the Krauncha weapon, and,0 Kākutstha, a couple of darts, And I will confer upon the Kankāla, and the dreadful Mashaia, and Kapāla, and Kinkini—all those that are intended for slaughtering Rākshasas. And, O mighty-armed one, son of the best of men, I will confer upon thee the mighty weapon Vidyādhara, and that excellent scimitar named Nandana, and the favorite Gandharba weapon, Mohana, and Praswāpana, and Pasamana, and Saumya, O Rāghava! And O best of men, do thou accept Varshana, and Soshana, and Santāpana, and Vilapana, and Mādana hard to repress, beloved of Kandarpa, and that favorite Gandharba weapon, Mānava, and the favorite Pichāsa weapon, O highly famous prince. And do thou, O mighty- armed Rāma, speedily accept the Tāmasa, O best of men, and the exceedingly powerful Saumana,and the irrepressible Samvarta and Maushala, O son of the king, and the Satya weapon, and the supreme Māyamaya, and the Saura. Tejaprabha, capable of depriving foes of energy, and the Soma, and the Sisira, and the Tāshtra, and the terrible Dāruna belonging unto Bhaga, and Sileshu, and Madana—all assuming forms at will, and endowed with exceeding prowess, and highly exalted." Then with his face turned towards the east, that foremost of ascetics having purified himself, gladly conferred the *mantras* upon Rāma. And the Vipra also bestowed upon Rāghava those weapons, of which even he celestials are incapable of holding all. As that intelligent ascetic, Viçwāmitra, recited *mantras*, all those invaluable weapons appeared before that descendant of Raghu. And, with clasped hands, they well-pleased, addressed Rāma, —"These, O highly generous one, are thy servants, O Rāghava. And whatever thou wishest, good betide thee, shall by all means be accomplished by us." Thus addressed by those highly powerful weapons, Kākutstha Rāma, with a delighted soul, accepting them, touched them with his hand, and said,—"Do ye appear before me as I remember you!" Then the exceedingly energetic Rāma, well pleased, paying everence unto the mighty ascetic, Viçwāmitra, prepared to set out.

---

[47] Chakra means discus. These enumerations specify different kinds of the discus.—T.
[48] Pāca means noose—T.

SECTION XXVIII.

Having accepted those weapons with purity, Kākutstha while proceeding, with a complacent countenance spake these words unto Viswāmitra,—"O adorable one, I have received these weapons, incapable of being repressed even by the celestials themselves. Now, O best of ascetics, I would acquire a knowledge of withdrawing them." Upon Kākutstha's representing this, Viçwāmitra of high austerities, endowed with patience, of excellent vows, and pure in spirit, communicated unto him the *mantras* for restraining the weapons. "Do thou, 0 Rāma, accept Satyavat, and Sataykirti, and Dhrishta, and Rabhasa, and Pratiharatara, and Parānmukha, and Avānmukha, and Lakshya, and Alakshya, and Drihanābha, and Sunābha, Dacāksha, and Satavaktra, and Dacacirsha, and Satodara, and Padranābha, and Mahānābha, and Indunābha, and Swanābha, and Jyotisha, and Sakuna, and Nairāshya, and Vimala, and Yaugandhara, and Vindra, and the two Daityapramathanas, and Suchivāhu, and Mahāvāhu, and Nishkali, and Virucha, and Archimāli, and Dhritimāli, and Vrittimān, and Ruchira, and Pitrya, and Saumansa, and Vidhuta, and Makara, and Karavira, and Rati, and Dhana, and Dhānya, O Rāghava, and Kāmarupa, and Kāmaruchi,and Moha, and Avarana,and Jrimbhaka and Sarpanātha, and Panthāna, and Varuna,—these sons of Kricāswa, O Rāma, effulgent, and assuming shapes at will. And, good betide thee, O descendant of Raghu, thou art worthy to receive these weapons." Thereupon, Kākutstha with a heart overflowing with delight, said,—"So be it!" And those weapons were furnished with celestial and shining persons, and endowed with visible shapes, and capable of conferring happiness. And some of them were like (live) coals; and some comparable unto smoke; and some were like unto the Sun or the Moon. And with folded hands, they spake unto Rāma in honied accents,—O chief of men, here we are! Do thou command as to what we are to do on thy behalf." Then the descendant of Raghu answered, saying,—"Repair whithersoever ye will! Recurring to my memory, do ye in time of need, render me assistance!" Thereupon paying homage unto Rāma, and having gone round him, they replied unto Kākutstha,—"Be it so!" and returned whence they had come. And having learnt all about those weapons, Rāghava, while proceeding spake sweetly unto that mighty ascetic, Viçwāmitra,—"What is yonder wood hard by the hill, appearing like clouds? Great is my curiosity. It is pleasing unto the sight, and abounds in beasts, and is exceedingly romantic, and is adorned with various birds singing sweetly. Now, O foremost of ascetics, we have come out of a wilderness capable of making one's hair stand on end. And from the pleasantness attaching to this place, I have come to a conclusion. Tell me, O reverend sir, whose hermitage is this? where, O eminent ascetic, is that hermitage where dwell those wicked-minded wretches of impious deeds, given to slaughtering Brāhmanas, who disturb thy sacrifice? Where, O adorable one, is that spot, repairing unto which, O Brāhmana, I am to protect thy sacrificial rites, and to slay the Rākshasas? All this, O foremost of ascetics, I desire to hear, O lord."

SECTION XXIX.

Hearing those words of Rāma of measureless prowess, vho had asked the question, the highly energetic Viçwāmitra answered, saying,—"Here, O mighty-armed Rāma, Vishnu of mighty asceticism worshipped of all the deities, for years upon years, and hundreds of *Yugas*, dwelt for carrying on his austerities and *Yoga*. This, O Rāma, was formerly the hermitage of the high-souled Vāmana. And this is famed as Siddhāçrama, in consequence of that one of potent asceticism having attained fruition there. And it came to pass that at this time Virochana's son, king Vāli, having vanquished the celestials with Indra and the Maruts, established that dominion of his, famous in the three worlds. And that mighty chief of the Asuras celebrated a sacrifice. And as Vāli was performing that sacrifice, the deities with Agni at their head, coming unto Vishnu himself at this asylum, addressed him, saying.—"Virochana's son, Vāli, O Vishnu, is celebrating a sacrifice. Do thou, before the ceremoney is finished, accomplish thy own end. He duly conferreth upon such as repair unto him from various quarters all those things that they ask for. And do thou thyself, O Vishuu, aided by thy power of illusion, assuming a Dwarf-form, accomplish the welfare (of the celestials.)" In the meantime, O Rāma, the wonderful Kasyapa resembling fire in splendour, and flaming in energy, having in company with, and with the assistance of, the divine Aditi, O Rāma, accomplished his vow, lasting for hundred years, began to hymn the destroyer of Madhu ready to confer boons. "By means of warm austerities, do I behold thee composed of penances, a mass of mortifications, and endowed with a form and a soul of austerities. And in thy person, O lord, do I behold this entire universe. And in Thee without beginning, and incapable of being pointed out, do I take refuge!" Thereupon exceedingly pleased, Hari spake unto Kaçyapa, with his sins purged off saying,—"Do thou mention the boon! Good betide thee. Methinks thou deservest a boon." Hearing these words of his, Marichi's son, Kaçyapa, said,—"A-diti, the gods and I myself, crave of thee this,—and, O bestower of boons, it behoveth thee well pleased to confer on us this boon, O thou of excellent vows! Do thou, O sinless one, become born as my son in Aditi, O adorable deity! Do thou become the younger brother of Sakra, O destroyer of Asuras. It behoveth thee to help the celestials afflicted with grief. And this place through thy grace will attain the name of Siddhāçrama. The work, O lord of the celestials, hath been accomplished. Do thou now, O thou of the six attributes, ascend from hence!" And accordingly Vishnu of mighty energy took his birth in Aditi. And assuming the form of a dwarf, he presented himself before Virochana's son. And then asking for as much earth as could be covered by three footsteps, that one ever engaged in the welfare of all creatures, with the object of compassing the good of all, stood occupying the worlds. And having by his power restrained Vāli, that one of exceeding energy, again conferred the three worlds upon the mighty Indra,—and made them subject to his control. Formerly he used to dwell in this asylum capable of removing fatigue. And through reverence for the Dwarf, I reside here. And this hermitage is infested by Rākshasas disturbing rites. And, O most puissant of men, here thou shouldst slay those ones of wicked ways. To-day, O Rāma, will I repair unto this supremely excellent Siddhāçrama. And this asylum, child, is as much thine as mine." Saying this, taking Rāma and Lakshmana, the mighty ascetic, experiencing exceeding delight, entered that asylum, and appeared graceful, like the Moon emerged from mist in conjunction with the Punarvasu stars. And beholding Viçwāmitra, the ascetics inhabiting Siddhāçrama, suddenly rising in joy, worshipped that intelligent one,—and extended unto the princes the rites of hospitality. And then having reposed for while, those unreproved princes, the descendants of Raghu, with clasped hands, addressed that foremost of ascetics,—"Be thou even to-day initiated unto the ceremony. Good betide thee, O best of ascetics! Let this Siddhāçrama verily attain fruition,—and let thy words be verified!" Thus addressed, that mighty saint of exceeding energy, with his mind subdued, and senses under restraint, caused himself to be initiated into the ceremony. And like unto the Kumāras,[49] Rāma and Lakshamana, having passed the night pleasantly, rose in the morning; and having finished their morning worship, and with purity and self-restraint recited the prime *mantras*, paid their obeisance unto the sacrificial fire and the sacrificer, Viçwāmitra, who was seated.

SECTION XXX.

Then those princes, repressors of foes, cognizant of place, and time, and words, thus spake unto Kuçika's son agreeably to time and place, saying,—"O adorable one do thou tell us as to the time when we should oppose those rangers of the night! Let not that hour pass away!" Upon the two Kākutsthas' saying this, and finding them prompt for the encounter, those ascetics well-pleased, fell to extolling the sons of the king. "For six nights from to-day, ye should protect us. This ascetic hath been initiated into the sacrifice, and must therefore, observe taciturnity." Hearing these words of theirs, those illustrious princes, renouncing sleep, began to guard the hermitage six days and nights; and those heroic and mighty archers with their armours on protected that best of ascetics and subduer of enemies. And when time had thus gone by and the sixth day had arrived, Rāma said unto Sumitrā's son,—"Being well equipped, be thou vigilant!" When Rāma, manifesting emotion, and being eager for encounter, had said this, the priests and spiritual guides lit up the altar. And along with Viçwāmitra and the family priests, they lit up the altar furnished with Kuça, and Kāca, and ladles, and faggots, and flowers. And as reciting *mantras*, they were about to duly engage in that sacrifice, there arose a mighty and dreadful uproar in the sky. And as in the rains, masses of clouds appear enveloping the firmament,[50] the Rākshasas, displaying illusions in that wise, began to rush onward. And Maricha and Suvahu together with their followers coming in dreadful forms, began to shower down blood upon the altar. And on seeing the altar deluged with gore, Rāma suddenly rushed forward, and beheld them in the sky. And suddenly seeing them rushing in amain, the lotus-eyed Rāma fixing his gaze at Lakshmana, said,—"Behold, O Lakshmana, by means of a *Mānava* weapon, I shall, without doubt, drive away the wicked, flesh-eating Rākshasas, even as the wind driveth away clouds before it. Surely I cannot bring myself to slay such as these." Saying this, that descendant of Raghu, Rāma, in vehemence fixing on his bow an exceedingly mighty and gloriously-dazzling Mānava weapon, discharged it in great wrath at Māricha's chest. And wounded by that foremost of Mānava weapons, Māricha carried off a sheer hundred Yojanas, dropped in the midst of the ocean. And finding Māricha senseless,

[49] Skanda and Visakha.—T.

[50] The text reads, *gamanam avaryya*—obstructing passage. Evidently the reading is vicious—it should run *gaganam avaryya*—enveloping the firmament.—T.

and whirling, and afflicted by the might of the weapon, and overcome, Rāma addressed Lakshmana, saying,—"Behold, O Lakshmana, this Mānava weapon first used by Manu, depriving him of his senses, hath carried him off,—and yet hath not taken his life! But these shameless, wicked, and blood-drinking Rākshasas, addicted to wrong-doing, these disturbers of sacrifices, will I slaughter." Having said this, anon showing unto Lakshmana his lightness of hand, Raghu's descendant took out a mighty Agneya weapon, and discharged it at the breast of Suvāhu. Thereat being pierced with that shaft, he fell down upon the ground. Then taking a Vāyavaya weapon, the illustrious and exceedingly generous Rāghava, bringing delight unto those ascetics, slew the rest. And having destroyed all those Rākshasas disturbing sacrifices, Raghu's descendant was honored by the saints, even as Indra in days of yore, after having vanquished the Asuras. And when the sacrifice had been completed, the mighty ascetic Viçwāmitra, beholding all sides cleared of Rākshasas, spake unto Kākutstha, saying,—"O mighty-armed one, I have obtained my desire; and thou hast executed thy preceptor's mandate. And, O illustrious hero, thou hast truly made this a Siddhacrama." Having thus extolled Rāma, he took Rāma and Lakshmana, to perform his evening devotions.

SECTION XXXI.

Those heroes, Rāma and Lakshmana, their interest secured, with glad hearts passed that night there. And when the night had passed away and the morning come, they together appeared before the saint, Viçwāmitra, and the rest. And having saluted that foremost of ascetics resembling flaming fire, they of honied speech spake unto him words exceedingly lofty.—"These servants of thine, O best of ascetics, have come before thee. Do thou command, O chief of anchorets, what command of thine are we to execute?" Thus addressed by them, the Maharshis with Viçwāmitra at their head spake unto Rāma, saying,—"A highly meritorious sacrifice, O foremost of men, is to be celebrated by Mithila's lord, Janaka. Thither shall we repair. And thou, O great among men, must accompany us, and there behold a wonderful jewel of a bow. And formerly this bow of immeasurable energy, and dreadful, and exceedingly effulgent at the sacrifice, had been conferred in court by the celestials (on king Devarāta). And neither gods nor Gandharbas, neither Asuras nor Rākshasas nor men, can fix the string upon it. And desirous of being acquainted with the prowess of this bow, many kings and princes came; but they in spite of their mighty strength, failed in stringing it. There, Kākutstha, thou wilt behold that bow belonging to the high-souled king of Mithilā,—as well as his exceedingly wonderful sacrifice. That rare bow, O foremost of men, furnished with an excellent device for griping it, had been solicited by Mithilā's lord as the fruit of his sacrifice; and the celestials conferred it upon him. And now, O descendant of Raghu, in the residence of king, the bow is worshipped like a deity with *aguru*, *dhupa*, and various other incenses." This having been said, that foremost of ascetics, in company with Kākutstha and the saints, departed. And on the eve of setting out, he addressed the sylvan deities, saying,—"Luck! I will, with my desire obtained, go from forth this Siddhāçrama unto the Himavat mountain on the north of the Jāhnavi." Having said this, that tiger-like ascetic, Kuçika's son, along with other anchorets having asceticism for their wealth, set out in a northerly direction.

And as that best of ascetics proceeded, he was followed by Brāhmanas upholding the Veda, carrying the sacrificial necessaries on an hundred cars. And birds and beasts dwelling in Siddhāçrama followed the high-souled Viçwāmitra having asceticism for wealth. And then followed by the body of devotees he dismissed the birds. And having proceded a longway, when the sun was sloping down, the ascetics rested on the banks of the Sona. And when the maker of day had set, having bathed and offered oblations unto the fire, those ascetics of immeasurable energy, placing Viçwāmitra in their front, sat them down. And Rāma also together with Sumitrā's son, having paid homage unto those ascetics, sat him down before the intelligent Viçwāmitra. Then Rāma of exceeding energy, influenced by curiosity, asked that foremost of ascetics, Viçwāmitra, having asceticism for his wealth, saying,—"O worshipful one, what country is this, graced with luxuriant woods? I am desirous of hearing this. Good betide thee, it behoveth thee to tell me this truly." Thus addressed by Rāma, that one of high austerities and excellent vows began in the midst of the saints to describe the oppulence of that region.

SECTION XXXII.

Once upon a time there was a mighty son of Brahmā, of high austerities, named Kuça. And he was cognizant of duty, and ever engaged in observing vows and honoring good men. And that high-souled one begat on Vaidarbhi, sprung from a respectable line, and endowed with all noble qualities, four sons like unto himself, and possessed of extraordinary prowess—Kucyāmva, and Kuçanābha, and Asurtarajas, and Vasu, resplendent and breathing exhaustless spirits. And with the deisre of enhancing Kshetrya merit, Kuça said unto his truthful and virtuous sons,—'Ye sons! do ye engage in the task of governing,—and thereby acquire immense merit.' Hearing Kuja's words, those four foremost of men and best of sons addressed themselves to founding seats for their government. And the highly energetic Kucāmva founded the city of Kaucāmvi; and the righteous Kuçanābha, the metropolis of Mahodaya; and the magnanimous Asurtarajas, Dharmāranya; and king Vasu, Girivraja, best of capitals. This city with these five mighty mountains shining around (otherwise) called Vasumati belongs to the high-souled Vasu. And the river known by the name of Sumāgadhi flows through the Magadhas. And in the midst of the five foremost of hills, it looks like a garland. And this Māgadhi, O Rāma, belongs unto the high- souled Vasu, taking, O Rāma, an easterly course, and flowing through fertile fields furnished with corn. And, O descendant of Raghu, the virtuous-souled Rājarshi Kuçanābha begat an hundred peerless daughters on Ghritāchi. And it came to pass that they endowed with youth, beautiful, and like unto the lightning in the rainy season, decked in excellent ornaments, coming to their garden, were merrily singing and dancing and playing on musical instruments, O Rāghava! And as they perfect in every limb, and unparalleled on earth in beauty, and endowed with all qualities, and furnished with youth and grace, were in the garden, like unto stars embosomed among clouds, that life of all, the air, beheld them and said,—"I seek for ye: do ye become my wives. Do ye renounce this human guise, and attain long lives. Youth verily is unstable, specially with the human beings: do ye attaining unfading youth, become immortal." Hearing this speech of the Air of ever fresh energy, the damsels ridiculing it, said,—"Thou rangest the hearts of all creatures, O foremost of celestials, and we also know thy influence. Wherefore, then, dost thou dishonor us? O foremost of celestials, we are the daughters of Kuçanābha, O divine one. And god as thou art, we can dislodge thee from thy place; but we refrain from doing so, lest thereby we lose our ascetic merit. May, O foolish one, that time never come, when disregarding our truthful sire, we following our inclination, shall resort to self choice. Our father verily is our lord and prime god. Of him even shall we become the wives unto whom our father giveth us away." At these words of theirs, that lord and adorable one, the Air, exceedingly enraged, then entered into their bodies, and broke all their limbs. Their bodies being thus broken by Air, those damsels, exceedingly agitated and overwhelmed with shame, with tears in their eyes entered the residence of the king. And finding his supremely beautiful and favorite daughters with their limbs broken, and woe- begone, the king bewildered, spake,—'Ye daughters, what is this? Who is it that thus disregards virtue? By whom have ye all come by this crooked form? And why demonstrating your grief, do ye not answer me?' Having said this, the king heaved a deep sigh and became eager to hear all about it."

SECTION XXXIII.

Hearing those words of the intelligent Kuçanābha, his hundred daughters touching his feet with their heads, said, —'O king, that life of all, the Air, was desirous of overcoming us, having recourse to an improper way; nor did he regard morality.—We have a father, good betide thee; and have no will of our own. Do thou ask our father about it, if he consent conferring us on thee.—But that wicked wight did not listen to our words; and as we were saying this, were we roughly handled by him.' Hearing those words of theirs, the highly pious and puissant king addressed his hundred beautiful daughters, saying,—'Ye have displayed a signal example of that forgiveness which is fit to be followed by the forbearing; and that ye have unanimously regarded the honor of my house, also conduces to your praise. Alike to men and women, forbearance is an ornament. And difficult it is for one to exercise that forbearance, specially in respect of the celestials. And may every descendant of mine possess forbearance like unto yours! Forbearance is charity; forbearance is truth; forbearance, O daughters, is sacrifice; forbearance is fame; forbearance is virtue,—yea,the universe is established in forbearance. Then dismissing his daughters, the king endowed with the prowess of celestials,and versed in counsel, began to consult with his counsellors about the bestowal of his daughters in respect of time and place and person and equality of lineage. And it came to pass that at this time an ascetic named Chuli, highly effulgent, with his vital fluid under control, and of pure practices, was performing Brāhmya austerities. And as the saint was engaged in austerities, good betide thee, Urmilā's daughter named Somadā—a Gandharbi—ministered unto him. And in all humility that virtuous one for a definite period was engaged in ministering unto him. And thereat, her spiritual guide was gratified with her. And, O descendant of Raghu, once he said unto her,—'I am gratified good betide thee! What good shall I render thee? Thereupon, concluding that the ascetic was gratified, the Gandharbi, cognizant of words, exceedingly delighted, sweetly addressed that one versed in speech,— 'Thou art furnished with the Brāhmya fire, art like Brahmā himself, and of mighty austerities. I desire of thee a righteous son endowed with the Brāhmya ascetic virtues. I am without a husband, good betide thee, and I am no one's wife. Upon me who am thy servant, thou shouldst confer such a son by help of Brāhmya means.' Thereupon, well pleased with her, the Brahmārshi Chulina conferred upon her an excellent Brāhmya mind-begotten son, named Brahmādatta. And that king, Brahmādatta, founded the flourishing city of Kampilyā,even as the sovereign of the celestials founded the celestial regions. And, O Kākutstha, the righteous king Kuçanābha finally decided on conferring his hundred daughters upon Brahmādatta. And inviting Brahmādatta that highly energetic lord of earth, with a glad heart conferred his hundred daughters upon him. And, O descendant of Raghu, king Brahmādatta resembling the lord himself of the celestials, by turns received their hands in marriage. And as soon as he touched them, the hundred daughters were cured of their crookedness, and became free from anguish, and were endowed with pre-eminent beauty, And upon beholding them delivered from (the tyranny of) the Air, the monarch Kuçanābha became exceedingly delighted, and rejoiced again and again. And he dismissed the newly married lord of earth, king Brahmādatta, in company with his consorts and the priests. And the Gandharbi Somadā rejoiced exceedingly at the completion of the nuptials of her son; and embracing her daughters-in-law again and again, and extolling her son, she expressed the fulness of her joy."

SECTION XXXIV.

'And, O Rāghava, when Brahmādatta was married, that sonless one, (Kuçanābha), with the intention of obtaining male offspring, took in hand a son-conferring sacrifice. And when the sacrifice had commenced, that son of Brahmā, the exceedingly noble Kuça, spake unto king Kuçanabha, saying, 'O son, there will be born unto thee a virtuous son like to thyself: thou wilt obtain even Gādhi,—and through him enduring fame in this world.' Having said this unto king Kuçanābha, Kuça, O Rāma, entering the welkin, went to the eternal regions of Brahmā. Then after sometime, an eminently virtuous son, named Gādhi, was born to the intelligent Kucanābha. O Kākutstha, even that highly pious Gādhi is my sire. And, O descendant of Raghu I, called Kauçika, am sprung from Kuça's line. And, O Rāghava, I had a sister of noble vows born before me. And her name was Satyavati; and she was bestowed upon Richika. And following her lord, she ascended heaven in her own proper person. And my highly generous sister, Kauçiki, hath finally assumed the form of a mighty river. And in order to compass the welfare of all creatures, my sister is now a noble and charming river of sacred waters, issuing from the Himavat mountains. And thenceforth, out of affection for my sister, Kauciki, I ever dwell happily in the vicinity of the Himavat, O Rāghava. And that virtuous Kauçiki, Satyavati, as well established in religion as truth, and chaste, and eminently pious, is now the foremost of streams. And, O Rāma it is only for the purpose of completing my sacrifice that leaving her behind, I have come to Siddhāçrama. And now by virtue of thy energy, have I attained fruition. Now, O Rāma, I have narrated unto thee the circumstances connected with the history of my line and myself, as also of this place, O mighty-armed one,—which thou hadst asked me to relate. But, O Kākutstha, while I was speaking, half the night hath been spent. Do thou now sleep, good betide thee,—so that thou mayst not feel any difficulty while on the journey. The trees stand motionless, and the beasts and birds are silent, and, O descendant of Raghu, all sides have become enveloped in nocturnal gloom. The midnight is gradually passing away; and the firmament thick-studded with stars resembling eyes, is illumined up with their light. And that dispeller of darkness, the mild-beaming moon, is rising, gladdening the hearts of all creatures with his splendour. And night-ranging beings—terrible carnivorous Yakshas and Rākshasas—walk hither and thither." Having said this, the mighty ascetic of exceeding energy paused. And those ascetics honoring him, said,—"Excellent! Excellent! This line belonging to the Kuçikas is ever exalted and devoted to virtue, And those foremost of men sprung in the Kuça race are high-souled and like unto Brahmārshis—and specially thou, O illustrious Viçwāmitra, art so. And that best of streams, Kauçiki, hath added lustre unto thy line." and the auspicious son of Kuçika having been extolled by those delighted ascetics—the foremost of their order—slept, like unto the sun, when setting. And Rāma too along with Sumitrā's son having in admiration praised that best of ascetics, enjoyed the luxury of slumber.

SECTION XXXV.

Having in company with the ascetics passed the remainder of the night on the banks of the Sona, Viçwāmitra, when the day broke, spake,—"O Rāma, the night hath passed away, and the morn hath come. The hour for performing the prior devotions hath arrived. Arise! arise! good betide thee! Do thou prepare for going." Hearing these words of his, Rāma, having finished his morning devotions and rites, and ready for departure said,—"This is the Sona, of excellent waters, fathomless, and studded with islets. O Brāhmana, by which way shall we cross?" Thus addressed by Rāma, Viçwāmitra replied,—"Even this path hath been fixed upon by me,—that, namely, which the Maharsais go." And having proceeded far, when the day had been half spent they beheld that foremost of streams, the Jahnavi, worshipped by ascetics. And having beheld that river furnished with sacred waters, and frequented by swans and cranes, the ascetics who accompanied Rāghava were exceedingly delighted. And they took up their quarters on the banks of the river. And then having bathed and duly offered oblations of water unto the gods and the manes of their ancestors, and performed Agnihotra[51] sacrifices, and partaken of clarified butter like unto nectar, those high-souled and auspicious ones, with glad hearts, sat down, surrounding Viçwāmitra. And the descendants of Raghu also sat down, occupying prominent places as befitted their rank. Then Rāma with a heart surcharged with cheerfulness spake unto Viçwāmitra, saying,—"O adorable one, I desire to hear how the Gangā flowing in three directions and embracing the three worlds, falls into the lord of streams and rivers." Influenced by Rāma's speech, the mighty ascetic Viçwāmitra entered upon the history of the Gangā's origin and progress, O Rāma, that great mine of ore, Himavat is the foremost of mountains. Unto him were born two daughters, unparalleled on earth in loveliness. And, O Rāma, their mother of dainty waist, the amiable daughter of Meru, named Menā, was the beloved wife of Himavat—she of whom was born Gangā

[51] Sacrifice with burnt offering—T.

the elder daughter of Himavat; and, O Rāghava, a second daughter was also born unto him, named Uma. And it came to pass that once upon a time, the deities, with the view of accomplishing some work appertaining to them as divine beings, in a body besought that foremost of mountains for that river flowing in three directions, Gangā. Thereupon, desirous of the welfare of the three worlds, Himavat in obedience to duty, conferred upon them his daughter flowing everywhere at will, and sanctifying all creatures. Thereat in the interests of the three worlds, accepting her, those having the welfare of the three worlds at heart, went away with Gangā, considering themselves as having attained their desire. The other daughter of the mountain, O descendant of Raghu, adopting a stern vow, began to carry on austerities, having asceticism for her wealth. And that best of mountains bestowed upon Rudra of unequalled form his daughter Uma, furnished with fiery asceticism, and worshipped of the worlds. And these, O Rāghava, are the daughters of that king of mountains, worshipped of all, *viz.*, Gangā, the foremost of streams, and the divine Umā. Now, O best of those endowed with motion, have I related unto thee how that sin-destroying one flowing with her waters in three diverse directions, first, O child, went to the firmament and then ascended the celestial regions."

SECTION XXXVI.

When the ascetic had spoken thus, both the heroes, Rāma and Lakshmana, saluting that first of anchorets, said,—"O Brāhmana, thou hast delivered this noble narration fraught with morality. Now it behoves thee to speak about the elder daughter of the mountain-king. Thou art extensively conversant with everything relative to men or gods. Why is it that that purifier of the worlds laveth three directions? And why is that foremost of streams, Gangā, famous as wending in three ways? And, O thou cognizant of morality, what are her performances in the three worlds?" Thereat Viçwāmitra having asceticism for his wealth, began to relate unto Kākutstha that history in detail in the midst of the ascetics. "In days of yore, O Rāma, the blue-throated one of mighty asceticism, having entered into matrimony, commenced upon knowing the goddess. And as that intelligent blue-throated god, Mahādeva, was thus engaged in sport, a devine hundred years passed away; and yet, O Rāma, chastiser of foes, no son was born of her. Thereat all the gods with the Grand sire at their head became exceedingly anxious. "Who will be able to bear the offspring of this union?" And thereupon the celestials repairing unto Mahādeva, thus addressed him, saluting low,—'O god of gods, O mighty deity, ever engaged in the welfare of all, it behoveth thee to be propitious at the humble salutations of the celestials. The worlds, O foremost of celestials, are incapable of bearing thy energy. Therefore, for the welfare of the three worlds, do thou, being furnished with Brahmā asceticism, in company with the goddess practise austerities, and rein in thy energy by thy native indomitableness. Do thou preserve these worlds; for it becometh thee not to destroy all.' Hearing the words of the deities, the great god of the worlds said unto them,—'So be it!' And addressing them again he said,—'Ye gods, by my own energy I will assisted by Umā bear my virile vigour,—therefore let the creation find rest! But tell me, ye foremost of celestials, who will sustain my potent virility rushing out from its receptacle?' Being thus addressed, the gods answered him having the bull for his mark,—'The earth will to-day bear thy vital flow.' Thus assured, the mighty lord of the celestials let go his vital fluid; and thereat the earth containing mountains and forests was over-spread with the energy. Then the gods spake unto the Fire, saying,—'Do thou in company with the Wind enter into this fierce and mighty energy!' And when the Wind had entered into it, it was developed into a white hill, and a forest of glossy reeds, resembling fire or the Sun. And here sprang from Fire Kārtikeya of mighty energy. And there- upon the celestials and the saints, with gratified hearts, began to pay enthusiastic adorations unto Umā aud Sivā. Then the Mountain's daughter, O Rāma, addressed the celestials, cursing them with eyes reddened in wrath,— 'While in association with Mahādeva for obtaining sons, I was broken in upon by ye,—for this, ye shall not be able yourselves to beget offspring on your wives. And from this day forth, your wives shall remain without issue.' Having thus spokeu unto the celestials, she cursed the Earth also, saying,—'O Earth, thou shalt have various forms, and many shall lord it over thee! Nor, stained because of my ire, shalt thou experience the pleasure that is felt on obtaining a son, O thou of wicked understanding, O thou that dost not wish me a son!' Witnessing the gods thus dis-tressed, the lord of the celestials set out in the direction presided over by Varuna.[52] And having repaired to the north side of that mountain,[53] Maheswara along with the goddess became engaged in austerities on the peak Himavatprabhava. I have now related unto thee, O Rāma, the spread of the Mountain's daughter, (Gangā). Do thou how together with Lakshmana listen to the narration of Bhāgirathi's po-tency."

SECTION XXXVII.

And on that celestial being engaged in austerities, the deities with Indra and Agni at their head, desirous of gaining over the generalissimo, appeared before the Grandsire. And, O Rāma, the gods with Agni at their head, bowing unto him, addressed that possessor of the six attributes, the Grand-sire, saying,—'0 God, that adorable one who had formerly consigned unto us the generalissimo, resorting to high asceticism, is practising austerities with Umā. Do thou now, O thou conver-sant with resources, so order as is advisable in the interests of the worlds! Verily thou art our prime way.' Hearing the words of the deities, the Grandsire of all creatures, consoling them with soft words, spoke unto them, saying,—'Even as the Mountain's daughter hath said, sons will not be born unto ye of your own wives. Her word is infallible of a certainty: there is no doubt about it. This is the celestial Gangā—she on whom Hutāsana[54] will beget a son—the foe-subduing generalissi-mo of the celestials. And the elder daughter of the Mountain will consider that son as brought forth by Umā; and Umā also will, without doubt, look upon him with regard.' Hearing these words of his, O descendant of Raghu, the gods bowing unto the Grand-sire, paid him homage. Then, O Rāma, repairing unto the Kailāça mountain teeming with metals, the deities commissioned Agni with the view of having a son (born unto him.) 'Do thou, O god, accomplish this work of the de-ities! O thou of mighty energy, do thou discharge thy energy into that daughter

---

[52] The West.—T.
[53] The Himalaya.—T.
[54] Fire.—T.

of the mountain, Gangā.' Thereupon giving his promise unto the gods, Pavaka[55] approached Gangā, saying, — 'Do thou, O Goddess, bear an embryo; for even this is the desire of the deities.' Hearing this speech, she assumed a divine appearance. And beholding her mightiness, Agni was shrunk up on all sides. And then Pavaka from all sides discharged his energy into her, — and thereat all her streams became surcharged with it, O descendant of Raghu. And unto him staying at the head of all the deities, Gangā spoke, saying, — 'O god, I am incapable of sustaining this new- sprung energy of thine: I am burning with that fire, and my consciousness fails me.' Thereupon that partaker of the oblations offered unto the gods, said unto Gangā, — 'Do thou bring forth thy embryo on the side of this Himavat!' Hearing Agni's words, Gangā of mighty energy cast her exceedingly effulgent embryo on her streams, O sinless one. And as it came out of her, it wore the splendour of molten gold; and in consequence of its fiery virtue, objects near and objects far were converted into gold and silver of unsurpassed sheen, — while those that were more distant were turned into copper and iron. And her excreta were turned into lead. In this wise, various metals began to increase on earth. And as soon as the embryo was brought forth, the woods adjoining the mountain, being overspread with that energy, were turned into gold. And from that day, O descendant of Raghu, gold of effulgence like unto that of fire, became known as Jātarupa, O foremost of men! And when the son was born, the deities with Indra and the Maruts enjoined ipon the Kirtikā stars to suckle him. 'Surely he shall be son into us all' — concluding thus, they as soon as he was born, by turns began to dispense milk unto him. Then the celestials called him Kārtikeya, saying, — 'Without doubt, this son shall become famed over the three worlds.' And hearing those words of theirs, the Kirtikās bathed the offspring that had issued from her womb, flaming like fire, and with auspicious marks. And, O Kākutstha, since Kārtikeya had issued from (Gangā's) womb, the celestials called that effulgent and mighty-armed one, Skanda.[56] And then the teats of the Kritikās were filled with milk; and thereupon assuming six mouths, he began to suck milk from the teats of those six. And having drunk the milk, that lord although then possessed of a tender frame, by virtue of his inborn prowess in one day vanquished the Danava forces. And him possessed of mighty effulgence, the celestials assembled with Agni as their leader sprinkled with water, by way of installing him as their generalissimo. He who, O Kākutstha, on the earth revereth Kārtikeya, is blessed, and attaineth righteousness, and being long-lived and obtaining sons and grand-sons, repaireth to the regions of Skanda."

SECTION XXXVIII.

Having said those words unto Rāma, composed of melodious letters, Kauçika again spoke unto Kākutstha, saying, — "Formerly there was a king—lord of Ayodhyā named Sagara. And it came to pass that righteous one, though eagerly wishing for children, was without issue. And Vidharbha's daughter, O Rāma, named Keçini, was the elder wife of Sagara. And she was virtuous and truthful. And the second wife of Sagara was called Sumati, who was the daughter of Arishtanemi

---

[55] Fire. — T.

[56] *Skanna* means *issuing from.* — T.

and the sister of Suparna.[57] And with those wives of his,that mighty king, coming to the Himavat, began to practise austerities on the mountain Bhriguprasravana. And when a full hundred years had been numbered, the ascetic that had been adored by means of these austerities, Brighu, best of those endowed with truth,- conferred a boon upon Sagara, saying, —'O sinless one, thou shalt obtain glorious offspring; and, O foremost of men, thou shalt attain unparalleled renown among men. And, O child, one of thy consorts shall bring forth a son who will perpetuate thy race; and the other give birth to sixty thousand sons.' As that best of men was saying this, those daughters of kings, exceedingly delighted, propitiating him, addressed him with clasped hands, —'Who of us, O Brāhmana, shall produce a single son, and who many? This, O Brāhmana, we wish to hear. May thy word prove true!' Hearing this, the highly pious Bhrigu said these pregnant words,—'Do ye unfold your minds. Who wishes for what boon,—between a single perpetuator of the line, and innumerable sons, possessed of mighty strength, and furnished with fame, and endowed with high spirits?' Hearing the ascetic's words, O descendant of Raghu, Keçini in the presence of the monarch chose, O Rāma, a single son to perpetuate the line; and Suparna's sister, Sumati, sixty thousand sons, high spirited and furnished with fame. And then, O son of Raghu, having gone round the saint and bowed down the head, the king went to his own capital, accompanied by his consorts. And after a length of time, the elder, Keçini, bore a son unto Sagara, known by the name of Asamanja. And Sumati, O foremost of men, brought forth a gourd. And when it burst open, out came from it sixty thousand sons. And the nurses fostered them by keeping them in jars filled with clarified butter. And after a great length of time, they attained to youth. And after a long lapse of time, Sagara's sixty thousand sons attained to youth and beauty. And O foremost of men,[58] the eldest son of Sagara, taking those children, would, O descendant of Raghu, often cast them into the Sarayu, and in mirth behold them sinking in the waters. Being thus evil-disposed, and injuring honest folks, and engaged in doing wrong unto the citizens, he was banished by his father from the city. And Asamanja had a son possessed of prowess, named Ansuman. And he was beloved of all men and fair-spoken towards every one.

"And, O foremost of men, it came to pass that after a long time had gone by, that lord of earth Sagara made up his mind, saying,—'I will sacrifice.' And having determined upon it, that one versed in the Vedas set about it, in company with his priests."

SECTION XXXIX.

When Viçwāmitra had ended, hearing his words, Rāma exceedingly pleased, spoke unto that ascetic resembling flaming fire, saying,—"I am anxious to hear in detail, good betide thee, how, O Brāhmana, my ancestor arranged for the sacrifice." Hearing those words of his, Viçwāmitra, smiling, eagerly spoke unto Kākutstha, saying,—"Do thou, O Rāma, hearken unto the story of the high-souled Sagara's sacrifice. Sankara's father-in-law is the far-famed Himavat. And approaching

[57] Garura.—T.

[58] The text has *Narasresthas*, put for Asamanja. Evidently this is an error. I make it a vocative.—T.

each other, the Himavat and the Vindhya beheld each other. And on the region lying between them took place, O foremost of men, that sacrifice of Sagara's. And that country, O best of men, is excellent as a sacrificial ground. And, O Kākutstha, equipped with a powerful bow, that mighty car-warrior, living under Sagara's sway, Ançumat, O child, followed the horse, for the purpose of protecting it. And it came to pass that with the intention of disturbing the sacrifice of that monarch, on a certain day Vāsava, assuming the form of a Rākshasi, stole away the sacrificial horse.[59] And, O Kākutstha, on the horse of that high-souled one being stolen, the priests said unto the king engaged in the ceremony,—'On this auspicious day, hath the sacrificial horse been stolen by violence. Do thou, O Kākutstha, slay him that steals the horse,—and bring it back. Otherwise the sacrifice will be defective, bringing us misfortune. Therefore, do thou, O king, act so, that the sacrifice may not be marred with defects.' Hearing the words of the priests, the king addressed his sixty thousand sons in the midst of his court, saying,—'Being, as this great sacrifice is, presided over by eminently pious Brāhmanas sanctified by mantras, I do not, ye foremost of men, ye sons, see how Rākshasas may find entrance into it. Therefore, repair ye, and seek for the horse, ye sons. Good betide you! Do ye search the entire earth engarlanded with oceans; and do ye search *Yoyana* after *Yoyana*, ye sons. And do ye delve the earth till ye light upon the horse, by my command following the track of that stealer of the horse. I have been initiated into this sacrifice with my grand-sons and priests.' And thereat the mighty princes, enjoined by their father, breathing high spirits, began to range the earth, O Rāma. Then they each fell to delving the bowels of the earth for the space of a *Yoyana* in length and breadth, with their hands resembling thunder-bolts in feel, and with darts like unto thunder-bolts, and with gigantic ploughshares. And being thus riven, the earth, O descendant of Raghu, began to send forth loud cries.

O Rāghava, O thou hard to repress, there arose an uproar from serpents, and Asuras, and Rākshasas, and other creatures, that were being slaughtered. And, O descendant of Raghu, they excavated the earth, O Rāma, for sixty thousand *Yoyanas*,—yea, as if they had intended to reach the lowest depths underground. Thus, O foremost of kings, those sons of the monarch dug all around Jamvudwipa, filled with mountains. Thereat, the gods together with the Gandharbas, and Asuras, and Pannagas, in trepidation appeared before the Grand-sire. And propitiating that high-souled one, they with melancholy countenances and in exceeding agitation, spoke these words unto the Grand-sire,—'O adorable one, the entire earth is being excavated by the sons of Sagara; and many are the high souled ones as well as the aquatic animals that are being slain in consequence.—This one is the disturber of our sacrifice, and by him hath the sacrificial horse been stolen,—saying this, Sagara's sons are committing havoc upon all creatures.''

SECTION XL.

Hearing the speech of the celestials, that possessor of the six attributes, the Grand-sire, spoke unto them exceedingly frightened and deprived of their senses on beholding the prowess of Sagara's sons like unto the Destroyer himself,—'This

---

[59] The Bengali edition reads this sloka differently.—T.

entire Earth belongeth unto the intelligent Vāsudeva, she being his consort. And that adorable one is indeed her lord. And assuming the form of Kapila, he unceasingly sustaineth the Earth. And the sons of king Sagara will be consumed by the fire of his wrath. The pre-ordained excavation of the Earth, as well as the destruction of Sagara's sons, had been foreseen by the far-sighted.' Hearing the words of the Grand-sire, those repressors of their foes, the three and thirty[60] celestials, being exceedingly rejoiced, went back to their respective quarters. And as the sons of Sagara were riving the Earth, there arose a mighty noise, like unto the bursting of thunder. Then, having riven the entire Earth and ranged it all around, the sons of Sagara together (returned to their father) and spake unto him, saying —'By us hath the Earth been extensively surveyed, and have powerful deities and Dānavas, Rākshasas, Piçāchas, Uragai and Pannagas been slain; and yet do we find neither the horse nor the stealer thereof. What are we to do now? Good betide thee, do thou consider it well.' Hearing those words of his sons, that foremost of kings, getting into a wrath, said, O descendant of Raghu, —'Do ye yet again, good betide ye, delve the earth, and having got at the stealer of the horse, cease.' Receiving this mandate of their sire, the sixty- thousand sons of the high-souled Sagara rushed towards the depths of the earth. And as they were engaged in excavating, they beheld the elephant of the quarter resembling a hill, named Virupāksha, holding the earth. And, O son of Raghu, that mighty elephant, Virupāksha, held on his head the entire earth with its mountains and forests. And, O Kākutstha, when on sacred days the mighty elephant, from fatigue, shaketh his head, then takes place the earthquake. Thereupon, O Rāma, going round that mighty elephant, and honoring him duly, they went on piercing the underearth. And having pierced the East, they pierced the South, — and in the Southern quarter also they beheld a mighty elephant—the high-souled Mahāpadma, resembling a huge hill, holding the earth on his head. And thereat they marvelled greatly. And having gone round him, the sixty- thousand sons of the high-souled Sagara began to penetrate into the Western region. And in the Western quarter also those highly powerful ones beheld the elephant of that quarter named Saumanasa, resembling a mighty mountain. And having gone round him, and asked him as to his welfare, they delving on, arrived at the Northern region. And on the North likewise, O foremost of the Raghus, they beheld Bhadra, white as snow, holding this earth on his goodly person. And having felt as well as gone round him, those sixty thousand sons of Sagara went on penetrating the depths of the earth. Then repairing to the famous North- eastern region, Sagara's sons becoming enraged, began to dig the earth. And there those high-souled, exceedingly powerful and vehement ones beheld the eternal Vāsudeva in the guise of Kapila. And there also, experiencing exceeding delight, O descendant of Raghu, they found his horse, browsing hard by. And knowing him to be the destroyer of the sacrifice, they bearing spades, and ploughs, and innumerable trees and crags, with eyes reddened with ire, furiously rushed against him, exclaiming, —'Stay! Stay! And thou it is that hast stolen our sacrificial horse. O thou of wicked understanding, know that thou hast fallen into the hands of the sons of Sagara.' Hearing this speech of theirs, Kapila, O descendant of Raghu, overwhelmed with rage uttered a tremendous roar. And then, O Kākutstha, the

---

[60] The eight *Vasus*, eleven *Rudras*, twelve *Adityas* and two *Acwins.*—T.

sons of Sagara were reduced to ashes by the high-souled and incomparable Kapila."

SECTION XLI.

Seeing the delay on the part of his sons, King Sagara, O son of Raghu, addressed his grandson, flaming in his native energy, saying,—Thou art heroic and accomplished and like unto thy uncles. Do thou enquire into the circumstances that have befallen thy uncles, as also about the way by which the horse hath escaped. And as there are stong and mighty creatures inhabiting the Earth's interior, with the view of resisting them, do thou take thy bow along with thy scimitar. And honoring those that deserve to be honored and slaying such as disturb thee, do thou, having attained thy end, come back, becoming the instrument for the completion of my sacrifice.' Thus duly enjoined by the high-souled Sagara, Ançumat endowed with fleet vigor, taking his bow as well as his scimitar, set out. And commanded by the monarch, O best of men, he found the underground way that had been carved out by those high-souled ones. And he found an exceedingly powerful elephant belonging to the cardinal point, worshipped by deities, and Dānavas, and Rākshasas, and goblins, and birds, and Uragas. And having gone round him, and asked him as to his welfare, he enquired after his uncles and the stealer of the horse. Hearing this, the mighty-minded elephant of that quarter answered—'O son of Asamanja, having attained thy object, thou wilt speedily return with the horse.' And hearing those words of his, Ançumat by turns duly asked the same question of all the elephants belonging to the cardinal points. And being honored by those guardians of the cardinal points, knowing words as well as their application in regard to time, place, and person, he was asked by them, saying,—'Do thou come with the horse!' Hearing those words of theirs, that one of fleet vigor repaired unto the spot where the sons of Sagara, his uncles, had been reduced to a heap of ashes. And (arriving there), Asamanja's son, smitten with grief, and being exceedingly afflicted at their destruction, bewailed in heaviness of heart. And exercised by grief and sorrow, that foremost of men espied there the sacrificial horse straying near. And desirous of offering oblations of water unto those princes, that highly powerful one in need of water, did not find any watery expanse in the neighbourhood. And it came to pass, O Rāma, that surveying wide, he descried the maternal uncle unto the princes, Suparna, the lord of birds, resembling the Wind. And thereupon Vinatā's son possessed of mighty strength spoke unto him, saying,—'Do not lament, O foremost of men. The destruction of these was for the welfare of all. These highly powerful ones had been consumed by the peerless Kapila,—therefore, thou ought not to offer water unto them in consonance with social usuage. Gangā, O foremost of men, is the elder daughter of Himavat. In her (streams) do thou perform the watery rites of thy uncles, O mighty-armed one: let that purifier of the worlds lave these, reduced to a heap of ashes. And on these ashes being watered by Gangā, dear unto all, the sixty thousand sons of Sagara will repair unto the celestial regions. Do thou, O highly pious one, go back, taking this horse, O foremost of men; and do thou complete the sacrifice of thy grand-father, O hero.' Hearing Suparna's speech, the exceedingly powerful Ançumat of mighty asceticism speedily taking the horse, retraced his steps. Then coming to the king who had been initiated into the ceremony, he, O descendant of Raghu, faithfully communicated unto him the words of Suparna, Hearing this sorrowful intelligence, the king duly finished the sacrifice agreeably to the scriptures. And having seen the completion of the sacrifice, that lord of earth entered his capital; but the king could not see how to bring Gangā on earth. And without being able to ascertain it, the mighty monarch after a long course of time, and having reigned for thirty thousand years, ascended heaven."

SECTION XLII.

When Sagara had bowed unto the influence of Time, the subjects selected the righteous Ançumat for their king. And, O descendant of Raghu, Ançumat proved a great ruler. And his sbn, the celebrated Dilipa, was also a great king. And, O Raghu's son, consigning unto Dilipa his kingdom, Ançumat entered upon rigid austerities on the romantic summit of the Himavat. And having for the space of thirty-two hundreds of thousands years carried on austeries in the woods, that highly famous one, crowned with the wealth of aceticism, attained the celestial regions. And the exceedingly powerful Dilipa, hearing of the destruction of his grand-fathers, was stricken with grief; yet he could not ascertain his course about it. And he constantly thought as to how Gangā could be brought down, how to perform their watery rites, and how to deliver them. And as that pious one furnished with self- knowledge was always meditating upon this, an eminently virtuous son was born unto him named Bhagiratha. And performing numerous sacrifices, the mighty king Dilipa reigned for thirty thousand years. And without having arrived at any definite decision in regard to their deliverance, the king, O puissant one, being attacked with an ailment, breathed his last. And having sprinkled his son Bhagiratha in the way of installing him in the kingdom, that prime of men, the king, by virtue of his own acts, repaired to the region of Indra. And, O descendant of Raghu, that royal saint Bhagiratha was possessed of righteousness, And being without issue, and desiring to obtain it, the mighty monarch consigned his kingdom and his subjects to the care of his counsellors, and engaged in bringing down Gangā. And, O Raghu's descendant, restraining his senses, and eating once a month, and surrounding himself with five fires, and with arms upraised, he for a long lapse of time performed austerities at Gokarna. And as he was performing his terrible austerities, a thousand years rolled away. And thereat that possessor of the six attributes and lord of all creatures, Brahmā, was well-pleased with that high-souled monarch. And presenting himself together with the celestials, the Grand-sire thus spoke unto the high-souled Bhagiratha engaged in austerities, —'0 Bhagiratha, O mighty monarch, pleased am I with thee, O lord of men, on account of thy ardent austerities; do thou, O thou of excellent vows, ask for the boon thou wouldst have.' Thereupon that great car-warrior, the highly powerful and mighty-armed Bhagiratha, with clasped hands, said unto the Grand-sire of all creatures, —'If, adorable one, thou art pleased with me, if thou wouldst grant me the fruit of my asceticism, may Sagara's sons receive water at my hands; and on the ashes of those high-souled ones being laved by the waters of Gangā, may my great-grand-fathers without fail repair unto heaven! And, O divine one, I beseech thee, may our line never languish for want of offspring. May, O God, this prime boon light upon Ikshwāku's race!' When the king had said this, the Grand-sire addressed him these sweet and auspicious words composed of melting letters,—'O mighty car-warrior Bhagiratha, high is this thy aim. Be it so, good betide thee, thou enhancer of the Ikshwāku line. This Haimavati Gangā, Himavat's elder daughter, even her to hold, O king, do thou employ Hara; for Gangā's fall, O king, Earth will not be able to sustain. And to hold her, O king, find I none save the weilder of the Trident." Having thus addressed the monarch, and greeted Gangā, the creator of the worlds repaired to heaven with the celestials.

SECTION XLIII.

When that god of gods had gone away, Bhagiratha, O Rāma, pressing the earth with his thumb, spent a year in adoring Sivā. And when the year was complete, Uma's lord, Paçupati, worshipped of all the worlds, spake unto the king, saying,—'O foremost of men, I am well-pleased with thee: I will do what will be for thy welfare. I will hold the Mountain's daughter on my head.' Then, O Rāma, that one bowed unto by all creatures, the elder daughter of Himavat, assuming an exceedingly mighty shape, with irresistible impetus precipitated herself from the welkin upon Sivā's gracious head. And that divine one, Gangā, exceedingly difficult to sustain, thought,—'I will enter the nether regions, carrying off Sankara by my streams.' Knowing her proud intention, the adorable Hara waxed wroth; and the three-eyed deity set his heart upon enveloping her. And, O Rāma, as that sacred one plunged upon Rudra's holy head of tangled locks, resembling Himavat, she could by no means reach the earth, despite all her endeavours; nor did she obtain egress from under the matted locks. And she wandered there for many a year. And finding Gangā in this plight, Bhagiratha became again engaged in high austerities. And thereupon Sivā, O descendant of Raghu, was exceedingly gratified; and cast Gangā off in the direction of the Vindu lake. And as she was let off, seven streams branched out from her. And the three streams of the excellent Gangā of auspicious waters went in an easterly direction; while the Suchakshu, the Sitā, and that mighty river the Sindhu flowed on the auspicious west. And the seventh followed Bhagiratha's car. And that royal saint, the exceedingly puissant Bhagiratha, mounted on a superb car, went before; and Gangā followed him. And she descended from the welkin upon Sankara's head, thence alighting upon the earth; and there her waters flowed with thundering sounds. And earth looked beautiful with swarms of fallen and falling fishes, and tortoises, and porpoises. And then celestials and saints and Gandharbas, and Yakshas and Siddhas mounted on excellent elephants and horses and cars resembling cities, looked on Gangā descending upon the earth. And the celestials stationed on cars were struck with surprise; and all creatures marvelled at the excellent descent of Gangā. And eager to witness the spectacle, celestial hosts of immeasurable energy came there. And in consequence of the celestials coming thither, and the effulgence of their ornaments, the firmament free from clouds, shone as if with an hundred suns. And the sky was graced with fast-fleeting porposies and serpents and fishes resembling playing lightning; and the welkin scattered with pale foam-flakes by thousands, appeared as if it was scattered with autumnal clouds swarming with cranes. And the river proceeded sometimes rapidly, and sometimes awry, and sometimes in volumes, and sometimes sloping, and sometimes ascending, and sometimes languidly; and sometimes water clashed with water; and sometimes ascending an upland, it descended into a dell. And the pellucid and pure water first descending upon Sankara's head, and thence on to the earth, appeared exceedingly beautiful. And there the saints and the Gandharbas, as well as the inhabitants of the earth, touched the sacred water flowing from Bhaba's body. And those that had fallen from the sky unto the earth in consequence of some curse or other, having bathed there, and thereby having their sins washed and removed by that sanctifying water, again ascended the sky and entered their respective regions. And through the agency of that shining water, all beings, feeling delight, rejoiced, and having bathed in Gangā, became cleansed from sin. And stationed on an excellent car that mighty king, the royal saint Bhagiratha, went first, and Gangā went at his back. And the gods, and the saints, and the Daityas, and the Dānavas, and the Rākshasas, and the foremost of Gandharbas and Yakshas, and the Kinnaras, and the mighty Uragas, and the Serpents, and the Apsarās, O Rāma and the acquatic animals in a body following Bhagiratha's car, with glad hearts went in the wake of Gangā. And withersoever king Bhagiratha went, the famous Gangā, foremost of streams, capable of destroying all sins, went. And Gangā flooded the sacrificial ground of the high-souled Jahnu, of wonderful deeds, as he was performing a sacrifice. Thereat, O Rāghava, reading her insolence, Jahnu, waxing wroth, drank up all her wonderful waters. Thereupon, the deities, and the Gandharbas, and the saints, struck with amazement, fell to worshipping that foremost of men, the high-souled Jahnu and brought Gangā into the daughtership of that high souled one. And that highly energetic lord, being propitiated, let Gangā off through his ears. Therefore it is that Gangā goes by the name of Jahnu's daughter Jāhnavi. Then Gangā again began to follow Bhagiratha's car. And having reached the ocean, that foremost of streams, with the object of accomplishing his work, entered into the subterranean regions. And having carefully brought Gangā, that royal saint, Bhagiratha, having his senses bewildered beheld his grand-fathers reduced to ashes. And the excellent waters of Gangā overflowed that heap of ashes; and thereupon, O best of the Raghus, they, their sins purged, attained heaven."

SECTION XLIV.

When having arrived at the Ocean, the king wending in Ganges wake, entered underneath the Earth, at that spot where those (sons of Sagara) had been reduced to ashes. And, O Rāma, on the ashes being washed by the waters of Gangā, Brahmā, the lord of all creatures thus spoke unto the monarch,—'O most puissant of men, the sixty three thousand sons of the high-souled Sagara have been delivered—and they have ascended heaven like unto celestials themselves. And, O lord of earth, as long as the waters of the ocean shall endure in the world, Sagara's sons shall reside in heaven like unto celestials. And this Gangā shall become thy eldest daughter; and she shall attain celebrity among all, being called after thy name. And Gangā is called both Tripathagā and Bhāgirathi. And she is known as Tripathagā, in consequence of her proceeding in three directions. Do thou now, O lord of men, here offer oblations of water unto thy grand sires,—and thereby, O king, make good thy promise. And, O king, that foremost of righteous ones, thy ancestor of exceeding renown, had failed to atain his desire. And, O child, Ançu-mat likewise unparalleled in the worlds in energy had failed in realising his cherished promise of bringing down Gangā. And then again that royal saint, crowned with qualities, of austerities like unto mine, ever abiding by his Kshatriya duties, even Dilipa's self—thy exceedingly puissant sire—O eminently righteous one—had failed in bringing down Gangā according to his cherished resolve, O sinless one. And now, O foremost of men, that promise having been fulfilled by thee, thou shalt attain signal glory in the world by the common consent of all. And, O vanquisher of thy foes, having brought about Gangā's descension, thou shalt from this act of thine also attain the regions of Brahmā. Do thou, O best of men, lave thyself in these waters incapable of being rendered worthless. O prime of men,—and thereby become purified, and attain sanctity. And do thou perform the watery rites of thy grand-sires. May luck be thine, I shall now repair to my own regions: do thou depart, O king.' Having said this, the illustrious lord of the celestials—the Grand-sire of all creatures—went unto the celestial regions. And the royal saint king Bhagiratha also of high fame having performed his ablutions and purified himself, and duly and in proper order offered oblations of water unto the sons of Sagara, entered his capital. And attaining exceeding prosperity, that foremost of men ruled his kingdom; and, O descendant of Raghu, having him as their sovereign, the people rejoiced greatly; and with their griefs removed, and prosperity secured, they lived in peace of mind. Thus, O Rāma, have I detailed unto thee the history of Gangā. Auspiciousness mayst thou obtain! Good betide thee, the evening draweth nigh. He that reciteth this story conferring prosperity, fame, long life, and heaven unto Vipras, Kshatriyas, and others, attaineth the good graces of his ancestors and the celestials; and, O Kākutstha, he that listeneth to the sacred history of Ganges descent, conferring length of days, attaineth all his desires, and all his sins are destroyed, and his life and fame increase.'

SECTION XLV.

Hearing the words of Viçwāmitra, Rāghava, together with Lakshmana, was struck with amazement,—and spoke unto Viçwāmitra, saying,—"O Brāhmana, wonderful is the story that thou hast recited unto us, *viz*; that of Gangā's sacred descension and the replenishing of the Ocean. And, O afflicter of foes, as we had been reflecting upon all this at length, the night hath passed away as if it were a moment. And the live-long night hath passed away as I in company with Sumitrā's son, was pondering over Viçwāmitra's auspicious speech." Then in the morning which happened to be bright, that subduer of his foes, Raghu's descendant, addressed the ascetic Viçwāmitra, who had finished his devotion,—"The auspicious night is past,—and we shall (again) listen to thy wonderful narrations. Let us now cross over this sacred stream—foremost of rivers—wending in three ways. And learning that thou hast arrived at this place, the pious ascetics have speedily come hither, and have also brought this barque with a spacious carpet." Hearing those words of the high-souled Rāghava, Kauçika crossed over the crowds of ascetics; and on reaching the north bank, he paid homage unto the saints. And when they had landed on the banks of tlie Gangā, they beheld a city named Viçāla. And thereupon speedily that foremost of ascetics in company with Rāghava, went towards

Viçāla,—beautiful and elegant like unto the celestial regions. Then the highly wise Rāma, with folded hands, asked that mighty ascetic Viçwāmitra concerning the excellent city of Viçāla,-"0 mighty ascetic, what royal line resideth in yonder large city? I desire to hear this, good betide thee; and great is my curiosity." Hearing those words of Rāma, that foremost of ascetics began to relate the history of Viçāla, saying,—"Do thou listen, O Rāma, to what I had heard from Sakra relating this history; and, O descendant of Raghu, do thou listen to all that befell in this city. Formerly in the Krita age, O Rāma, Diti's highly powerful sons, as well as those of Aditi, possessed of prowess, and virtuous and pious—high-souled ones both—O foremost of men, fell to reflecting,—'How can we become exempt from decrepitude and disease, and immortal.' And as they reflected, it struck them,— 'By churning the ocean of milk, we must obtain ambrosia.' Then deciding upon churning (the ocean), those ones of immeasurable energy making Vāsuki the cord, and the Mandara (hill), the stick, began to churn the deep. And after a thousand years had gone by, the hoods (of the serpent) serving as the churning cord, began to vomit virulent venom and to bite at the crags, with their fangs. And thereat there came out powerful poison like unto fire; and in consequence the entire universe with celestials, and Asuras, and men, began to burn. And thereupon, intending to seek refuge, they appeared before that mighty god, Sankara, or Paçupati, or Rudra,—hymning him,—'Save us.' 'Save us.' When that master, the lord of the celestials, was being thus addressed by the deities, there appeared before them Hari bearing the conch and the discus. And smiling Hari said unto the trident-bearing Rudra,—'O chief of the celestials, since thou art the foremost of the gods, this that hath come out of the ocean churned by the celestials, is thine. Remaining here, O lord, do thou receive the first offering in the form of this poison.' Having said this, that best of celestials vanished there. Witnessing the dismay of the celestials, and hearing also the words of Sarngin, Sivā took in that dreadful poison as if it were nectar; and then leaving the deities, the worshipful Hara went away. And then, O descendant of Raghu, as the celestials resumed the churning, that foremost of hills serving as the cord, entered the subterranean regions. Thereupon the gods and the Gandharbas fell to extolling the slayer of Madhu, saying,—'Thou art the way of all beings, of the celestials in especial. Do thou, O mighty-armed one, protect us, and recover the mountain.' Having heard this, Hrishikesa, or Hari, assuming the form of a tortoise, stood in the sea, supporting the hill on his back; and that Soul of all, Keçava best of male beings, taking hold of the top of the hill by his hand, began to churn the deep, stationed in the midst of the celestials. And after a thousand years had rolled on, arose a male being impregnated with the Ayurveda,[61] of exceedingly righteous soul, called Dhanwantari, bearing in his hands a stick, and a Kamandalu. And there arose also, from the cream of the churning waters, those magnificent dames the shining Apsarās. And, O foremost of men, as they had emerged from water, they are called *Apsarās*.[62] And there sprang sixty *Kotis* of shining Apsarās. And, O Kākutstha, the female attendants of those are numberless. And neither the deities nor the Dānavas would accept them,—and in consequence of this non-acceptance, they are known as women belonging to all.

---

[61] Science of Medicine.—T.

[62] Ap means water.—T.

And then, O Raghu's descendant, arose the eminently pious daughter of Varuna, Vāruni, who fell to looking for acceptance. And Diti's sons, O Rāma, did not accept the daughter of Varuna,—and Aditi's sons, O hero, accepted that one of blameless limbs. And hence Diti's sons go by the name of Asuras; and Aditi's by that of Suras. And the celestials became exceeding glad, on having accepted Vāruni. And, O foremost of men, next arose Uchhaiçravā—best of horses, and also Kaustubha; and next, the excellent ambrosia. And,0 Rāma, tremendous was the carnage for the porsession thereof (ambrosia); and Aditi's and Diti's sons fought together. And the Asuras assembled together with the Rākshasas; and, O hero, mighty was the battle that was fought, striking terror into the three worlds. And when a great havoc had been committed, the highly powerful Vishnu, assuming a captivating form speedily stole away the ambrosia. And those that came forward before that best of male beings, Vishnu, knowing no deterioration, were crushed in conflict by Vishnu in a different form. And in that exceedingly dreadful battle between the sons of Diti and Aditi, those heroic ones, *viz.*, Aditi's heroic sons slaughtered those of Diti. And having slaughtered the sons of Diti and regained his kingdom, Purandara, happily began to rule the worlds, containing saints and Chāranas."

SECTION XLVI.

And on those sons of her being slain, Diti afflicted with great grief, thus addressed her husband, Maricha's son, Kaçyapa,—'O adorable one, thy high-souled sons have slain mine. I now wish for a son, who, obtained through long austerities, will be able to slay Sakra. And I will engage in austerities: it behoves thee to grant me such an embryo,—such a slayer of Sakra it behoves thee to promise me.' Hearing those words of hers, Maricha's son, Kaçyapa of exceeding energy answered the deeply aggrieved Diti, saying,—'Be it so.' Good betide thee, do thou become pure, O ascetic. If thou remain pure, when a full thousand years shall be complete, thou wilt give birth unto a son who will slay Sakra in battle. And through me, thou wilt give birth to a son that will destroy the three worlds.' Having said this, that highly energetic one rubbed her person with his palm. And having rubbed her, he said,—'Luck!' and then went away to carry on austerities. And when he had gone, Diti, O foremost of men, becoming exceedingly delighted, went unto Kuçaplava[63] and began to practise rigid mortifications. And, O foremost of men, as she was practising austerities, the thousand-eyed deity most dutifully ministered unto her. And the thousand-eyed one provided for her fire, and *Kusa*, and faggots, and water, and fruits, and roots, and other things that she wanted. And at all times, Sakra served Diti by rubbing her person, and removing her fatigue. And when ten years only were wanting to complete the thousand years, Diti, O descendant of Raghu, being exceedingly delighted, thus spoke unto the thousand-eyed one,—'O best of those endowed with prowess, of me engaged in austerities, ten years only remain (to complete the period.) And after that time, good betide thee, thou wilt behold thy brother. I will, O son, bind him unto thee in affection, whom I had besought for to compass thy destruction,—so that, the fever of thy heart removed, thou wilt with him enjoy the victory of the three worlds. On thy high-souled sire having been besought by me, he, O foremost of celestials, granted me

[63] An asylum on the cast, otherwise called Beshalaksha.—T.

the boon that after a thousand years, I shall obtain a son.' And it came to pass that having said this, the sun being in his meridian, the worshipful Diti with her feet placed at that part of the bed which should contain her head, was overpowered by sleep. And thereupon seeing her resting her feet at the place where she should place her head,—and consequently unclean, Sakra was exceedingly delighted, and smiled. And, O Rāma, Purandara entered into her womb, and that highly self-controlled one severed the embryo in seven parts. And the embryo being pierced by the thunder-bolt of an hundred knots, cried at the top of its voice, and thereat Diti awoke. 'Do not cry, do not cry,'—exclaimed Sakra: and even while it was crying, the mighty-minded Vāsava continued piercing it 'Do not slay it; do not slay it,' said Diti. Thereupon, in consideration of the honor of his mother, Sakra went out.

Then he with clasped palms accosted Diti, saying,—'O worshipful one, thou didst sleep with thy feet placed where thy head should have lain, and hast therefore become impure. And finding this opportunity, I severed in seven pieces that would be slayer of mine in battle. Do thou, O worshipful one excuse me.

SECTION XLVII.

When the embryo had been sundered in seven, Diti exceedingly aggrieved humbly spoke unto the irrepressible thousand-eyed deity, saying,—'By my fault it is that the embryo hath been sundered in seven. O chief of the celestials, herein thou art guilty of no transgression, O destroyer of Vala, And since calamity hath befallen the embryo, I wish to do thee a good turn. Let the seven parts become the guardians of the seven Maruts. And, O son, let my sons having noble forms, becoming famous as Mārutas range the Vātaskandha regions in heaven. And let one range Brahmā's regions, and another Indra's, and the highly illustrious third also range around, being known as Divya Vayu.[64] And, O best of celestials, by thy command, let the four remaining sons of mine known by the name which thou hast mentioned, range about in appointed periods.' Hearing her words, that destroyer of Vala; the thousand-eyed Purandara, with clasped palms said,—'All this that thou hast said must come to pass; there is no doubt about it. Good betide thee, thy sons endowed with celestial forms, shall range about. And it hath been heard by us that having thus ascertained in that hermitage, the mother and the son, O Rāma, went to heaven, their desire obtained. Even this, O Kākutstha, is the place where formerly the mighty Indra sojourned, and where he attended upon Diti of accomplished ascetic success. And, O most powerful of men, Ikshwāku had an exceedingly righteous son born unto him of Alamvushā, known by the name of Viçāla. And here stood a palace, built by him, called Viçālā. And Viçāla's son, O Rāma, was the mighty Hemachandra. And after Hemachandra comes the celebrated Suchandra. And, O Rāma, the son of Suchandra was Dhumrāswa. And then was born Srinjaya, son unto Dhumrāswa. And Srinjaya's son was the powerful Sahadeva. And Sahadeva's son was the pre-eminently pious Kuçāçwa. And Kuçāçwa's son was the puissant Somadatta. And now, O Kākutstha, Somadatta's son the effulgent and invincible and renowned Sumati resideth in this city. And by the grace of Ikshwāku, all the sovereigns of Viçālā are long-lived, and high-

---

[64] Etherial air.—T.

souled, and puissant, and pious. And here will we happily spend a night; and on the morning of the morrow thou wilt, O foremost of men., behold Janaka.' And having heard that the illustrious Viçwāmitra had come, that best of kings, the effulgent Sumati, appeared before him. And having paid Viçwāmitra high homage together with his priests and friends, and with clasped hands enquired after the former's welfare, he addressed Viçwāmitra, saying, — "Blessed are we, and obliged are we, whose domains, O ascetic, have been graced with thy presence. Surely none is more blessed than I am."

SECTION XLVIII.

Having met together, they enquired after each other's welfare. And then Sumati spoke unto the mighty ascetic, saying, — "Good betide thee, boasting of the prowess of celestials of elephantine or leonine gait, heroic resembling tigers or bulls, possessed of expansive eyes like lotus-petals, bearing scimitars and bows and quivers, like unto the Açwinis in grace, endowed with youth, like unto celestials fancy-led, descended from etherial regions to the earth beneath, whose sons, O ascetic, are these boys, and what for have they come hither, and why also is it that they journey on foot? And adoring all directions, like unto the Sun or the Moon adorning the firmament, and resembling each other in personal proportions, and expressions, and gestures, and equipped with excellent weapons, and war-like, how have these paragons cf men come into this impracticable way? I wish to hear all this related truly." Having heard his words, Viçwāmitra faithfully related all about it. Hearing Viçwāmitra's words, the king was extremely surprised and having those sons of Daçarātha as his all-worthy guests, received with becoming respect those highly powerful ones deserving of hospitality. And meeting with such splendid reception from Sumati, those descendants of Raghu spent there a night, and the next day set out for Mithila. And beholding Janaka's beauteous city, the ascetics exclaiming, — 'Excellent, excellent' fell to admiring Mithila. And in a grove at Mithila, Rāghava saw an ancient, lonely, and romantic asylum, and asked that foremost of ascetics, saying, — "What is this that looketh like an asylum, though without any ascetics? I wish to hear, O worshipful one, to whom this asylum belonged in time past." Hearing this speech addressed by Raghu's descendant, that one versed in speech, the highly energetic and mighty saint, Viçwāmitra, answered, — "Ah! Do thou listen. I will tell thee through the wrath of what high-souled one this hermitage came to be cursed. O foremost of men, this excellent asylum honored by ths celestials themselves, formerly belonged to the high- souled Gautama. And here, O illustrious prince, in days of yore Gautama in company with Ahalyā carried on austerities for a long series of years. And perceiving occasion, Sachi's lord, the thousand-eyed deity, assuming the form of that ascetic thus addressed Ahalyā, — '0 exceedingly beautiful one, those bent upon sport, do not stay for the menstrual season. And, O graceful one, I desire to enjoy thy company (on the instant). Thereupon, out of curiosity, that one of perverse understanding consented to the proposals of the chief of the celestials. Then, having attained her object, she spoke unto that foremost of the celestials, saying. — 'O best of the immortals, I have obtained my desire, — do thou speedily go from his place, O lord. Do thou, O lord of the celestials, from a sense of repectibility preserve thyself and me also.' Indra too smiling, said unto Ahalyā, —'O thou of shapely hips, pleased am I. Now I repair unto my own place.' Having known her thus, Indra, Rāma, exceedingly apprehensive of Gautama, then hurriedly sallied out of the thatched cottage. Just at this time, Indra saw that mighty ascetic Gautama entering—that foremost of anchorets, incapable of being repressed by the deities and the Dānavas, and equipped with ascetic energy, having bathed in the waters of holy spots, and flaming like fire, carrying faggots and *kusa* grass. And seeing him, the countenance of the lord of the celestials turned pale. And seeing the wicked thousand-eyed deity in the guise of an ascetic, the well-behaved anchoret fired with rage said, —'And since, O thou of wicked understanding assuming my form, thou hast done this foul deed, thou shalt lose thy scrotum.' And soon as the high-souled Gautama had said this in ire, the scrotum of the thousand-eyed one dropped to the earth. And having seen Sakra in this plight, he cursed his wife also, —'For a thousand years thou shalt live here feeding upon air, without food, tormented with repentance and thou shalt remain in this hermitage unseen of any. And when the irrepressible son of Daçarātha Rāma, shall come to this deep wood, thou shalt be cleansed of thy sin. And, O wicked one, ministering unto him the rites of hospitality, with a mind free from ignorance and covetousness, thou shalt in thy own form with joy regain my side.' Having said this to that wicked woman the highly energetic Gautama of rigid austerities, forsaking this hermitage, began to carry on penances on the romantic summit of the Himavat, inhabited by Siddhas and Charanas."

SECTION XLIX.

"And having been deprived of his scrotum, Sakra with eyes tremulous with fear, addressed the celestials with Agni at their head, as well as the Siddhas and the Gandharbas and the Chāranas, saying, —'I have accomplished the work of the celestials by stirring the ire of the high- souled Gautama, and thereby disturbing his austerities. And in doing so, I have been deprived of my scrotum; and Ahalyā also hath been put down. And I have deprived him of his ascetic energy by causing him to utter a mighty curse,—and, therefore, ye celestials, and saints, and Chāranas, ye should restore my scrotum unto me who have served the gods.' Hearing Satakratu's[65] words, the deities along with the Maruts led by Agni, presented themselves before the divine Pitris.[66] And then Agni addressed the latter, saying, —'This ram is possessed of a scrotum; while Sakra hath been deprived of his. Do ye taking the scrotum of the ram furnish Sakra with it. And although deprived of the scrotum, the ram will be able to grant consummate satisfaction unto ye. And on those that will offer such a ram for your entertainment, ye will bestow undying and profuse merit.' Hearing Agni's speech, the assembled Pitris, rooting up the scrotum of the ram, joined it unto the person of the thousand-eyed deity. Thence- forth, Kākutstha, the divine Pitris together feast upon scrotumless rams, for their scrotum had been joined unto the person of Indra. And thenceforth, O Rāghava, Indra also through the high-souled Gautama's ascetic energy, hath been bearing the scrotum of a ram. Therefore, O highly powerful one, do thou enter the

[65] Lit. the performer of an hundred sacrifices, one of the appellations of Indra.
[66] The ancestors.

hermitage of that pious one, and deliver the dignified and divinely fair Ahalyā.' On hearing Viçwāmitra's words, Rāghava in company with Lakshmana, placing Viçwāmitra in their front, entered the asylum; and they beheld that magnificent dame flaming in ascetic energy; and incapable of being gazed at too near even by the celestials and the Asuras; as if created by the Deity to be the divinely charming Woman; like a flame hid in smoke; or the brightness of the full moon clouded and dimmed in mist; or the solar splendour incapable of being beheld on account of clouds. And by virtue of Gautama's word, she had been incapable of being seen by any in the three worlds, till the sight of Rāma. And now the curse having come to an end, she could be perceived by them. And the two descendants of Raghu then took hold of her feet; but remembering Gautama's words, she on her part took hold of theirs. And with a collected mind she gave them water for their feet as well as *Arghya*, and extended unto them the rites of hospitality. And the Kākutsthas accepted the homage thus rendered according to the ordinance. And blossoms began to shower copiously to the sounds of kettledrums; and the Gandharbas and the Apsarās began to rejoice greatly. And exclaiming, 'Excellent, excellent,' the celestials honored Ahalyā, as with a person purified by penance, she again came under Gautama's governance. And the highly energetic Gautama also happy on his union with Ahalyā, honored Rāma highly, and that one of mighty mortifications then became engaged in austerities. And having duly received signal honors from the great ascetic Gautama, Rāma set out for Mithilā.

SECTION L.

Then proceeding north-east Rāma in company with Sumitrā's son, placing Viçwāmitra at their head, appeared before the sacrificial ground. And Rāma and Lakshmana said unto that puissant ascetic,—"Great is the pomp and splendour of the high-souled Janaka's sacrifice. And, O pious one, many thousand of Brāhmanas inhabiting various regions, and well-read in the Vedas (have come to this sacrifice); and the abodes of ascetics are thronged with hundreds of cars. Do thou, O Brāhmana, arrange for some place where we may put up." Hearing Rāma's words, the mighty ascetic Viçwāmitra selected for their abode a well-watered spot free from bustle and tumult. And hearing of Viçwāmitra's arrival, the best of monarchs without blame, placing the priests Satānanda before him, as well as the high-souled family priests, speedily taking the *arghya*, at once went out in humble guise, and offered it unto Viçwāmitra according to the ordinance. Having accepted that homage of the high-souled Janaka, the ascetic enquired after the king's welfare, and the uninterrupted performance of his sacrifice. And the king together with his priests, having enquired of the ascetics as to their welfare, cheerfully embraced them all in a proper way. Then he with clasped hands, spoke unto that foremost of anchorets, saying,—"O worshipful one, do thou along with these eminent ascetics, take thy seat." Hearing Janaka's words, the mighty ascetic sat him down. And the king also, in company with his priests and counsellors sat down around in order of rank. And then the monarch looking into Viçwāmitra's face, said.—"To-day by the grace of the gods, hath my sacrifice been crowned with success—to-day have I reaped the fruit of my saciifice by beholding thy worshipful self. Blessed and obliged am I whose sacrificial ground, O Brāhmana, hath been graced by thee along with these ascetics. Twelve days, O Brahmārshi, have been fixed for the period of initiation by the sages. On the expiry of that term, thou wilt, O Kauçika, behold the celestials come unto the sacrifice for claiming their respective shares." Having said this, the king with a cheerful countenance, with folded hands, again intently asked that foremost of ascetics,—"These youths, good betide thee, like unto celestials in prowess, of the gait of lions or elephants, heroic, and resembling tigers or bulls, of expansive eyes like unto lotus-petals, bearing scimitars, quivers and bows, graceful like unto the Açwins, endowed with youth, resembling immortals fancy-led from heaven unto the earth—whose sons, O ascetic, are they and what for have they come, and why again have they come afoot? And bearing excellent arms, whose sons, O mighty anchoret, are these heroic ones, who grace this place even as the sun and the moon do the welkin, and resemble each other in bodily proportions, expression, and gestures; wearing side-locks and of warlike mien? This I would hear truly related." Hearing this speech of the high-souled Janaka, that ascetic of immeasurable soul related all about Daçarātha's sons,—their sojourn in Siddhāçrama, and the slaughter there of the Rākshasas, their undaunted journey, the sight of Viçāla, the encounter with Ahalyā and Gautama, Rāma's curiosity about the mighty bow, and visit there for beholding the same. Having related all this unto the high-souled Janaka that one endowed with exceeding energy, the mighty ascetic Viçwāmitra, paused.

SECTION LI.

Hearing the narration of the intelligent Viçwāmitra, Gautama's eldest son, the exceedingly energetic Satātnanda of rigid austerities, highly effulgent by virtue of his asceticism, with his down standing on end wondered greatly at the sight of Rāma. And seeing the king's sons seated at their ease, he said unto that foremost of ascetics, Viçwāmitra, —"O most powerful of anchorets, by thee was my illustrious mother, grown old in asceticism, shown unto the king's son. Did my famous and exalted mother entertain with the produce of the woods Rāma worthy of every one's homage? And, O highly energetic one, hath that old story relative to my mother having been wronged by that celestial, been communicated unto Rāma? And, O Kauçika, good betide thee, hath my mother, in consequence of beholding Rāma, been united with my revered sire? And, O son of Kuçika, hath the highly energetic Rāma come hither, after having been rendered homage by my high- souled revered sire? And, O Kuçika's son, was my revered sire of quiescent soul, saluted by Rāma when he arrived there?" Hearing those words of his, the mighty ascetic Viçwāmitra, skilled in speech, replied unto Satānanda, cognizant of words, saying,—"O best of ascetics, nothing necessary was omitted by me,—but everything hath been done. And the ascetic's wife hath been united with him, even as Renuka with Bhrigu's son."[67] Hearing the speech of the intelligent Viçwāmitra, the exceedingly energetic Satānanda said unto Rāma,—"Art thou well come, O chief of men? It is by our luck that, O descendant of Raghu thou hast come unto us, headed by the respected Maharshi Viçwāmitra. This highly energetic Viçwāmitra, this Brahmārshi is of prowess measureless; and deeds inconceivable, by virtue of his asceticism. Him thou knowest as the prime way. O Rāma, there existeth on this

[67] Jamadagni, father of Parusurama.—T.

earth not one that is more fortunate than thyself. Thy protector is even Kuçika's descendant, by whom mighty austerities have been performed. Do thou listen as I faithfully describe unto thee the ascetic power of the high-souled Kauçika. Do thou listen unto me relating this. This righteous one was for a long time a king, subduing his enemies, cognizant of morality, acomplished, and intent upon the welfare of his subjects. And there was a king named Kuça, the son of Prajāpati. And Kuça's son was the powerful and pious Kuçanābha. And Kuçanābha's son was Gādhi. And Gadhi's son is the highly energetic and mighty ascetic Viçwāmitra who ruled the earth. And that king reigned for thousands of years. And it came to pass that once with his four-fold forces marshalled, he set out for ranging the earth. And the king went on by turns ranging cities and kingdoms, rivers and mountains and asylums. And at length that foremost of conquerers, the mighty Viçwāmitra, came upon Vasishtha's asylum furnished with various blossoming plants and trees; abounding in animals; inhabited by Siddhas and Chāranas; graced by celestials and Dānavas and Gandharbas and Kinnaras; and filled with mild deer; frequented by the feathered tribes; crowded with Brahmārshis; with Devarshis inhabiting it; aye teeming with high-souled ones of accomplished ascetic success and resembling fire; like another region of Brahmā; graceful; and adorned on all sides with high-soulded saints and Vālakhilyas and Vaikhānasas resembling Brahmā, feeding on water or air, or living on withered leaves, or subsisting on fruits and roots, and self- controlled, and free from faults, and of vanquished senses, and engaged in reciting *mantras* and performing *homas*.

SECTION LII.

Upon seeing that foremost of those reciting *mantras*, the highly powerful and heroic Viçwāmitra, exceedingly delighted, bowed unto him in humility. And having enquired as to the pleasantness of Viçwāmitra's journey, the high- souled and adorable Vasishtha ordered a seat for the former. And on the intelligent Viçwāmitra having been seated, that best of ascetics properly entertained him with fruits and roots. And having accepted Vasishtha's hospitality, that foremost of monarchs, the exceedingly energetic Viçwāmitra, then enquired of Vasishtha as to the welfare of his asceticism, his *Agnihotrās*, and his disciples, and his trees. Thereupon Vasishtha communicated the welfare of all unto that best of kings. Then Brahmā's son, Vasishtha, of fierce austerities, the best of those reciting mantras, asked Viçwāmitra, seated at his ease, saying, — '0 king, is it well with thee? And, O king, dost thou rule thy subjects, pleasing them consistently with royal duties? And, O virtuous one, are thy retainers maintained on salaries from the kingdom? Do they abide by thy mandates? And, O destroyer of foes, hast thou vanquished thy enemies? And, O repressor of foes, is it well with thee as to, O most powerful of men, thy forces, exchequer, and friends, and, O sinless one, sons and grand- sons?' Thereupon, the highly powerful king, Viçwāmitra, with humility communicated unto Vasishtha his complete welfare. And having conversed for a long time, those virtuous ones, experiencing exceeding joy, ministered unto each other's delight. Then, O descendant of Raghu, after the conversation had ended, the adorable Vasishtha, smiling, addressed Viçwāmitra, saying, — 'O highly powerful one, I desire to properly entertain thee of immeasurable power, as well as thy forces, — do thou, therefore, accept my hospitality. Do thou receive the hospitality which I extend unto thee. O king, thou art the foremost of guests, and art worthy of assiduous homage.' Being thus addressed by Vasishtha, that mighty ascetic, king Viçwāmitra, said,—'Even by this word of thine relative to receiving me, hast thou in fact done so. And, O worshipful one, even with the fruits and roots that are in thy asylum, with the water for washing my feet, and sipping,—yea, with the sight of thy revered self, have I been, O profoundly wise one, excellently entertained by thee, who art thyself worthy of homage. I bow unto thee. I will go now. Do thou regard me with a friendly eye.' As the king was speaking thus, the righteous-souled and generous Vasishtlia again and again pressed him to accept his hospitality. Then Gadhi's son answered Vasishtha, —'Very well. O potent ascetic,—let that be which findeth favor in thy sight.' This having been said by him, Vasishtha, the best of those reciting *mantras*, joyfully called his sacrificial dappled cow, whose sins had been washed away,—'O Savalā! do thou come soon; and hear my words. I intend to entertain this royal saint together with his forces. Do thou enable me to entertain him, by yeilding excellent viands. And, O divine one, O thou that conferrest everything that is desired, do thou grant everyone whatever he asketh among edibles impregnated with the six tastes. And do thou, O Savalā, speedily create sapid viands to be chewed, sucked, licked or drunk'."

SECTION LIII.

Thus addressed by Vasishtha, that bestower of all that was desired, Savalā, O destroyer of thy foes, brought forth everything that was desired by everyone. And she produced sugarcanes, and honey, and fried rice, and excellent *Maireyas*,[68] and costly drinks,and various viands, and heaps of warm rice resembling hills, and other kinds of edibles, and soups, and *Dadhikulyās*,[69] together with silver plates by thousands filled with meats of diverse tastes. And, O Rāma, that army of Viçwāmitra consisting of cheerful and stout men being superbly entertained by Vasishtha, became exceedingly gratified. And the royal saint, Viçwāmitra himself, together with the priests and Brāhmanas and the inmates of the inner apartment, was also heartily filled. And being hospitably entertained with his courtiers and counsellors and retainers, he, exceedingly delighted, spoke unto Vasishtha, saying, —'Received and excellently entertained have I been by thee,0 Brāhmana, who thyself art worthy of being honored. Do thou, O thou conversant with speech, listen to me. I will tell thee a word. Do thou bestow on me Savalā for an hundred thousand kine. O worshipful one, varily this one is a jewel; and as it is the function of kings to acquire jewels, do thou confer on me Savalā; for, O twice-born one, this one by right belongs unto me.' Thus addressed by Viçwāmitra the righteous and adorable Vasishtha—best of ascetics—replied unto that lord of earth,—'O king, neither for an hundred thousand nor for an hundred *koti* of kine, nor yet for heaps of silver, will I part with Savalā. O subduer of enemies, this one deserves not to be separated from my side. Even like unto the fame of the mighty, this Savalā is ever joined with me. My oblations to the gods and the Pitris as well as my subsistence itself

[68] A kind of wine prepared from molasses.—T.
[69] A preparation of milk and rice.—T.

are established even in her. And my *Agnihotras*,[70] *Vali*,[71] and *Homa*[72] depend uper her; and, O royal saint, my *Svāhākāras* and *Vashatkāras*[73] as well as my various lore depend upon her. All this is so: there is no doubt about it. Verily she is my all; and in her do I find my delight. And many are the reasons, O king, why I cannot give unto thee Savalā.' Thus addressed by Vasishtha, that one versed in speech, Viçwāmitra, eagerly rejoined,—'I shall confer upon thee fourteen thousand elephants decked in gold chains and gold neck-ornaments and hooks; and I will confer upon thee eight hundred golden cars furnished with bells and each yoked with four white horses; and, O thou of auspicious vows, I will confer upon thee one thousand and ten high-mettled horses of noble breeds; and I will confer upon thee a *koti* of youthful and variegated kine,—do thou grant unto me Savalā. And as much of gems and gold, O best of regenerate ones, as thou wilt ask for, shall I bestow upon thee: do thou grant me Savalā.' Thus besought by the intelligent Viçwāmitra, that adorable one replied, saying,—'O king, Savalā I will not by any means give. This is verily my jewel: this is verily my riches: this is verily my all: this is verily my subsistence. And this is my *Darsa*[74] and this my *Paurnamasa*,[75] and this my various sacrifices with *dakshinas*;[76] and, O king, this my various rites. This, O king, is without doubt, the root of all my rites. And what need of dilating? This one bestowing everything that is desired will I not part with.'''

SECTION LIV.

"When the ascetic Vasishtha would not part with the cow of plenty then Viçwāmitra, O Rāma, forced Savalā away. And, O Rāma, carried away by that high- souled king, Savalā, stricken with grief and afflicted with sorrow, bethought herself, weeping,—'Have I been forsaken by the high-souled Vasistha that the royal retainers carry me off thus aggrieved? What wrong have I done unto that mighty ascetic of concentrated spirit, that, knowing me to be faultless, that righteous one leaveth her that was devoted unto his service?' Revolving this in her mind and sighing again and again, she darted unto where the pre- eminently energetic Vasishtha was; and defeating those servants (of the king), she with the speed of the wind, appeared at the feet of that high-souled one. And weeping Savalā having the voice of clouds, standing before Vasishtha, spoke in distressful accents,—'O Brahmā's son, wherefore have I been forsaken by thee,—that the servants of the king were carrying me from off thy presence?' Thus addressed the Brahmārshi said these words unto that one aggrieved,and of heart afflicted with sorrow, and like unto a sister,—'O Savalā, not that I forsake thee; nor hast thou done me any wrong. But this mighty king proud of his prowess hath been carrying

---

[70] Maintainance of the perpetual fire.—T.

[71] Offerings to the spirits of air.—T.

[72] Burnt offerings.—T.

[73] Sacrifices performed with the exclamation of *Swāhā* and *Vashat* respectively.—T.

[74] Bi-monthly sacrifice, performed at change of the moon by persons maintaining a perpetual fire.—T.

[75] A ceremony performed at the full of the moon by persons maintaining a perpetual fire.—T.

[76] Gifts to Brāhmanas on occasions of sacrifice.—T.

thee away. Surely, my strength is not equal to his. More specially, he is a king,a powerful king,—more particularly,this day he should not be slain by me (inasmuch as he is my guest): he is a Kshatriya and lord of earth. And he is foremost in might by virtue of possessing this entire Akshauhtni abounding in elephants and horses and cars and standards, and pennons on elephants.' Thus addressed by Vasishtha, that one cognizant of words humbly said in reply unto that Brahmārshi of incomparable power,—'The might of the Kshatriyas is not great,—the Brāhmanas are more mighty than they. O Brāhmana, superhuman is the power of the Brāhmanas, excelling that of the Kshatriyas. Thy power is immeasurable; and the exceedingly energetic Viçwāmitra is not as powerful as thyself. Thy energy is unequalled. O highly energetic one, do thou command me bursting with Brāhma forces: the pride, power and endeavours of that wicked one will I bring down.' Thus accosted by her, the highly famous Vasishtha, O Rāma, said,—'Create thou forces capable of crushing the forces of the enemy.' Hearing those words of his, Suravi created (an army). And, O king, Pahlavas by hundreds brought into being by her lowing, begin even in Viçwāmitra's sight to commit havoc upon his forces. Thereat, exceedingly angered, with eyes expanded in ire, that king commenced to slay the Pahlavas with various weapons. And beholding the Pahlavas by hundreds afflicted by Viçwāmitra, she again created grim-visaged Sakas mixed with Yavanas. And the field became thronged with the Sakas mixed with Yavanas, of dazzling splendour,exceedingly fierce resembling golden filaments, bearing sharp scimitars and adzes, and clad in yellow apparel. And that entire host (of Viçwāmitra) was being consumed by them like unto flaming fires. Then the exceedingly powerful Viçwāmitra hurled weapons at them; and with these the Yavanas, Kāmvoyas and Varvaras[77] became sore afflicted."

SECTION LV.

"And beholding them sore harassed, and overwhelmed by Viçwāmitra's weapons, Vasishtha directed (Savali) saying,—'O cow of plenty, do thou create (fresh troops), through thy *Yoga* power.' And from her roar, there came into being Kāmvojas, resembling the Sun. And from her udders sprang Varvaras, arms in hand; and from her mysterious parts, Yavanas; from her anus, Sakas; and from the pores of her skin, those barbarians,—Hāritas and Kirātas. And, O descendant of Raghu, anon Viçwāmitra's entire host consisting of foot, and elephant, and horse, and car, was exterminated by them. And seeing the army annihilated by the high- souled Vasishtha, the hundred sons of Viçwāmitra, equipped with various weapons, rushed in high ire against that best of *mantra*-reciting ones. Thereupon, uttering a roar, that mighty ascetic consumed them quite. And in a moment, Viçwāmitra's sons together with horse and car and foot were reduced to ashes by the high-souled Vasishtha. And witnessing them all destroyed, together with the army, the illustrious Viçwāmitra, covered with shame, became plunged in thought; and like unto a tideless ocean or a fangless snake, he instantly became shorn of his effulgence, like unto the sun overwhelmed by Rāhu.[78] And deprived of his forces and sons,

---

[77] Barbarians.—T.

[78] A Daitya with the tail of a dragon, whose head was severed from his body by Vishnu; but being immortal, the head and tail retained their separate existence, and being

he appeared like a bird bereft of its wings; and losing his entire army and with it the high spirits that it had inspired him with, his heart died within him. Then entrusting one of his (remaining) sons with the sovereignty, saying,—'Do thou rule the earth agreeably to the duties of the Kshatriya,' he went into the forest. And repairing to the side of the Himavat inhabited by Kinnaras and Serpents, that one of mighty asceticism began to perform austerities with the view of propitiating Māhadeva. And on a certain occasion that lord of the celestials, Vrishadwaja,[79] intending to confer a boon, appeared before the mighty ascetic Viçwāmitra,—'What for, O king, art thou performing penance? Do thou unfold what thou hast to say. I am for conferring a boon: do thou express what boon thou wouldst obtain.' Thus addressed by that god, that performer of mighty austerities, Viçwāmitra, bowing down unto him, addressed him, saying,—'If, O mighty god, thou art pleased (with me), do thou confer upon me the science of archery with all its mysteries and *mantras*, as well as its virtues of helping from far and near. And, O sinless one, may all those weapons that are with the celestials and the *Dānavas* and the *Maharshis* and the Gandharbas and the Yakshas, and the Rakshas, shine on me! May this my desire be granted me through thy grace, O god of gods! There- upon, saying,—'Be it so'—the lord of the celestials vanished. And obtaining the arms from the lord of the celestials, the mighty Viçwāmitra, naturally haughty became swelled with insolence. And surcharged with energy, like unto the sea during the equinox, he considered, O Rāma, as if that foremost of saints, Vasishtha, was already slain. And repairing to Vasishtha's asylum, the king began to discharge weapons, capable of burning down the hermitage. And beholding those weapons discharged by the intelligent Viçwāmitra, the ascetics, overtaken by fear, by hundreds began to fly. And Vasishtha's disciples as well as the animals and birds inhabiting there, fled in all directions by thousands. And for a time the hermitage of the high-souled Vasishtha was bare of living beings, and still like unto a wilderness, though Vasishtha cried again and again,—'Do not fear. To-day will I slay Gādhi's son, even as the sun (destroys) mist.' Having said this, that best of *mantra*-reciting ones, Vasishtha, in high wrath, addressed Viçwāmitra, saying,—'Since, O fool, thou hast destroyed this hermitage that had been prospering for a long time, thou of execrable ways shalt not live long.' Saying this, he, transported with wrath, and like unto the smoking flame at universal dissolution, speedily upraised a staff resembling another mace of Yama itself."

SECTION LVI.

Thus addressed by Vasishtha, the mighty Viçwāmitra, aiming a fiery weapon, said,—'Stay! Stay!' The worshipful Vasishtha also on his part, raising a Brahmā staff resembling another staff of Kāla, exclaimed in wrath,—'Wretch of a Kshatriya! here am I,—do thou display the might thou ait master of. To-day, O Gādhi's son, will I humble thy pride of arms. Thou disgrace of thy race, where is thy Kshatriya might, and where my high Brahmā energy? Do thou behold my superhuman Brahmā energy.' And even as water allayeth the fierceness of a flame, the Brahmā staff quenched the energy of the powerful fiery weapon discharged by Gādhi's

transfered to the stellar sphere, became the author of eclipses.—T.

[79] An appellation of Sivā; meaning, who hath the bull for his vehicle.—T.

son. Then Gādhi's son, waxing wroth, discharged Varuna and Raudra and Aindra and Pāsupata and Aishika weapons. And, Mānava, and Mohana, and Gāndharba, and Swāpana, and Jrimbhana, and Mohana, and Santāpana, and Vilāpana, and Soshana, and DSruna, and Vajra hard to baffle, and Brahmāpāça, and Kalapāça and Varunapāça, and Pināka (favorite of Sivā), and the two *Asanis*, wet and dry, and the Danda weapon, and Paiçācha, ani the Krauncha weapon, and Dharmachakra, and Kālachakra, and Vishuchakra and Vāyavya, and Mathana, and the Haraçiras weapon, and the twin Saktis, hurled he, and Kankāla, and Mushala, and the mighty weapon Vidyādhara, and the terrible Kāla weapon, and the dreadful Trisula weapon, and Kāpāla, and Kankana,—all these weapons hurled he (Viçwāmitra), at that best of *mantra*-reciting ones, O descendant of Raghu. And it was wonderful to behold. But Brahmā's son baffled all those by means of his staff. And on those (weapons) being resisted, the son of Gādhi hurled a Brahmā weapon. And on that weapon being discharged, the deities with Agni at their head, and the Devarshis, and the Gandharbas, and the mighty Serpents, became afflicted with fear. And on that Brahmā weapon being discharged, all the three worlds became exceedingly alarmed. And, O Raghu's descendant, Vasishtha by virtue of his Brahmā energy completely baffled that terrible Brahmā weapon. And when the high-souled Vasishtha had baffled the Brahmā weapon, his form became fierce and terrible, capable of striking terror into the three worlds. And from the pores of his body, resembling a smoking flame, darted out scintillations of fire. And resembling another staff of Yama, the Brahmā staff raised by Vasishtha's arm flamed like unto the smokeless fire at the universal dissolution. Then the ascetics in a body fell to eulogizing that best of *mantra*-reciting ones, Vasishtha, saying,—'Thy might, O Brāhmana, is infallible. Do thou rein in (the Brahma) energy, by thy own. O Brāhmana, Viçwāmitra of mighty strergth hath been subdued by thee. Infallible is thy extraordinary might. Let the creatures now be relieved from their distress.' Thus addressed, that highly energetic one of rigid austerities, became pacified. And Viçwāmitra, being put down, heaving a sigh, said,—'Fie upon the Kshatriya might: the strength begot of Brahmā energy, is might indeed. By one Brahmā staff hath all my weapons been put to the rout. Beholding this, I with a placid mind and senses will engage in mighty austerities,—which shall earn for me Brāhmanahood."

SECTION LVII.

"Then with his heart burning, in consequence of the remembrance of his humiliation, and having made enemies with that high-souled one, Viçwāmitra of mighty asceticism sighing, and sighing, went towards the south, in company with his queen, and became engaged in dreadful austerities, O Rāghava. And subsisting on fruits and roots, and restraining his senses, he performed the most rigid austerities. And four sons engaged in observing truth and duty—Havishpanda, Madhushpanda, Drihanetra, and Mahāratha[80] were born unto him. And when a thousand years had been completed, the Grand-sire of all, Brahmā, addressed the ascetic, Viçwāmitra in sweet words , saying,—'O son of Kuçika, the regions of the Rājarshis have been won by thee through thy austerities. And on account of

[80] Some texts have *Mahodara*.—T.

this thy asceticism, we recognize thee as a Rājarshi.' Having said this, the highly energetic prime Lord of all creature went to the celestial regions in company with the celestials.

Hearing this, Viçwāmitra hanging down his head from shame and possessed by a mighty sorrow, said, in piteous accents, —'I have performed rigid austerities,—yet the deities and the saints recognise me only as a Rajarshi. I do not consider the fruit of my asceticism as gained.' Ascertaining this in his mind, that righteous and highly composed one of high austerities, O Kākuststha, again engaged in penances. And, O Rāghava, it came to pass that at this time, that enhancer of Ikshwāku's line, the celebrated and truthful Trisanku of subdued sense made up his mind, saying,—'I will perform a sacrifice, and in body win the prime way of the celestials.' And summoning Vasishtha, he unfolded his mind into him. And on the high-souled Vasishtha saying,—'I am incapable of doing this,' and disregarded by the latter, the King went towards the southern quarter. And with the view of securing success to his endeavours, the king repaired where Vasishtha's sons had for a long time been performing austerities. And the highly energetic Trisanku saw the hundred exceedingly effulgent sons of Vasishtha engaged in austerities with fixed faculties. And approaching all those high-souled sons of his spiritual guide, and paying them reverence he, hanging down his head from shame, with clasped hands, addressed those mighty spirits, saying —'I seek protection of ye; and I take refuge in ye capable of conferring it. Disregarded have I been, good betide ye, by the high-souled Vasishtha. I have set my heart upon celebrating a mighty sacrifice: it behoveth ye to command me. And, with the view of propitiating ye, I, lowly bowing down my head, beseech the sons of my spiritual guide,—Brāhmanas ever staying by asceticism,—do ye with collected minds officiate in this sacrifice, so that success may be secured unto me; and that in body I may attain the regions of the celestials. Disregarded by the ascetic Vasishtha, other way find I none, ye anchorets, except the sons of my spiritual guide. To the Ikshwākus, their preceptor is their prime way. Therefore after him (Vasishtha), even ye are the objects of my adoration.

SECTION LVIII.

"Hearing Trisanku's speech, the hundred sons of the saint, O Rāma, excited by wrath, said these words unto the king,—'Disregarded hast thou been, O thou of perverse understanding, by our truth-telling sire,—why, then, having passed him by, do thou seek for others' help? To the Ikshwākus, their spiritual guide is their prime way; nor art thou capable of setting at naught the words of that truth- telling one. That worshipful saint said, that he was incapable (of accomplishing this),— how can we then undertake that sacrifice? Thou art ignorant, O foremost of men. Do thou speedily retrace thy steps. And, O king, that adorable one is competent to officiate at the sacrifice itself of the three worlds, how can we then contribute to his dishonor?' Hearing those words of theirs, that king, with accents tremulous with passion, again addressed them, saying, —'Disregarded by that worshipful one as well as by the sons of my spiritual guide, I will go after another way,—so peace be unto ye, ascetics.' The saint's sons, on their part, hearing that speech couching a fierce intent, cursed him in exceeding wrath, saying, — Thou shalt come by Chandāla-hood.' Having said this, those high-souled ones entered each into his dwelling. And when the night had gone by, the king came by Chandālahood. And clad in a blue garb, blue and rough of person, having a short head of hair, wearing a garland composed of materials culled from a cemetery, his body bedaubed with ashes from the same quarter, he was decked out with iron ornaments. And, O Rāma, beholding him in the guise of a Chandāla, his counsellors as well as followers, renouncing him, fled in a body. And, Kākutstha, maintaining himself in patience, the monarch burning day and night, all alone went unto the ascetic Viçwāmitra. And beholding the disappointed king in the guise of a Chandāla, the ascetic O Rāma, was touched with pity. And from commiseration, that pre-eminently pious and exceedingly energetic one said unto that king frightful to behold, saying, — 'Good betide thee, O heroic lord of Ayodhyā, thou hast fallen into Chandāla-hood through a curse, what is the purpose of thy coming, O highly powerful prince?' Hearing him, the king conversant with words, fallen into Chandāla-hood, with folded hands, said unto that one versed in speech, — Disregarded had I been by my spiritual guide as well as his sons. And far from attaining my desire,I came by this calamity. O thou of placid presence, I had desired to repair unto heaven in body. By me have an hundred sacrifices been performed, — but yet do I not obtain the fruit thereof. I have never before told an untruth; and I swear by my Kshatriya morality, that albeit fallen on evil days, I will never do so in future, O gentle one. And sacrifices I have celebrated many, — and I have ruled my people in righteousness; and I have pleased my preceptors by my character and conduct. But, O best of ascetics, now endeavouring to do my duty and intending to perform a sacrifice, I have failed in enlisting the good graces of my spiritual guides. Therefore do I consider Destiny as supreme; and action as nothing. Destiny overtaketh all: Destiny is the prime way. Therefore it behoveth thee to grant thy favor unto me extremely distressed, who crave thy favor, and, good betide thee, whose endeavours have been baffled by Destiny. Other way will I wend none; nor is there any other refuge for me. It behoveth thee to meet Destiny with exertion'."

SECTION LIX.

"When the king had spoken thus, Kuçika's son, moved with pity, said these sweet words unto the king who had undergone Chandāla-hood, — 'O descendant of Ikshwāku, hast thou had a pleasant journey? I know thee well, O highly virtuous one. Refuge will I grant thee, — so fear not, O best of monarchs. I shall summon all the pious Maharshis, who shall assist at the sacrifice, O king, — and then thou wilt be able to accomplish thy purpose easily. And should the guise thou hast come by in virtue of thy preceptor's curse, cling to thee yet, thou wilt bodily repair unto heaven in this form. And since appearing before Kuçika's son, thou hast taken his refuge, I consider heaven, O lord of men, as if within thy grasp.' Having said this, that exceedingly energetic one ordered his highly virtuous and profoundly wise sons to provide the sacrificial necessaries. And summoning his disciples, he said, — 'Do ye by my command bring hither all the saints together with Vasishtha's sons; and our friends and their disciples and the family priests variously versed in lore. Aud should any summoned by my mandate, say aught, do ye fully represent unto me the expression of slight.' Hearing his speech, they set out in different directions; and Brahmavādis[81] began to pour in from various countries. And the disciples (of Viçwāmitra) returning, fully communicated unto that ascetic of flaming energy the words of the Brahmavādis, saying,—'Hearing thy message, the regenerate ones resident in every part will come hither,—and some have already arrived—all save Mahodaya and the hundred sons of Vasishtha. Do thou, foremost of ascetics, listen to the words that they said with accents tremulous with emotion,—How can celestials and saints partake of offerings in the court of him that in addition to being a Chandāla, hath for his priest a Kshatriya? And how can high-souled Brāhmanas, patronized by Viçwāmitra, attain to heaven, having partaken of a Chandāla's fare?—These cruel words, O powerful ascetic, did Vasishtha's sons together with Mahodaya, utter with reddened eyes.' Hearing those words of theirs, that foremost of ascetics, with eyes reddened in anger, wrathfully cried,—'Since blameless as I am, those wicked-minded ones censure me practising fierce austerities, they shall, without doubt, be reduced to ashes. And this very day bound by the noose of Kāla, meeting with destruction at the hands of Vivaswata's son,[82] they shall for seven hundred births range these worlds, procuring dead men's clothes, always feeding on dogs' flesh, going by the name of Mushtikas, void of abhorrence, and of frightful, distorted forms and foul practices. And wicked Mahodaya also hath blamed me although undeserving of blame; therefore, reproved of all, he shall undergo Nishadahood. And becoming cruel and engaged in taking life, he shall through my ire fare wretchedly for a long lapse of time.' Having uttered this in the assembly of saints, that mighty ascetic, the highly powerful Viçwāmitra of fierce asceticism paused."

SECTION LX.

And knowing (by virtue of his *Yoga* power) Vasishtha's sons together with Mahodaya as destroyed in consequence of his ascetic energy, the highly powerful Viçwāmitra said in the midst of the saints,—'This descendant of Ikshwāku, the famous Trisanku, is virtuous and munificent and hath taken refuge in me, with the view of attaining the celestial regions in his own person. Therefore do thou engage with me in the sacrifice, so that he may bodily repair unto heaven.' Hearing Viçwāmitra's words, the pious Maharshis readily spoke in harmony with duty, saying,—This descendant of Kuçika is a highly irascible ascetic,—therefore what he saith should, without doubt, be performed. The worshipful one is like unto fire, and, if angered, may curse us. Therefore, let us engage in this sacrifice, so that Ikshwāku's descendant through the potency of Viçwāmitra may repair unto heaven in person. Then let us engage in this sacrifice.' Saying this, the sages entered upon the ceremony; and in that sacrifice the highly energetic Viçwāmitra acted as the priest. And Ritwijas versed in *mantras* performed every thing in order with *mantras*, in accordance with scripture and prescription. Then after a long time, Viçwāmitra of mighty austerities invoked thither all the celestials for receiving their respective shares; but the deities did not come to receive them. Thereupon, getting into a wrath, the mighty ascetic Viçwāmitra, lifting up a ladle, wrathfully

[81] A Brahmavādi is one who maintains that all things are Spirit.—T.
[82] Yama.—T.

spoke unto Trisanku, —'O lord of men, do thou witness the prowess of my self-earned asceticism. I shall by dint of my asceticism take thee bodily unto heaven. And, O king, do thou in person repair unto heaven hard to attain. Something yet remains in me of the self-earned fruit of my asceticism; and, O king, through the energy of that asceticism, do thou repair unto heaven in person.' And on the ascetic saying this, Kākutstha, that lord of men bodily ascended heaven in the very sight of the anchorets. And beholding Trisanku risen to heaven, the subduer of Pāka[83] together with all the celestials said,—'O Trisanku, turn thee back. Thou hast not earned abode in heaven. O fool, thou hast been blighted by the curse of thy spiritual guide. Do thou therefore drop down headlong.' The great Indra having spoken thus, Trisanku fell down, crying unto the ascetic Viçwāmitra,—'Save me, save me.' Thereupon, hearing his distressful cries, Kauçika waxed mightily wroth, and exclaimed,—'Stay, stay.' And in the midst of the ascetics, like unto another Prajāpati, he created other seven Rishis[84] on the Southern way; and also, overwhelmed with wrath created another set of stars. And collied[85] with passion, that illustrious one in the midst of the ascetics created another system of stars in the southern direction. And, saying,—'I will create another Indra, or the world (that I create) shall be without an Indra.' And in anger, he went the length of creating celestials. Thereupon, in trepidation, the saints and the celestials and the Asuras humbly addressed the high- souled Viçwāmitra thus,—'This king, O highly exalted one, hath been visited with the curse of his preceptor,—therefore, O ascetic, he deserves not to ascend heaven in person.' Hearing those words of theirs, that best of anchorets, Kauçika, in company with the celestials, said these pregnant words,—'Good betide ye, I have vowed unto this king, Trisanku's bodily ascension unto heaven,—therefore, I dare not falsify my vow. Let Trisanku evermore dwell in heaven in person, and let these stars created by me verily endure as long as the worlds. This it behoveth ye, ye gods, to ordain. Thus addressed, the deities answered that best of ascetics, saying,—'So be it, good betide thee! All these innumerable stars, O foremost of anchorets, shall remain in the firmament outside the path of Vaicwanara;[86] and shining in their splendour, Trisanku shall dwell with bended head, like unto an immortal. And all these luminous bodies shall follow that best of kings, illustrious and successful, as if he had attained heaven itself.' And the virtuous and exceedingly energetic Viçwāmitra, thus assured by the celestials, said in the midst of the saints,—'Ye gods, excellent well.' Then, after the sacrifice had concluded, the high-souled celestials and the saints of ascetic wealth went to their respective regions, O foremost of men."

SECTION LXI.

"And, O puissant one, seeing those saints gone, the highly energetic Viçwāmitra addressed those inhabitants of the forest, saying,—'A mighty disturbance hath happened in regard to the southern quarter: let us therefore repairing to another

[83] Indra.—T.

[84] Ursa major.—T.

[85] "And passion having my best judgment collied."—T.

Othello.

[86] The Zodiac—T.

region, carry on austerities. Ye high-souled ones, in the west there are extensive tracts; and there in Pushkara will we peaceably carry on our austerities. That asylum is really pleasant.' Having said this, that exceedingly energetic and mighty Muni[87] began to perform terrible austerities subsisting on fruits and roots. And it came to pass that at this time that mighty lord of Ayodhyā, Amvarisha, prepared for celebrating a sacrifice. And as he was sacrificing, Indra stole away his sacrificial beast. And on the beast being stolen, the priest said unto the king,—'O king, the beast hath been stolen (away); and it hath been lost through thy dereliction. And, O lord of men, his own fault destroyeth the king that faileth to protect (the subjects). And, O best of men, even this is the expiation: do thou, while the ceremony lasts, speedily bring back the beast, or bring a man (in its stead).' Hearing the priest's words, that highly intelligent king began to range various countries and provinces, cities, forests, and holy asylums, searching for the beast, with a thousand kine (as the price thereof). And, O child, it came to pass that arriving at Bhrigutunga,[88] he beheld Richika seated, there in company with his wife and sons, O descendant of Raghu. And bowing unto that Brahmārshi flaming in asceticism, and propitiating him; the exceedingly energetic royal saint of unparalleled effulgence having enquired as to his complete welfare, addressed Richika, saying,—'O highly pious one, O Bhrigu's son, if, in order that I may have a substitute for my sacrificial beast, thou sell thy son, my desire I shall attain. I have ranged every country; but the beast I do not find. Therefore, it behoveth thee to part with one of thy sons for price.' Thus addressed the exceedingly energetic Richika replied,—'O best of men, my first-born I will in no wise dispose of.' Hearing the words of the high-souled Richika, their mother spoke unto that foremost of men, Amvarisha, saying,—'The worshipful son of Bhrigu hath said that his first-born cannot be disposed of,—do thou, O lord, also know that the youngest, Sunaka, is my favorite. Therefore my youngest son will I not give unto thee. O foremost of men, the eldest sons are generally the best beloved of their fathers; and the youngest, of their mothers,— therefore the youngest I would retain.' And when the ascetic as well as his wife had spoken thus, the second son, Sunasepha, O Rāma, himself said,—'My father would not sell the eldest; nor my mother the youngest,—therefore I consider even the second as disposable. Do thou then, O prince, take me.' When that one versed in the Veda had ended, that lord of men, O mighty-armed descendant of Raghu, taking possession of Sunasepha, by paying kotis of kine, and heaps of jewels, and gold and silver by hundreds and thousands, went away exceedingly delighted. And that royal saint, the exceedingly energetic and highly famous Amvarisha, placing Sunasepha on his car, speedily set out."

SECTION LXII.

"And, O foremost of men, taking Sunasepha, that illustrious king at noon rested in Pushkara, O descendant of Rāghu. And having arrived at the excellent Pushkara, as the king was resting, the famous Sunasepha with an aggrieved heart saw his maternal uncle Viçwāmitra in company with some saints engaged in asceticism. Thereupon, with a woe-begone countenance, and sore afflicted with fa-

[87] Ascetic.—T.
[88] A mountain peak.—T.

tigue and thirst, he, O Rāma, flung himself into (Viçwāmitra's) lap, and said—'I have neither father, nor mother, nor relatives, nor friends anywhere. It therefore behoves thee, O gentle one, to save me in the interests of virtue, O foremost of ascetics. And, O best of men, thou art the protector of all, and their refuge. May the king have his desire and may I at the same time, attaining long life, and undc-teriorating, gain heaven, having performed meritorious austerities! Do thou with a delighted heart become a lord unto me that am without one. And, O righteous one, even as a father rescueth a son, do thou deliver me from this peril.' Hearing his words, Viçwāmitra of mighty austerities, pacifying him by every means, spoke unto his sons, saying,—'That in view of which fathers beget well-wishing sons—the compassing of welfare in the next world—is at hand. This youthful son of the ascetic craveth my protection. Do ye, ye sons, accomplish my desire by saving his life. Ye are all of virtuous deeds, ye are all engaged in the observance of righteous-ness,—do ye confer satisfaction upon Agni by one of ye becoming the (sacrificial) beast of the lord of men. Thus Sunasepha will obtain protection, the sacrifice will be freed from hinderance, the deities will be propitiated, and finally my word will be made good.' Hearing the ascetic's words, his sons, Madhuchchhanda and others, O foremost of men, haughtily and tauntingly answered,—'O lord, how, neglecting thy own sons, thou desirest to deliver that of another? This we consid-er as heinous, even like unto eating one's own flesh.' Hearing this speech of his sons, that best of anchorets, with eyes reddened with anger, said,—'Disregarding my words, ye have uttered this audacious and shocking speech, disclaimed by morality, and capable of causing one's hair to stand on end. Therefore, becoming Mushtikas, and living on dogs' flesh, do ye all, even like Vasishtha's sons, inhabit the earth for a thousand years.' Having cursed his sons, that best of ascetics then, by all means cheering up the distressed Sunasepha as to his protection, addressed him, saying,—'Do thou donning on a zone made of Kuça, and wearing a garland of red flowers, and bedaubing thy person with red sandal paste, hymn Agni with *mantras*, approaching the Vaishnava sacrificial stake; and, O ascetic's son, (at the same time) chaunt these two verses in that sacrifice of Amvarisha. Then thou wilt attain success.' Thereupon, with a concentrated mind securing those two verses, Sunasepha speedily presented himself before that leonine monarch, saying,—'O lion of a king, O thou endued with high intelligence, let us without delay repair hence. And, O foremost of monarchs, do thou engage in the sacrifice and com-mence upon the initiation.' Hearing those words of the ascetic's son, the king, filled with delight, readily at once repaired to the sacrificial ground. And with the consent of his court, the king fastened Sunasepha with a Kuça cord, and investing him with a crimson apparcl, tethered him to the stake as the (sacrificial) beast. And, being bound (to the stake), the ascetic's son first of all duly hymned Agni, and next those deities, Indra and his younger brother. Thereupon, gratified with the excellent eulogy, the thousand-eyed Vāsava conferred upon Sunasepha long life. And, O foremost of men, that king also, having completed the sacrifice, ob-tained the manifold fruit thereof through the grace of the thousand-eyed deity, O Rāma. And, O best of men, the righteous Viçwāmitra of mighty asceticism again carried on austerities at Pushkara for ten hundred years."

SECTION LXIII.

And when the thousand years had been completed and the mighty ascetic had accomplished his vow, the celestials in a body desirous of conferring upon him the fruit thereof, appeared before him. And the exceedingly effulgent Brahmā. addressed him in soothing words; saying, — 'Thou art henceforth a saint, good unto thee, — and (this eminence) thou hast attained through thy own laudable exertions.' Having spoken thus unto him, the lord of celestials returned to heaven. And Viçwāmitra of mighty energy became again engaged in rigid austerities. And, O foremost of men, it came to pass that after a long lapse of time that prime of Apsarās, Menakā, was at that time performing her ablutions in Pushkara, and she was observed by Kuçika's son, like unto lightning among clouds. And coming under the control of *Kandarpa*,[89] the anchoret spoke unto her, saying, — 'O Apsari, hath thy journey been a pleasant one t Do thou abide in my asylum. Do thou favor me; for, good betide thee, I have been rendered senseless by Madana.'[90] Thus addressed, that one of shapely hips began to dwell there. And mighty was the hinderance that befell Viçwāmitra as regarded his asceticism, as she, O Rāghava, staying in that asylum of his, pleasantly spent five and five years, O gentle one. And after this period had gone by, overwhelmed with shame and afflicted with anxiety and grief, the mighty ascetic Viçwāmitra impatiently thought, O son of Raghu, that all this mighty loss of austerities was the work of the celestials. And deprived of his senses by lust, the decade had passed away imperceptibly as if it were one day and night; and this impediment stood in the way of his austerities. And heaving a sigh, that best of ascetics burned in repentance. And with sweet words, renouncing the terrible and trembling Menakā standing wuh clasped hands, Kuçika's son, Viçwāmitra, O Rāma, went to the northern mountains. And practising the Brahmacharyya mode of lite with the intention of subduing lust, that highly famous one engaged in arduous austerities on the banks of the Kauçiki. And as he was thus engaged in profound austerities on the northern mountain, a thousand years, O Rāma passed away. Then taking counsel together, the celestials and the saints appeared before (Brahmā), saying, — 'Let Kuçika's son obtain the title of Maharshi.' Hearing the words of the celestials, the Grand-sire of all addressed the ascetic Viçwāmitra, in these sweet words, — O mighty saint, hast thou had a pleasant journey? Satisfied with thy fierce austerities, O Kauçika, I confer upon thee the eminence of the foremost saintship.' Hearing Brahmā's speech, the anchoret Viçwāmitra bowing down thus answered the Grand- sire with clasped hands, — 'The incomparable title of Brahmarshi is to be won by one by performing sterling works. And since thou hast not addressed me (by that title) it appears that I have not yet succeeded in subduing my senses.'[91] Thereupon Brahmā said unto him, — 'Do thou exert thyself until thou conquer thy senses? Saying this, Brahmā went to heaven. And when the celestials had gone, the mighty ascetic, Viçwāmitra, with upraised arms, and without any support, and subsisting on air, began

---

[89] Cupid. — T.

[90] Cupid. — T.

[91] The text is very faulty. The literal meaning would be, "since thou hast not I have subdued my senses" which would be absurd. I have therefore rendered the passage freely. — T.

to perform penances. And in summer, the ascetic surrounded himself with five fires, and in rains remained in an uncovered place, and in winter day and night stood submerged in water. Thus passed by a thousand years of terrible penances. And on the mighty ascetic Viçwāmitra being engaged in austerities, great was the agitation that exercised the celestials and Vāsav, in particular. And Sakra together with the Maruts spoke unto Rambha these words, fraught with weal unto himself, and woe unto Kauçika'."

SECTION LXIV.

"'O Rambha, this mighty service thou wilt have to perform in the interest of the celestials!—even to take Kauçika with the witchery of love.' Thus addressed by the intelligent thousand-eyed deity, the Apsari, O Rāma, with clasped palms, thus bashfully answered the chief of the celestials,—'O lord of the celestials, this mighty ascetic, Viçwāmitra, is a terrible person; and, without doubt, he will, O divine one, waxing wroth, curse me. And O god, even this is ay fear, and therefore it behoveth thee to favor me.' Thus apprehensively addressed by her in fear, the thousand-eyed one answered that damsel trembling and staying with clasped hands,—'Never fear, O Rambhā, good unto thee! Do thou perform my bidding. Assuming the form of a coel, captivating the heart, I will in this spring crowned with graceful trees, stay by thy side in company with Kandarpa. And do thou adding unto thy beauty, diverse blandishments bewitch this ascetic, Kuçika's son, O gentle one?' Hearing Indra's words, that comely damsel of luminous smiles, heightening her charms exceedingly, inspired Viçwāmitra with desire. And he listened to the mellifluous strains of the coel; and with a delighted heart, he beheld the fair one. Anon, listening to the warbling of the coel and her own incomparable singing, as well as beholding Rambhā, the ascetic began to entertain doubts. And knowing for certain that it was the thousand-eyed deity who had devised all that, that foremost of anchorets, Kuçika's son, overwhelmed with anger, cursed Rambhā, saying,—'Since, O Rambhā, thou endeavourest to seduce me who is bent upon subduing his anger and lust, thou shalt, O luckless one, remain as a stone for ten thousand years. And a highly energetic Brāhmana equipped with ascetic energy, will, O Rambhā, deliver thee, stained because of my ire.' Thus said that exceedingly energetic and mighty ascetic Viçwāmitra, and was filled with remorse unable to contain his anger of heart. And in consequence of his mighty curse, Rambhā was turned into a stone. Hearing the curse of the mighty saint, both Kandarpa and Indra left the place. And, O Rāma, on account of his anger, and his sense remaining still unsubdued he found no rest from deterioration of ascetic merit. And coming by decrease of ascetic merit, he thought within himself,—'No more shall I suffer anger to exercise me, —nor will I ever say anything to any. And I shall not breathe for an hundred years; and controlling my sense, I shall dry up my body. And so long as I do not attain Brāhmanahood as earned by my austerities, I shall suspending my breath and abstaining from food, stay for a long lapse of time. And engaged in austerities, my form will not undergo any deterioration.' That foremost of ascetics bound himself by this unparalleled vow to lead a life of such self-denial."

SECTION LXV.

"And forsaking the northern direction, the mighty *Muni*, O Rāma, betaking himself to the Eastern quarter, became engaged in dreadful austerities. And adopting the high vow of taciturnity for a thousand years, he, O Rāma began to perform the most signal and arduous austerities. And when the thousaud years had been complete, many an impediment tried the mighty *Muni* staying like the trunk of a tree, yet could not anger enter his heart; and firmly determined to shut out anger, he, O Rāma, kept his asceticism from deterioration. And, O foremost of the Raghus, when his vow of a thousand years had been observed, that one of mighty vows became desirous of feeding on boiled rice. And it came to pass O best of the Raghus that at this time Indra assuming the guise of a regenerate one, asked for the rice. Thereupon he gave it away unto the Vipra; and when the rice had been thus exhausted, that worshipful one of mighty austerities went without food. Nor, abiding by the vow of reticence, did he say aught unto the Vipra. And he then again resumed his dumb guise, restraining his breath at the same time. And that puissant ascetic did not breathe for a thousand years. And as he restrained his breath, vapours began to issue out of his head. And, at this, the three worlds being on fire became as if afflicted with fear. And bewildered on account of the energy of his asceticism, and shorn of their brightness, and afflicted with anguish, the Devarshis and the Gandharbas and the Pannagas and the Uragas and the Rākshasas in a body addressed the *Pitamaha*,[92] saying, — 'O divine one, various were the means by which we endeavoured to affect the mighty *Muni* Viçwāmitra with covetuousness and lust; but for all that he increaseth in asceticism. Nor do we perceive in him ever so little of anger or lust. And if thou do not confer upon him what his mind desireth to have, he will annihilate the thre worlds with all that is mobile and immobile in them. And the ten cardinal points are disconsolate: and nothing can be discovered therein. And the seas are vexed, and the mountains riven. And the earth shaketh, and the winds keep steadily blowing. And, O Brāhmana, we do not know how to remedy, this. And every one is inactive like an infidel. And the three worlds look as if stupified, with their minds exceedingly exercised. And by virtue of that mighty saint's energy, the sun itself hath been deprived of his splendour.

Therefore, god, against the mighty *Muni* bending his mind upon destruction, and consuming the three entire worlds like unto the fire raging at the universal dissolution, that exalted one of exceeding effulgence resembling a flame, should be pacified. Even should he desire the dominion of the celestial regions, do thou grant him his wish.[93] Then the celestials with Pilāmaha at their head, addressed the high-souled Viçwāmitra in sweet-words, saying, — 'welcome, O Brahmārshi! well pleased have we been with thy penances. And, O son of Kuçika, in consideration of thy fiery asceticism, thou hast obtained Brāhmana-hood. And, O Brāhmana, I will in company with the Maruts confer on thee long life. Hail unto thee! Do thou accept this, good betide thee. Go thou, O gentle one, as thou likest? Hearing Pitamaha's speech, the mighty ascetic, bowing down unto the celestials, said in delight, — 'If Brāhmana-hood hath really been obtained by me together with length of days, let *Omkāra* and *Vashatkāra* and the Vedas crown me; and let, ye gods, that

[92] *Lit.* grand-father. Here, a name of Brahmā meaning, *the great father of all.* — T.
[93] Some texts read *matam*, for *manas* — meaning the same. — T.

foremost of those versed in Kshatra Veda as well as of those cognizant of the Brah-maveda, even Brahmā's son, Vasishtha, recognize me. Having granted this prime desire of mine, do ye go away, ye gods.' Then pacified by the celestials, that best of reciters, the Brahmārshi Vasishtha, made friends (with Viçwāmitra), saying, — 'So be it.' 'Thou art a Brahmārshi. There is no doubt about this. And every thing hath been compassed in thy behalf,' — having said this, the deities went to their respec-tive regions. And that Brahmārshi, the righteous Viçwāmitra also, having attained excellent Brāhmana-hood, paid his homage unto that best of reciters, Vasishtha; and having secured his end, began to range the entire world, staying in asceticism. In this wise, O Rāma, was Brahmānya actually obtained by the high-souled one. This, O Rāma, is the foremost of ascetics, — this one is Asceticism incarnate. This one ever abideth by duty; and he is the stay of ascetic energy."

Having said this, that best of regenerate persons paused. Hearing Satānan-da's narration delivered in the presence of Rāma and Lakshmana, Janaka with clasped hands addressed the son of Kuçika, saying, — 'Blessed and favored am I, that thou, O Kauçika, accompanied with Kākutstha, hast arrived at my sacrifice, O puissant anchoret. Purified am I, O Brāhmana, by thy very sight, O mighty *Muni*. And from thy sight have I received various qualities. O Brāhmana, thy mighty austerities have been related in detail; and myself as well as the high-souled Rāma have listened to the narration relative to thy formidable ascetic energy; and the assembled courtiers have heard of thy various perfections. Immeasurable is thy asceticism; and immeasurable thy power; and ever immeasurable thy qualities, O Kuçika's son. I never, O lord, am tired of listening to that wonderful narration. Now, O foremost of ascetics, the hour for performing the daily devotions hath arrived, and the solar disc hangeth aslope. To-morrow morning, O highly ener-getic one, thou wilt see me again. Welcome, best of reciters. It behoveth thee to favor me." Thus addressed, that best of ascetics, extolling that powerful one, well pleased, dismissed the delighted Janaka. Thus accosted, Mithilā's lord, Vaideha, in company with his priests and friends, went round that foremost of ascetics. And the righteous Viçwāmitra also together with Rāma and Lakshmana, having been honored by the high-souled ones, took up their quarters there.

SECTION LXVI.

The next morning, which happened to be bright, the lord of men, having per-formed his daily devotions, welcomed Viçwāmitra and Rāghava. And having, in accordance with the scriptures, paid homage unto the former as well as the two high-souled Rāghavas, that virtuous one said, — "Hail, O worshipful sir! What shall I do unto thee, O sinless one?" Do thou command. Surely, I deserve to be commanded by thee. Thus addressed by the high-souled Janaka, that first of as-cetics endowed with a righteous soul, well versed in speech, answered, — "These sons of Daçaratha — Kshatriyas — famed among men, are eager to behold that best of bows, that lies with thee. Do thou show it unto them, may it be well with thee! Having obtained a sight of that bow, the king's sons, their desires crowned with success, will return as they list." Thus accosted, Janaka replied unto the mighty *Muni*, saying, — "Listen to why the bow lieth here. There was a king known by the name of Devarāta. He was the elder brother of Nimi. And, O worshipful one, this bow was consigned unto the hands of that high-souled one as a trust. Formerly with the view of destroying Daksha's sacrifice, the puissant (Sivā), drawing this bow, sportively spoke unto the celestials in ire, saying,—'Since, ye gods, ye deny me the shares (of this sacrifice), which I lay claim to, I will with my bow even sever those beads of yours.' Thereat, O powerful ascetic, with agitated hearts, the deities fell to propitiating that lord of the celestials,—and Bhava was pleased with them. And well-pleased with them, he conferred this upon those high-souled ones. And even this is that jewel of a bow belonging to the high-souled god of gods, and which was ultimately, O lord, consigned as a trust unto our ancestor. And as I was ploughing the mead, arose a damsel,—and as I obtained her while hallowing the field (for sacrifice), she hath come to be known by the name of Sitā. And arising from the earth, she grew as my daughter. And unsprung from the usual source, she was then established here as my daughter, whose hand must be obtained by bending the bow. And O foremost of ascetics, many a king, coming here, had saught to obtain my growing daughter arisen from the earth. But, O worshipful one, in consideration of her being one whose dower must be prowess in bending the bow. I would not bestow my daughter upon those lords of earth seeking for the damsel. Thereupon O puissant anchoret, all the kings in a body began to flock to Mithilā, desirous of being acquainted with the strength of the bow. And on their being curious (as to the bow), I showed it unto them; but they could neither hold nor wield it. And, O mighty *Muni*, finding those powerful kings to be but endowed with small prowess, I parsed them by. Hear what then befell, O thou of ascetic wealth. Then, O powerful anchoret, in high ire, the kings, doubtful as to their strength in stringing the bow, laid siege to Mithilā. And those potent princes, conceiving themselves as frustrated by me, began to harass the city of Mithilā, waxing wondrous wroth. And when a year had been completed, my defensive resources were entirely exhausted,—and at this, I was exceedingly aggrieved. Then I sought to propitiate the deities; and well- pleased, the celestials granted me a *Chaturanga* army. At length those wicked kings, meeting with slaughter, broke and fled in all directions, together with their adherents, bereft of vigor, and confidence in their strength. And, O puissant ascetic, this highly effulgent bow will I show unto Rāma and Lakshmana, O thou of excellent vows. And, if, O ascetic, Rāma succeeds in fixing string to it, I will confer upon Daçarātha's son my daughter Sitā, unsprung from the usual source."

SECTION LXVII.

Hearing Janaka' s words, the mighty *Muni* Viçwāmitra said unto the king,—"Do thou show the bow unto Rāma." Thereupon the king Janaka commanded his ministers, saying,—"Do ye bring the wonderful bow furnished with unguents and garlands." Commanded by Janaka, the ministers entered the city; and placing the bow in their front, those, endowed with immeasurable energy, came out And deposited in a case on a cart borne upon eight wheels, it was with difficulty drawn along by five thousand stalwart persons of well-developed frames. And having brought that case of iron, wherein lay that bow, the royal counsellors spoke unto Janaka resembling an immortal, saying,—"Here is the best of bows, O king, worshipped of all sovereigns. O foremost of kings, O lord of Mithila, if you think it worth showing (shew it)." Hearing their speech, the king with clasped palms said unto the high-souled Viçwāmitra well as Rāma and Lakshmana, — "This best of bows, O Brāhmana, hath always been worshipped by the Janakas; as also by mighty kings incapable (of wielding and stringing it.) And neither the celestials, nor the Asuras, nor the Rākshasas, nor the Gandharbas nor the Yakshas, nor the Kinnaras, nor the mighty Uragās, — how shall men fare? — have succeeded in stringing or stretching it, or fixing the arrow to it, or pulling its string, or wielding it. This foremost of bows hath been brought here, O chief of ascetics. Do thou, O exalted one, show it unto these sons of the king." Hearing Janaka,s words, the righteous Viçwāmitra said unto Rāghava, — "O Rāma, do thou, my child, behold the bow." At the words of the Maharshi, Rāma, opening the case, wherein lieth the bow took a sight of it and said, — "This divine bow will I touch with my hand, — and shall I also strive to wield and draw it?" Thereat both the king and the ascetic said, — "Excellent well." At the words of the anchoret, in the sight of countless thousands of spectators, the righteous son of Raghu with exceeding ease took hold of the bow by the middle, and fixed the string upon it, — and having fixed the string, drew it. And that foremost of men enjoying high fame, snapped the bow in the middle. And mighty was the sound that was heard on the occasion, like unto the bursting of a thunder-clap: and the earth trembled terribly, as it doth in the vicinity of a mountain splitting; and overwhelmed by the noise, all rolled head over heels, with the exception of that best of ascetics, the king, and the two Rāghavas. And on the people being re-assured, the king conversant with speech, his apprehension removed, with folded hands addressed that puissant ascetic, saying, — "O worshipful one, I have beheld the prowess of Daçarātha's son. This is verily wonderful and inconceivable; and I did not think this was possible. And my daughter, Sitā, being united with her lord, Daçarātha's son, Rāma, will shed lustre on Janaka's line. And my promise *viz.*, that I will confer Sitā upon him that will bend the bow, hath been fulfilled, O son of Kuçika. And this Sitā, this my daughter, dearer unto me than life will I confer upon Rāma. And, O Brāhmana, by thy permission let my counsellors speedily post hence, O Kauçika, good betide thee unto Ayodhyā, in cars; and with humble speech bring the king unto my capital. And let them communicate unto him all about the bestowal of Sitā upon Rāma, in consequence of his having bent the bow. And let them acquaint the monarch with the welfare of the Kākutsthas protected by the ascetic; and let them, speedily posting here, bring the delighted king." And thereupon Kuçika's son said, — "So be it." And the righteous king, summoning his counsellors, despatched them to Ayodhyā with his letter, to communicate all duly unto the king, and bring him thither.

SECTION LXVIII.

Thus commissioned by Janaka, the envoys, having spent three nights on the way, entered the city of Ayodhyā, with their conveyance afflicted with fatigue. And in accordance with the royal commission, entering the king's residence, they saw the aged king Daçarātha, resembling a celestial. And freed from apprehension, the envoys with clasped hands addressed the monarch in sweetly humble accents, saying, — "O mighty monarch, Mithilā's lord king Janaka, in company with his priests, in sweet and affectionate words, repeatedly enquires after the complete welfare of thyself along with thy priests and servants. And having enquired after thy complete welfare, Mithilā's lord, Vaideha, by permission of Kauçika addresses thee thus,—'Thou knowest the vow I had made formerly—*viz*, to confer my daughter upon him that would bend the bow,—and the kings, in consequence of their having been deprived of prowess, and being baffled, have come to entertain spite against me. And that daughter of mine, O king, hath been won by thy son arrived here at will, headed by Viçwāmitra. And, O mighty-armed one, that divine, jewelled bow hath been snapped in the middle by the high-souled Rāma in the midst of a large assembly. And upon that high-souled one should I confer Sitā, having prowess assigned for her dower, And in this wise will I free myself from my vow; and this thou shouldst permit. And, O mighty king, do thou, good betide thee, come speedily, headed by thy priests. It behoveth thee to see the Rāghavas; and, O foremost of kings, to see me delivered from this vow. And do thou attain the joy incident to the nuptials of both thy sons,'—thus spoke sweetly the lord of Videha, permitted by Viçwāmitra and staying by the opinions of Satānanda." Hearing the words of the envoys, the king, exceedingly rejoiced, addressed Vasishtha and Vāmadeva, as well as his counsellors, saying,—"Protected by Kuçika's son, that enhancer of Kauçalyā's joy stayeth in Videha in company with his brother Lakshmana. And the high-souled Janaka hath witnessed the prowess of Kākutstha; and he wisheth to bestow his daughter upon Rāghava. If this alliance with the high-souled Janaka is relished by ye, we shall speedily repair to his capital. Let there be no waste of time." Thereupon, the counsellors along with the Maharshis said,—"Excellent!' And the king highly delighted, said unto the counsellors,—"Our journey commenceth on the morrow." And excellently ministered unto, the counsellors of that foremost of monarchs (Janaka), endowed with every excellent quality, spent that night in joy.

SECTION LXIX.

Then when the night had been spent, king Daçaratha accompanied with his priests and adherents, well pleased spoke unto Sumantra, saying,—"To-day let the officers in charge of the treasury, taking plenty of excellent wealth, and furnished with various gems, go in advance under proper escort. And let the four-fold forces sally out with speed. And at my command let horses and conveyances and elegant vehicles march out. And let Vasishtha and Vāmadeva and Jāvāli and Kaçyapa and Mārkandeya endowed with long life and the saint Kātyāyana—let these regenerate ones go forward. And do thou also yoke my car. Let not the proper time pass away; for the envoys urge speed upon me." At these words of the king, the four-fold forces together with the saints went in the wake of the monarch. And after bar- ing passed four days on the way, they arrived at Videha.

And hearing of Daçaratha's arrival, the auspicious king Janaka experienced great delight, and having obtained the aged king Daçaratha, he honored him duly.[94] And that best one (Janaka) spoke words unto that delighted chief of men.

[94] The text: *And hearing of Dasaratha's arrival, the auspicious king Janaka honored him duly; and having obtained the aged monarch Dasaratha, he being delighted experienced the excess of joy.*—T.

"Hath thy journey been a pleasant one, O best of men? By luck have I obtained thee, O descendant of Raghu. Do thou experience the joy earned by the prowess of thy sons. And by luck it is that I have obtained the highly energetic and worshipful saint Vashistha accompanied by the foremost regenerate ones, like him of an hundred sacrifices, by the celestials. By luck it is that I have overcome the obstacle; by luck it is that my race hath attained renown, in consequence of alliance with those endowed with prowess, the exceedingly potent Rāghavas. O lord of men, to-morrow morning, after the completion of the sacrifice, do thou perform the nuptials, in company with the foremost of the saints." Hearing his speech in the midst of the saints, that best of those conversant with words, the lord of men, replied unto the monarch, saying, — "A gift should be accepted, — this I heard formerly. And what thou sayest, O thou cognizant of duty, will we accomplish." Hearing these words of the truthful (king), chiming in with morality and conducive to fame, the lord of Videha was filled with admiration. Then the ascetics experiencing great delight, passed the night happily in each other's company. And the king, overjoyed on beholding his sons, the Rāghavas — passed (the night) in exceeding delight, splendidly entertained of Janaka. And the exceedingly energetic Janaka also, versed in men and things, having in accordance with the ordinance completed the sacrifice and performed all the preliminary rites relative to the nuptials of his daughters, reposed for the night.

SECTION LXX.

Then next morning Janaka skilled in speech, having in company with the Maharshis performed his daily duties, addressed the priest Satānanda, saying, — "My highly energetic, puissant and eminently righteous brother known by the name of Kusādhwaja dwelleth in the auspicious city, Sānkāçyā, whose ramparts are ranged round with pointed weapons, and which is laved by the river Ikshumati, and which resembles the celestial regions or the aerial car, Pushpaka. I wish to see him, and he is in charge of my sacrifice. And that highly energetic one will partake with me the joy of this occasion." This having been said unto Satānanda, some competent persons presented themselves; and Janaka commanded them (to set out) for Sānkāçyā. And commanded by the monarch, off they went, mounting on fleet coursers, with the view of bringing over that best among men, like Vishnu at the mandate of Indra. And arriving at Sānkāçyā, they presented themselves before Kuçadhwaja, and faithfully delivered unto him the intention of Janaka. And hearing the tidings conveyed by those foremost of envoys endowed with great fleetness, Kuçadhwaja set out at the mandate of the monarch. And on coming to Videha, he appeared before the high-souled Janaka addicted to righteousness. And saluting Satānanda as well as the eminently virtuous Janaka, he sat down on an excellent and superb seat worthy of a king. And having been seated, both the heroic brothers of immeasurable splendour addressed that foremost of counsellors, Sudāmana, saying, — "Go, foremost of counsellors, and speedily bring over the irrepressible Ikshwāku of immeasurable splendour along with his sons and ministers." Thereupon, repairing to the camp he saw that enhancer of the race of the Raghus, and saluting him with bended head, addressed him, — "O heroic lord of Ayodhyā, Vaideha, the master of Mithilā, hath wished to see thee along with thy priests." Hearing the words of that best of counsellors, the king accompanied by the saints and his adherents came to Janaka. And in company with his counsellors, and preists and adherents, the king-foremost of those skilled in speech—spoke unto Vaideha, saying,—"O mighty king, tbow knowest that the worshipful saint Vasishtha is the spiritual guide of our race; and in every ceremony that we undertake, he it is who serves the function of a spokesman. And permitted by Viçwāmitra along with all the Māharshis, even this one of a righteous soul will relate my genealogy." And on Daçarātha resuming silence, the worshipful saint Vasishtha, versed in speech, spoke unto Vaideha in company with his priests, saying—"The perpetual, everlasting, and undeteriorating Brahmā sprang from the Unmanifest (Brahmā). From him sprang Maricha; and Kaçyapa is son unto Maricha. And from Kaçyapa sprung Vivaswat; and Manu is son unto Vivasvvat.[95] This Manu is otherwise called Prajipati; and Ikshwāku is Manu's son. And this Ikshwāku, thou must understand, was the first king of Ayodhyā And Ikshwāku's son, it is well known, was the graceful Kukshi. And Kukshi's son was the graceful Vikukshi.[96] And Vikukshi's son was the exceedingly energetic and powerful Vāna. And Vāna's son was the highly energetic and powerful Anaranya. From Anaranya sprang Prithu; and from Prithu, Trisanku. And Trisanku's son was the highly famous Dhundumāra. And from Dhundumāra sprung the Mahāratha, Yuvanaçya. And from Yuvanācya sprung Māndhātā, lord of earth. And Māndhātā's son was the graceful Susandhi. And Susandhi's two sons were Dhruvasandhi and Prasenajit. And from Dhruvasandhi sprung the famous Bharata. And from Bharata sprung Asita; to fight whom were born as hostile kings, those heroes, the Haihayas, the Tālajanghas, and the Sasavindas. And engaged in conflict with them, that king fled (from his kingdom); and repairing to the Himavat in company with his two consorts, the feeble Asita there paid his debt to Nature. The story runs that his two wives were in the family-way; and that with the intention of destroying the embryo of the other, one of them administered poison unto the former mixed in her food. And it came to pass that at this time, Bhrigu's son, the ascetic Chyavana, had become addicted to the romantic Himavat—foremost of mountains. And here one of these exalted dames with eyes resembling lotus-petals, saluting Bhrigu's son shining like a celestial, desired of him an excellent son. And drawing near unto that sage, Kālindi saluted him. And that Vipra said unto her, who was desiring of having a son born of her,—"In thy womb, O exalted one, will be speedily born an excellent son mixed up with poison, highly powerful, and exceedingly energetic, and possessed of mighty strength, and graceful. Therefore, do thou not grieve, O thou of lotus-eyes." And having paid reverence unto Chyavana, that chaste and worshipful princess, although bereft of her husband, gave birth to a son. And since intending to destroy her foetus she that was co-wife with her had administered poison unto her, *Sagara*[97] was born together with the poison.

And Sagara's son was Asamanja,and Asamanja's Ançumāt. And Dilipa was son unto Ançumāt, and Bhagiratha unto Dilipa. And from Bhagiratha sprang Kā-

[95] The Bengal Text reads: *From Maricha sprang Angiras; and his son was Prachetas; and Manu is Prachetas' son.*—T.

[96] The Bengal Text: *From Ikshwāku sprung Vikukshi.*—T.

[97] *Gara, poison. Sagara means, with poison,* i. e. here, *one born with poison.*—T.

kutstha, and from Kākutstha, Raghu. And Raghu's son was the puissant Pravridha, feeding on human flesh; and he came finally to be known by the name of Kalmāshapāda.[98] And from him sprung Sankhana. And Sudarçana was Sankhana's, and Agnivarna was Sudarçana's son. And Sighraga was Agnivarna's, and Maru was Sighraga's son. And Maru's son was Praçucruka, and from Praçucruka sprung Amvarisha. And Amvarisha's son was Nahusha, lord of earth. And Nahusha's son was Yayāti, and Yayāti's was Nābhāga. And Nābhāga's son was Aja, and from Aja sprung Daçaratha. And from this Daçaratha have come the brothers Rāma and Lakshmana. And it is in the interests of Rāma and Lakshmana belonging to the heroic and truthful and pious Sovereigns sprung in the Ikshwāku line, and possessing purity of race even from the time of their founder, that, O king, we solicit the hands of thy daughters. And, O foremost of men, it behoveth thee to confer like brides upon like bridegrooms."

SECTION LXXI.

When Vasishtha had spoken thus, Janaka with clasped hands answered unto him, saying, —"It behoveth thee to listen unto our genealogy as related by myself. In the matter of disposal of daughters, O foremost of anchorets, one's own line should be described by one boasting of a noble ancestry. Do thou then, O mighty-minded one, listen to the same. There was a king famed over the three worlds by his own acts—Nimi—eminently pious and the foremost of those endowed with strength. And his son was named Mithi, and Mithi's son was Janaka. And from this king Janaka have we derived that word as applied to every one of us. And from Janaka sprang Udāvasu; and Udāvasu's son was the pious-souled Nandivardhana. And Nandivardhan's son was the heroic Suketu. And Suketu's son was the mighty and righteous Devarāta. And the Rajarshi Devarāta's son was Vrihadratha. And Vrihadratha's son was the heroic and puissant Mahāvira. And Mahāvira's son was Sudhriti, endowed with fortitude and having truth for prowess. And Sudhriti's son was the pious-spirited and eminently righteous Dhritaketu. And the Rajarshi Dhritaketu's son was Haryyaçya. And Haryyaçya's son was Maru; and Maru's son was Pratindhaka. And Pratindhaka's son was the righteous king Kirtiratha. And Kirtiratha's son was Devamirha, and Devamirha's, Vibudha, and Vibudha's Mahidhraka. And Mahidhraka's son was king Kirtiratha endowed with great strength. And the Rājarshi Kirtiratha had Mohāromā born unto him; and Mohāromā, the virtuous Sarnaromā. And the Rājarshi Sarnaromā had Hraswaromā born unto him. And this high-souled king conversant with morality had two sons: the elder, myself, the younger, even my brother, the heroic Kuçadhwaja. And installing in the kingdom myself, who was the elder son, and consigning unto my care Kuçadhwaja, our father sought the forest. And on my aged sire ascending heaven, I righteously ruled the kingdom and cherished my brother Kuçadhwaja resembling a celestial, with the eye of affection. And it came to pass that on one occasion a certain powerful king named Sudhanwā came from the city of Sankaçya before Mithilā intending to lay seige to it. And he sent word unto me, saying, —'Do

---

[98] He incurred Vasishtha's curse, and was turned into Rākshasa. He took up water, intending to clear scores with Vasishtha; but at the request of his wife, desisted, pouring down the water at his own feet. Hence the name of Kalmashapada.—T.

thou give me the all-excellent bow of Sivā, as well as thy daughter, the lotus-eyed Sitā'. And in consequence of my not granting him either, king Sudhanwā, O Brahmarshi, entered into hostilities with me; but he was both defeated and slain by me in the encounter. And, O foremost of ascetics, slaying king Sudhanwā, I installed in Sankaçya my heroic brother Kuçadhwaja. This one, O mighty anchoret, is my younger brother, and I am his elder. O powerful ascetic, well pleased will I confer on thee these as thy daughters-in-law,—Sitā on Rāma, good betide thee, and Urmilā on Lakshmana. And, I take oath thrice that, without doubt, I will with a glad heart confer upon thee, O potent ascetic, as thy daughters- in-law my second daughter Urmilā and also Sitā resembling the daughter of a celestial, having prowess assigned for her dower. Do thou now, O king, perform the ceremony *Godana* of the nuptials of Rāma and Lakshmana; and also perform their ancestral rites, good unto thee; and then complete the marriage ceremony. To-day the star Maghā is on the ascendant. On the third day, my master, when the Phālguna will be on north, do thou, O monarch, perform the marriage ceremony. Do thou now, however, dispense gifts for invoking blessings upon Rāma and Lakshmana."

SECTION LXXII.

When Vaideha had spoken thus, the mighty ascetic Viçwāmitra in company with Vasishtha addressed that heroic king, saying,—"O puissant one, the lines of the Ikshwākus and the Vaidehas are exceedingly noble and incomparable. No other race can by any means compare with them. And, O monarch, this youthful union of Rāma and Lakshmana with Sitā! and Urmilā is fit by all means; and it is worthy of their wealth of grace. Now do thou, O foremost of men, listen to my words. This youthful brother of thine, king Kuçadhwaja, O thou versed in morality, this pious-souled one, O king, hath, O prime of men, a couple of daughters, unparalleled on earth in beauty, whom we would ask for, to become wives unto the prince Bharata and the intelligent Satrughna; as we, O king, ask for thine own daughters in the interests of those high-souled ones (Rāma and Lakshmana). And these sons of Daçarātha are endeued with youth and beauty, resembling the Lokapālas, and possessed of the prowess of celestials. Therefore do thou, O foremost of sovereigns, by this alliance with both the brothers, bind the Ikshwāku race. And in this may thy mind never waver!" Hearing Viçwāmitra's words embodying' the sentiments of Vasishtha, Janaka with clasped hands addressed both the potent ascetics, saying,—"I consider my line as blessed; since such puissant ascetics wish for such a desirable alliance. Whatever ye wish, even that shall be done, good betide ye. Let these daughters of Kuçadhwaja together become the wives of Satrughna and Bharata. On the same day, O mighty Muni, let the four highly powerful princes espouse the hands of the four princesses. The learned consider bridal celebrated on the day succeeding those on which the Phalgunis are on the ascendant,—and having for its presiding deity Bhaga—as the most auspicious." Having said these amiable words, king Janaka arose, and with clasped hands addressed both the foremost of ascetics, saying,—"I have reaped high religious merit (by these nuptials), and I also am your disciple. And do ye, ye anchorets, occupy these best of thrones, (belonging to us). And even as this kingdom is unto Daçarātha, is Ayodhyā unto myself. Do ye not therefore entertain any doubts as to your lordship. Do ye therefore do as it behoveth ye." And as Vaideha Janaka was speaking thus, Raghu's son, king Daçaratha, well pleased answered that monarch, saying, —"Countless are the excellences that pertain to ye brothers, lords of Mithilā"; and saints and sovereigns are ever honored by ye,[99] auspiciousness be yours. Good betide ye, I will repair unto my own quarters, there to duly perform the Srāddha ceremonies." Then having greeted that king of men, the illustrious Daçaratha, placing those foremost of ascetics in his front, went away. And reaching his quarters, the king performed the Srāddha according to the ordinance, arose the next morning, and completed *Godana* ceremony in consonance with the time. And to Brāhmanas the monarch severally gave away kine by hundreds and by thousands, for the welfare of his sons. And that puissant one gave away unto the regenerate ones four hundred thousands of kine furnished with horns plated with gold, and each having her calf, —together with bell-metal vessels for milking them. And that descendant of Raghu addicted to his sons made presents of various other valuables unto the Brāhmanas, on behalf of his sons. And having given away kine, the king surrounded by his sons looked like unto the amiable Prajāpati[100] surrounded by the Lokapālas.

SECTION LXXIII.

And it came to pass that the day on which the king made excellent presents of kine, the heroic Yudhājit, son unto the lord of the Kekayas and maternal uncle unto Bharata, presented himself before Daçaratha. And having seen the king and enquired after his welfare, he said unto him, —"The lord of the Kekayas hath from affection enquired after thy welfare, saying, —'They of whose peace thou art anxious, are at present well.' And, O foremost of kings, desirous of seeing my nephew (Bharata) that lord of earth repaired to Ayodhyā, O descendant of Raghu. And learning at Ayodhyā that thy sons for the purpose of marriage had, O monarch, come to Mithilā with thyself, I have speedily hied hither, with the intention of seeing my sister's son."

Then king Daçaratha, on having that dear guest with him, rendered unto him all the respect that he deserved. Then having passed the night in company with his high-souled sons, that one versed in men and things arose in the morning, and having disposed of his daily duties, approached the entrance of the sacrificial ground, headed by the saints. Then at an auspicious moment called Vijaya, Rāma with Vasishtha as well as other Maharshis at his head, and accompanied by his brothers adorned with various ornaments, who had all performed the rites relative to their nuptials, (approached the entrance of the sacrificial ground). Then the worshipful Vasishtha, coming unto Vaideha, spake as follows, —"King Daçaratha, O foremost of sovereigns—that chief among the best of men—accompanied with his sons, who have performed all the rites relative to their nuptials, stayeth the orders of the bestower (of the bride); for the meeting of the giver and the receiver is indispensable to every transaction (of this nature). Do thou therefore maintain thy

[99] The commentator here seems to be in fault. He explains, —"By you have your royal ancestors been honored." Evidently an error. I differ from him. The particle *cha (and)* makes the point clear.—T.

[100] The Bengal text—*Like Prajāpati himself.*—T.

merit by accomplishing this excellent nuptial ceremony." Thus addressed by the high-souled Vasishtha, that exceedingly generous and energetic one versed in morality answered, saying,—"Who acts as my warder there? And whose commands doth he stay? And what need of exercising judgment in entering one's own house? As this kingdom is mine, so it is verily thine. O foremost of anchorets, my daughters resembling flames of fire, having performed all the rites relative to the incoming nuptials, are at the foot of the dais; and, sitting beside the dais, I myself had been expecting thee every moment. Do thou perform everything without let. What need of delaying further?" Hearing those words uttered by Janaka, Daçarātha entered in together with his sons and the body of saints. Then unto the king of the Videhas, Vasishtha spake as follows,—"O saint, do thou, O pious one, in company with the saints perform, O master, the nuptial ceremonies of Rāma charming unto all." Thereupon, saying,—"So be it" unto Janaka, the worshipful saint Vasishtha of mighty austerities with Viçwāmitra and the pious Satānanda in his front, constructed a dais agreeably to the scriptures, decking it out with fragrant flowers all around, and golden ladles, and variegated water- pots, and platters with ears of barley, and censers filled with *Dkupa*, and conchs, and sacrificial spoons, and vessels furnished with *Arghyas*, and those containing fried paddy, and sanctified *Akshatas*. And over the dais, Vasishtha with due *mantras* and rites spread an awning consisting of *Darvas* of equal proportions. And with prescribed rites and·*mantras* placing fire upon the dais, the highly energetic one commenced upon offering oblations. Then bringing Sitā adorned with various ornaments near the fire, and placing her before Rāghava, king Janaka addressed the enhancer of Kauçalya's joy, saying,—"This Sitā, my daughter, do thou accept, good betide thee, as thy partner in the observance of every duty: do thou take her hand by thine. May she be of exalted piety, and devoted to her husband; ever following thee like thy shadow!" saying this, the king sprinkled Rāma's palm with water sanctified with *mantras*; with the celestials and saints exclaiming,—"Excellent! Excellent!" And the celestial kettle-drums sounded, and blossoms began to shower down copiously. Having thus given away his daughter Sitā, with water and *mantras*, king Janaka overflowing with delight, said,—"Come forward, O Lakshmana, good unto thee. Receive thou Urmilā ready to be bestowed by me upon thee. Do thou accept her hand: let there be no delay about it." Having addressed Lakshmana thus, Janaka spake unto Bharata, saying,—"Do thou, O descendant of Raghu, take Mandavyā's hand by thine own." And the righteous lord of Mithilā spake also unto Satrughna, saying,—"Do thou, O thou of mighty arms, take Srutakirti's hand by thine own. May ye all be good, and vowed unto excellent life! and be, ye Kākutsthas, ye united with your wives. Let there be no delay about it." Hearing Janaka's speech, those four perpetuators of Raghu's line, staying by Vasishtha's opinions, taking the hands of the four brides with their owil, went round the sacrificial fire, and the dais, and the king, and the high-souled saints; and in company with their wives, agreeably to direction entered into matrimony in accordance with the ordinance. And there was a mighty shower of shining blossoms from the firmament accompanied with the sounds of celestial kettle-drums, and choiring and instrumental music. And the Apsarās danced and the Gandharbas sang melodiously, at the bridal of the foremost of the Raghus. And this seemed wonderful to witness. And to the blowing of trumpets, those exceedingly puissant ones, thrice going round the fire, in company with their wives went to the encampment. And the king,having seen that all the auspicious ceremonies were performed, went in their wake, accompanied by the sages and his adherents.

SECTION LXXIV.

Then when the night had passed away, the mighty *Muni* Viçwāmitra, having greeted the monarch, set out for the Northern mountains. And when Viçwāmitra had gone away, king Daçarātha, greeting Mitbila's lord, Vaideha, actively prepared for setting out for his own capital. And then the king of the Videhas gave a dower consisting of various things. And Mithilā's lord gave many hundred thousands of kine, and excellent woolen stuffs, and *Kotis* of common cloths; and elephants, and horses, and cars, and foot men, as well as an hundred damsels adorned, endowed with elegance, to form goodly waiting-maids. And well- pleased the king gave as a noble dower gold and silver and pearls and coral. And having given divers kinds of articles, that king, the lord of Mithilā, bidding adieu to the monarch (Daçarātha), re-entered his own capital. And the master of Ayodhyā accompanied with his high-souled sons, and headed by the saints in a body, started on the journey, followed by his army and attendants. And as that tiger-like one was on his way, in company with Rāghava and the saints, the fowls began to utter frightful cries all around, and the beasts on earth to stream in a Southern direction. And beholding them, that tiger like monarch asked Vasishtha, saying,—"Those birds of fierce aspects emit frightful cries and beasts stream in a Southerly direction. What is this? My heart trembleth and my mind is not at ease." Hearing the speech of king Daçarātha, that mighty saint spake sweetly, saying, "Hear what would be the result of it. These fowls of the air by their cries presage some dreadful impending evil; but these beasts betoken peace restored. Therefore do thou renounce anxiety." And as they were thus conversing, there blew a strong wind, shaking all the earth, and breaking down the trees. And a deep gloom enveloped the sun; and no quarter could be discovered. And enveloped in ashes, that host became stupified. And at that dreadful hour, Vasishtha and the other saints and the king with his sons alone retained their senses, all else were deprived of their senses, and the army was enveloped with ashes. And the king saw that repressor of kings, the decendant of Bhrigu, Jamadagni's son, dreadful to behold, wearing a head of matted locks, irrepresible like unto Kailāça, and unbearable like unto the fire at the universal dissolution, flaming fn energy, incapable of being looked at by the unrighteous, with his axe on his shoulder, equipped with a bow like unto the lightning, and fierce arrows, looking like Sivā the slayer of Tripura. And beholding him of dreadful appearance like unto flaming fire, the Vipras headed by Viçwāmitra, engaged in reciting *mantras* and offering oblations unto the fire,— those saints assembled together—began to converse with each other., saying,—"Is this one, enraged because of the slaughter of his sire, intent upon exterminating the Kshatriyas? Formerly, having slaughtered the Kshatriyas, he pacified his ire and mental ferment,—therefore, to annihilate the Kshatriyas once again can never be his endeavour." Having said this, the saints offered *Arghya* unto Bhrigu's son of dreadful appearance; and addressed him in soothing words, saying,—"O Rāma! O

Rāma." Accepting that homage rendered unto him by the saints, that puissant one, Jamadagni's son, Rāma, addressed Rāma, the son of Daçaratha.

SECTION LXXV.

"O Rāma, son of Daçaratha, I have, O hero, heard of thy wonderful prowess; and I have also heard all about thy breaking of the bow. And having heard of that wonderful and inconceivable breaking of the bow, I have bent my steps hither, taking another auspicious bow. Do thou stretch it, fix the arrow upon this mighty and dreadful bow, belonging to Jamadagni; and thus display thy prowess. Then, having witnessed thy might in stretching the bow, I shall offer thee combat, laying under contribution our utmost strength." Hearing his words, king Daçaratha with a blank countenance, and clasped hands, said,—"Thou hast quenched thy ire against the Kshatriyas; and, moreover, thou art a Brāhmana boasting of high austerities. It therefore behoveth thee to dispel the fears of my sons who are boys. Thou bringest thy life from the race of the Bhargavas engaged in observing vows, and studying the Veda; and thou hast renounced arms vowing in the presence of the thousand-eyed one. And embracing a life of righteousness, thou didst confer the earth upon Kāçyapa; and repaired to the forest, making the Mahendra hill thy home. O mighty *Muni*, thou hast come here to compass the destruction of my all; but if Rāma be slain, we shall never live." Thus addressed by Daçaratha, the powerful son of Jamadagni, disregarding his words, thus addressed Rāma,—"These two foremost of bows, extraordinary, and worshipped of all the worlds, and stout, and powerful, surpassingly excellent, were constructed with care by Viçwakarmā. And, one of these, O foremost of men, for the destruction of Tripura, the celestials gave unto Tramvaka, desirous of encounter,—even that which, O Kākutstha, thou hast snapped. And this second, which is irrepressible, was given to Vishnu, by the chiefs of the celestials. And, O Rāma, this bow belonging unto Vishnu, capable of conquering hostile cities, is, O Kākutstha, equal in energy unto the bow belonging unto Rudra. Once on a time the deities, with the object of ascertaining the respective prowess of Vishnu and the blue-throated one, asked the great father, about it. Thereupon the great father, foremost of those abiding by truth —reading the intention of the deities, fomented a quarrel between them. And upon that quarrel breaking out among the deities, there took place a mighty contest capable of making one's hair stand on end, between Vishnu and the blue-throated one, each burning to beat the other down. Then on Vishnu uttering a roar, Siva's bow of dreadful prowess became flaccid. And thereupon the three-eyed Mahādeva became moveless. And upon the assembled gods with the saints and the Charanas beseeching those two foremost of celestials, they became pacified. And upon beholding that bow of Siva rendered flaccid by Vishnu's prowess, the deities with the saints acknowledged Vishnu as the more powerful. And the enraged Rudra of high fame made over the bow along with its shafts unto the hands of the Rājarshi, Devarata of Videha. And, O Rāma, this bow belonging to Vishnu, capable of conquering hostile cities, Vishnu consigned to Bhrigu's son, Richika, as a worthy trust. And the exceedingly energetic Richika made over the divine bow unto his son of immeasurable prowess, my sire the high-souled son of Jamadagni. And once on a time, on my sire surcharged with ascetic energy, renouncing the bow, Arjuna, under the influence of unrighteous sentiment, compassed the death of my father. Thereupon, learning of the lamentable and untoward slaughter of my sire, I from ire, annihilated the Kshatriyas, springing up afresh by numbers, then bringing under sway the whole earth, I, O Rāma, on the sacrifice being over, conferred it upon the righteous Kaçyapa as Dakshina. Having made this gift, I was dwelling in the Mahendra hill equipped with ascetic energy, when, hearing of thy snapping of the bow, I have speedily come hither. Do thou now, O Rāma, agreeably to the cannon of the Kshatriya morality, take this excellent and mighty bow of Vishnu, that had belonged to my father and grand-father. And do thou set upon this best of bows an arrow capable of conquering hostile cities. And, O Kākutstha, if thou succeed, I shall then offer thee combat."

SECTION LXXVI.

Hearing Jamadagni's words, the son of Daçaratha, in consideration of the presence of his father, said these words in subdued tone,—"O Bhrigu's son, I have heard of the deeds thou hast performed, resolved on avenging thy sire. O Brāhmana, I acknowledge that. But, O Bhārgava, thou insultest me abiding by the Kshatriya duties, as pusillanimous or devoid of prowess. Do thou to-day witness my energy and vigor." Saying this, the enraged Rāghava, endowed with fleet vigor, took up Bhrigu's noble bow, together with the shaft, from his hand. And fixing the string upon it he set the arrow. And then Rāma enraged addressed Jamadagni's son, Rāma, saying,—"Thou art a Brāhmana and through Viçwāmitra, art worthy of my homage. Therefore it is, O Rāma,that I cannot let go this life-destroying shaft. Which of these shall I reduce to aught, O Rāma,—thy aerial course, or the merit thou hast attained through thy asceticism of ascending unto certain incomparable regions? This celestial arrow sprung from Vishnu, capable of conquering hostile towns, never hiteth fruitless, with energy destroying the pride of prowess of foes." And with the object of beholding Rāma holding that foremost of weapons, there assembled in a body the celestials and the saints, with the great father at their head. And the Gandharbas and the Apsarās and the Siddhas and the Charanas and the Kinnaras and the Yakshas and the Rākshasas and the Nagas assembled to behold that mighty wonder. And on Bhārgava's energy having passed into Rāma bearing that best of bows, Jamadagni's son became bereft of prowess, and Rāma (Paraçurāma) kept steadily eying Rāma. And rendered inert in consequence of his energy having been dispelled by Rāma's own, Jamadagna mildly addressed Rāma of eyes like lotus petals, saying,—"When formerly I gave away the earth unto Kāçyapas he said unto me,—Thou must no longer stay in my dominions. And in consonance with the words of my spiritual guide, ever since that time I have never spent a night on earth. Even this had been promised by me, O Kākutstha. Therefore, O hero, it behoveth thee not to destroy my course, O descendant of Raghu. With the speed of the mind shall I now wend my way to the Mahendra, best of hills. And, O Rāma, the regions I have conquered by my asceticism do thou destroy with that foremost of arrows: let there be no delay about it. Even from thy handling of this bow I know thee to be the chief of the celestials even that eternal one, the slayer of Madhu. Hail to thee, O vanquisher of foes! And all these celestials assembled are beholding thee, of unparalleled deeds, and without an antagonist in fight.—And,

O Kākutstha, neither ought I to be ashamed (because of this discomfiture); I have been baffled by the lord himself of the three worlds. And it behoveth, O Rāma to disengage this peerless shaft (from the bow), O thou—of noble vows; and on thy shooting the shaft, I shall repair to that foremost of mountains, the Mahendra. When Jamadagni's son, Rāma, had said this, the puissant and graceful son of Daçarātha shot that excellent arrow. And witnessing the destruction by Rāma of his regions earned by his own austerities, Jamadagni's son speedily started for that best of mountains, the Mahendra. And then all the quarters became cleared of gloom; and the celestials and saints fell to extol Rāma when he had shot the arrow. And that lord, Jamadagni's son Rāma, having gone round Rāma, the son of Daçarātha, and honored (by all), set out (for his own quarters).

SECTION LXXVII.

"When Rāma had departed, Daçarātha's son the illustrious Rāma, of serene soul, made over the bow unto the hands of Varuna of immeasurable strength. Then saluting the saints headed by Vasishtha, Rāma, the descendant of Raghu, seeing his father stupified, addressed him, saying—"Now that Jamadagni's son Rāma hath gone away, let the four-fold forces maintained by thee as their lord, march in the direction of Ayodhyā." Hearing Rāma's words, king Daçarātha embraced his son with his arms, and smelt Rāghava's crown; and hearing that Rāma had gone, the monarch became exceedingly delighted,—and considered himself and his son as having attained a second birth. And he urged on his army, and speedily arrived at the city, graced round with standards bearing pennons, and lovely to behold, and resounding with the sounds of trumpets, with its high-ways watered, and beauteous, and sprinkled around with flowers, crowded with citizens looking cheerful on account of the king's approach, bearing auspicious articles in their hands, and beautified with the vast concourse of people. And receivced by the citizens as well as the regenerate ones inhabiting the city coming forward a long way, and followed by his graceful sons, the handsome Majesty of ilustrious name, entered his own dear residence, like unto the Himāvat. And entertained by his own relatives with all objects of enjoyment, the monarch rejoiced exceedingly. And Kauçalya and Sumitrā and the slender waisted Kaikeyi, together with other wives of the king, were busy, receiving the brides, with the necessary ceremonies. And the royal spouses received the exalted Sita and the famous Urmila and both the daughters of Kuçadhwaja, graced with silken apparel, with *homas* performed and blessings invoked, on their behalf. And having paid reverence at the abodes of the gods, and rendered homage unto those that deserved the same, the daughters of the kings, well pleased, in private, took joy with their husbands. And having attained brides, and arms, with wealth and friends, those foremost of men, engaged in ministering unto their father.

And once on a time that descendant of Raghu, king Daçarātha addressed Bharata, saying,—"O son, this son of the king of the Kekayas thy uncle, Yudhajit stayeth here, that hero, having come to take thee over." And hearing these words of Daçarātha, Kaikeyi's son, Bharata, prepared for the journey, together with Satrughna. And having greeted his father, and Rāma of unflagging energy, and his mothers, that foremost of men, the heroic (Bharata) departed with Satrughna. And having Bharata as well as Satrughna, the heroic Yudhajit, with a delighted heart, entered his own city; and his father rejoiced exceedingly. And on Bharata having departed, Rāma and the exceedingly mighty Lakshmana, tended their sire resembling a celestial. And paying the utmost regard to the command of his father, Rāma discharged all the duties of the city, having for his object the pleasure or welfare (of the citizens). And needfully rendering every service to his mothers, he on proper occasions observed the duties pertaining to his superiors. And Daçarātha was exceedingly delighted; as also the Brāhmanas, and the traders, and the inhabitants generally, at the conduct and behaviour of Rāma. And Rāma having truth for prowess, by virtue of his excellence appeared unto every one the most meritorious of (Daçarātha's son's) like unto the self create Himself unto all being. And in the company of Sitā, the wise Rāma, bending his mind to Sitā with his heart dedicated unto her, passed many a season in delight. And Rāma's beloved Sitā, as having been bestowed upon him by his sire, by her loveliness, and her perfections as much as by her loveliness, went on enhancing his joy. And her lord came to excercise a double influence on her heart. And by her own heart, the daughter of Janaka, Mithilā's lord, resembling a goddess in grace, and like unto Sree (goddess of wealth) herself in loveliness, completely read his inmost sentiments. And experiencing delight, Rāma, receiving the Rājarshi's daughter, exercising her own will—the excellent princess—looked graceful, even like the lord Vishnu the chief of celestials on being joined with Sree.

END OF BĀLAKĀNDAM.

Lector House believes that a society develops through a two-fold approach of continuous learning and adaptation, which is derived from the study of classic literary works spread across the historic timeline of literature records. Therefore, we aim at reviving, repairing and redeveloping all those inaccessible or damaged but historically as well as culturally important literature across subjects so that the future generations may have an opportunity to study and learn from past works to embark upon a journey of creating a better future.

This book is a result of an effort made by Lector House towards making a contribution to the preservation and repair of original ancient works which might hold historical significance to the approach of continuous learning across subjects.

HAPPY READING & LEARNING!

LECTOR HOUSE LLP
E-MAIL: lectorpublishing@gmail.com